NEW BEGINNINGS BY THE SUNFLOWER CLIFFS

BOOK 1 OF THE SUNFLOWER CLIFFS SERIES

GEORGINA TROY

Boldwood

First published in Great Britain in 2023 by Boldwood Books Ltd.

Copyright © Georgina Troy, 2023

Cover Design by Alexandra Allden

Cover Illustration: Shutterstock and Getty Images

The moral right of Georgina Troy to be identified as the author of this work has been asserted in accordance with the Copyright, Designs and Patents Act 1988.

Every effort has been made to obtain the necessary permissions with reference to copyright material, both illustrative and quoted. We apologise for any omissions in this respect and will be pleased to make the appropriate acknowledgements in any future edition.

A CIP catalogue record for this book is available from the British Library.

Paperback ISBN 978-1-80426-108-8

Large Print ISBN 978-1-80426-107-1

Hardback ISBN 978-1-80426-109-5

Ebook ISBN 978-1-80426-106-4

Kindle ISBN 978-1-80426-105-7

Audio CD ISBN 978-1-80426-114-9

MP3 CD ISBN 978-1-80426-113-2

Digital audio download ISBN 978-1-80426-110-1

Boldwood Books Ltd
23 Bowerdean Street
London SW6 3TN
www.boldwoodbooks.com

To Rob, James, Saskia and Max.

1

JUNE – BLOWING DANDELION CLOCKS

'I'm coming, I'm coming,' Bea shouted breathlessly, stepping out of the shower and almost losing her balance as she slipped on the mat. She grabbed hold of the shower curtain, snapping it from its rings, before wrapping the nearest towel around her dripping body and running down the stairs.

'Bloody builders,' she cursed, stubbing her toe on the oak banister. Why did they choose today to arrive early, the one time she was running late? She pulled open the heavy front door.

'Sorry, love,' a man in paint-spattered overalls said, his eyes widening as he took in her lack of clothing. 'We, um, seem to have caught you on the 'op.'

'Yes, well, I'm in a bit of a rush.' She held the door open for the builder and his apprentice to enter the hallway. Holding on tightly to the front of her towel with one hand, Bea pushed back a stray lock of blonde hair with the other. 'I'll take you up to my bedroom.' The spotty-faced boy stifled a giggle, raising a pierced eyebrow at his boss until he was nudged sharply in the ribs. Bea cleared her throat, adding quickly, 'So that I can show you the work to quote for.' Her face flushed in embarrassment.

'Right you are, love.'

She could hear the builder grumbling to his apprentice as she led them up the carved oak staircase, trying not to think about how little her towel was covering, flushed at the thought of what she'd just said. 'My bathroom is en suite, or at least I hope it soon will be,' she explained. 'So, I thought the best place to start would be my room.'

'Righty oh.'

'I'll need the wall from this room knocked through, and a doorway put in down that end.' She pointed across the room, noticing her knickers and bra on the floor. Kicking them under the bed, she took a breath to continue.

'Can't be done,' said a gruff voice from the hallway.

Surprised, she took a backwards step out of her room to see who was talking. 'Why not?' she asked, her intended rant immediately catching in her throat when she came face-to-face with the most piercing blue eyes she'd ever seen. Bea was sure he must be handsome under all that facial hair, and despite her annoyance with him couldn't help staring.

'This is a very old house, and that, young lady, is a load-bearing wall,' he said, his perfect lips drawing back into a slight smile she instinctively knew was more amusement than appreciation of her appearance. He cleared his throat before tapping the wall for emphasis. 'I wouldn't advise knocking through it.'

Young lady? He couldn't be much older than her, she mused. Then again, thought Bea, he could be almost any age under all those whiskers. 'But I'd planned to,' Bea argued, not liking his condescending manner or his amused gaze. He may be used to women being stunned into submission by his overpowering presence, but she had just got rid of a bullying husband and wasn't about to replace him with a bossy builder.

'Anyway, and you are?' she asked, wishing she wasn't in such a compromising position. Running late was one thing, but not being dressed in front of this scowling builder was another entirely.

'Luke Thornton,' he said, studying the wall. 'I was a bit delayed and asked Bill to come ahead.' He motioned for Bea to follow him and walked down the hallway to another bedroom the other side of hers. 'This would be a better option.' He narrowed his eyes, contemplating the wall in front of him. 'This box room would make a perfect en suite.' He peered out of the window. 'Imagine soaking in your bath and staring across the fields at that view of Corbière Lighthouse.' He stepped back so Bea could have a look. She leant forward and gazed at the uninterrupted view across the fields to the white tower perched at the edge of the sea. He was right. She always enjoyed looking at this majestic building on the rocks at one end of St Ouen's Bay.

'Pretty spectacular, don't you think?' he said, standing behind her.

Bea gripped her towel, wishing she'd at least taken the time to put on her underwear, and nodded. He was right of course.

'Then,' he continued without waiting for her to answer, 'you could keep the other as the house bathroom. It's bigger, after all, and closer to the rest of the bedrooms.'

She thought through his suggestion for a moment. 'I see what you're saying, but I'd got the whole set up planned out in detail,' she said, not wishing to give in to him too readily, but desperate to put on some clothes. 'It doesn't sound like I have much of a choice really, so I suppose I'll have to go with your suggestion.'

Luke shrugged. 'You can do as you like, it's your house.' He studied the clipboard Bill handed to him. 'According to my secretary, apart from replacing the house bathroom and creating an en suite, you also want the downstairs cloakroom refitting, some plastering in the hall, and a bit of painting and decorating throughout the rest of the house.'

Bea nodded silently. It sounded as if this was going to be mammoth when he listed everything like that. Luke withdrew a biro from the top of the clipboard and began making notes. He nodded to the other men. 'You two can get going if you like, I'll catch up with you later.' He walked slowly down the stairs, his hand grazing paint surfaces as he passed the walls.

'Don't mind him, love,' whispered Bill from behind her. 'He doesn't mean to be so abrasive, it's just his manner.'

'He's had a lot goin' on,' the apprentice added, before receiving another nudge in his bruised ribs. 'Ouch, what was that one for?'

'You can get in the van.' The builder shook his head and frowned. 'Bloody kid is too ready to give his opinion when it's not needed.' He tilted his head in Luke's direction. 'He's a grand chap though.'

Bea glanced at Luke's broad back as he stepped into the down-stairs cloakroom. 'He hides it well, doesn't he?' she murmured, before hurrying to her bedroom to dress. Once clothed, she slipped on her shoes and went to wait for Luke in the kitchen at the back of the house. What was his problem with her, anyway? He made her earlier moodiness seem positively chirpy.

Bea checked the time and wished he would hurry up. She didn't have long. It would take at least fifteen minutes to get to her appointment, even if she took the open road all the way past Sunflower Cliffs, to the sand dunes on the other side of the bay and over by the golf course to St Brelade's Bay. She took out a small mirror from her handbag and re-applied her cherry lip-gloss. Butterflies jackhammered in her stomach; she wasn't looking forward to this meeting. Business associates were one thing, but dealing with the spoilt wife of her biggest client was another entirely.

'Wow, this room's a shrine to orange Formica,' Luke announced from the doorway.

Bea frowned. He was right, but there was no need to be rude. 'It is a bit, but I can't afford to do everything I want with the house, unfortunately. It's functional, even if it is a little, um, orange, so it'll have to wait until I can find enough money to fit a new one.'

Luke raked a hand through his messy brown fringe. 'It's not too bad.'

She noticed the glint of merriment in his eyes. 'I think that's a matter of opinion.' Bea raised her eyebrows, unable to help glancing up at the kitchen clock again.

'Right,' he said, smiling down at her. 'You obviously have to be somewhere, and I've made all the notes I should need. I'll pass this on to my secretary in the morning, and she'll sort a quote for you.'

Bea couldn't help noticing how his smile seemed to light up his entire face, or what she could see of it through his stubble. Her stomach did an involuntary flip when his dark blue eyes gave away his amusement, and looking away from him she pushed her hand deep into her bag. She wished her aunt was still with her; they'd have laughed about his stunned expression on seeing the kitchen for the first time. 'I can never find anything in here,' she said, aware of him watching her as she rummaged around trying to locate her car keys.

'I know better than to comment on women's handbags.' He shrugged. 'Was there anything else you need me to add to this list before I go?'

She remembered the time and tried not to panic. 'Right, about that work?' Bea mulled over what work she'd asked Luke to price for. Picking up her suit jacket from the back of her chair, she hesitated. 'This is a bit awkward,' she said. 'I'm not sure I'll be able to afford to have all the work done at once.' She chewed her lower lip. 'When I spoke to my sister about contacting you I'd hoped to be able to take out a loan for the work.'

His expression softened. 'I was sorry to hear about your aunt. I heard she was a remarkable lady.'

Bea swallowed. It was too soon to hope to be brave when talking about Aunt Annabel, but she needed to at least try. 'She was.' She cleared her throat, determined to draw her mind away from her heartache. She couldn't afford to mess up her mascara now; she didn't have time to fix her face before leaving. 'If you wouldn't mind quoting just the bathrooms and plastering for now, I'll probably have to do the rest myself.'

Luke nodded and scribbled something in his notebook. 'Not a problem. Give me a call if you're happy with the quote. The guys should be able to start early next week.'

Bea was surprised they could start so soon, but didn't like to say so. 'Okay, thank you.' She walked through to the front door with him. He'd seemed so gentle for a moment. 'Sorry to rush you, but I'm a little late for an appointment and need to get a move on.'

She waited for him to get into his blue pickup truck and watched in silence as he disappeared down her long gravel driveway in a cloud of dust. It was like blowing a dandelion clock, she mused – you never knew where the seeds would end up. She sighed heavily. This was no time to start panicking about the massive responsibility she was taking on. How many people would swap places with her in a second if they could own a house and garden as grand as The Brae? she wondered. Bea glanced around the large, panelled hallway. This house should be enjoyed by a family though, not a solitary, newly separated, grieving thirty-year-old. Was she mad to try so hard to keep this place?

As she walked through the hallway to the front door, Bea looked up at the assortment of paintings on the wall. 'Are any of you A Jersey Kiss?' she asked, doubting it very much. None of them looked like they could be. What was A Jersey Kiss anyway, and why hadn't her aunt left some sort of clue in her will?

2

JULY – A THORNY ISSUE

'Have you discovered what A Jersey Kiss is supposed to be yet?' Mel asked. 'Do you think it could be a painting or something?'

Bea wished she knew. Ever since her aunt's lawyer had told her that she'd inherited something called A Jersey Kiss, she'd been trying to figure out what it was. 'I've no idea. I've never seen anything where the name might fit, and I've checked all the paintings in the house.'

'Mum said it could possibly be a piece of jewellery. Didn't Antonio used to buy your aunt lovely pieces? She said they sometimes have names, if they're extra special.'

'Maybe,' Bea said, trying once again to picture the contents of her aunt's jewellery box and wondering why her stepmother Joyce – Mel's mum, who had never shown any interest in anything either she or her aunt had ever done before – was now trying to unlock this mystery. 'Then again, the lawyer told me that Aunt Annabel made her will over twenty years ago. She always needed money for her garden projects, so maybe she sold it during that time?'

'Probably,' Mel said, looking disappointed. 'Well, if it isn't the long-lost kiss thing that's making you look so thoughtful, what is it?'

'If you must know, I was thinking about Luke Thornton.' Bea dragged a black chiffon top over her chest, wishing, not for the first time, that her boobs were a couple of cup sizes smaller. Maybe she'd been a little over optimistic to think that she could fit into the clothes Mel had kindly brought round for her to try on.

'Oh yes, the famous Luke Thornton. I've never met him, but Grant tells me he's a pretty forceful guy.'

'Now why doesn't that surprise me?' Bea said raising an eyebrow. 'Although does your soon-to-be fiancé also explain why Luke's so moody?'

'Problems with his partner, I think.' Mel tilted her head to one side and studied Bea's torso thoughtfully.

'You mean she had the sense to leave him?' Bea couldn't help asking.

Mel shook her head. 'Not his girlfriend – a bloke, his business partner. I think he disappeared taking Luke's money, or something. Someone said he's been struggling a bit with it all.' Mel narrowed her eyes. 'You seem very interested in someone you said was horrible.'

'I'm only asking,' Bea said, pulling on a different top and scowling at her reflection in the cheval mirror. 'It's too tight. I knew this would be a waste of time. There's no way I can fit into any of your clothes, and I've worn all mine to death.'

Mel tugged at the hem from behind her to pull the top into shape. 'Will you hurry up and get ready?'

'I can't wear this.' With difficulty, Bea dragged off the offending article and dropped it on her crumpled duvet cover with the ten or so other outfits lying there in a heaped mess.

'We're going to have to think of something,' Mel said, folding the top angrily.

'This is my first time out since Aunt Annabel, well... you know.'

'She died, Bea. Yes, I know and I'm sorry, but you have to get a grip and move on.' Mel rummaged through Bea's wardrobe, checking for a suitable top. 'I know it was shit of Simon to leave so soon after, but tonight's my engagement party and I'm not going to let you mope at home.'

'You just don't want to have to deal with Joyce if I don't turn up.' Bea raised an eyebrow and grabbed hold of a purple silk peplum top that she seemed to wear to every smart occasion.

'Listen, we may not share the same mother, and I know she's a bit of a pain, but she only wants the best for me.'

Bea nodded. It wasn't Mel's fault her mother seemed so intent on pushing Mel forward in their father's affections. Poor man. How he coped with such determination, Bea could never understand.

'Anyway, it's been months since Annabel told you about Simon getting all hot and heavy with that slutty assistant of his, slimy git.'

Aunt Annabel, thought Bea. She'd have known what to say to cheer her up. 'I think the hardest part is that Claire's already pregnant with his baby.' She took a deep breath and held her arms out. 'What do you think?' she asked, holding the top up over her chest. 'It's not perfect, but it'll have to do.'

'Great! Now try this lipstick. It's a different shade to the cherry one you always wear. I think it'll suit you.'

Bea pouted in front of the mirror, concentrating on turning her full lips from their natural pale pink to a searing shade of fuchsia, when someone banged forcefully on her front door. Bea jumped, inadvertently rouging half her cheek. 'Shit.' She placed the lipstick down onto her dressing table and went downstairs, Mel following.

'What the hell are you supposed to be?' Simon asked, looking her up and down as she opened the front door, stepping back as he made his way into the hall.

'Come in, Simon,' Mel invited sarcastically.

He ignored her and kept his attention on Bea. She grabbed an old Barbour jacket from behind the heavy front door, dragging it on over her underwear. She really needed to stop answering the door wearing so little, she thought, annoyed at not thinking before answering the door.

'I don't believe this.' He swung round, staring down at Bea's chest encased in the new black satin push-up bra Mel had persuaded her to buy. 'You two are going out together. Aunt Annabel would have been delighted.'

Bea crossed her arms to hold the coat in place and swallowed. 'You leave her out of this.'

'She never liked me, did she?' He peered down at Bea, his irritation at her barely hidden.

'Probably because your angelic looks and charm hid the ugliness of a toad,' Mel said.

'What the hell is she on about?' He raised his eyebrows, ignoring Mel.

'You know perfectly well my godmother liked you, until she realised I wasn't the only woman you were sleeping with,' Bea snapped. 'She changed her mind then, of course.'

'We weren't getting on. It wasn't just my fault that our marriage broke down, you know. It takes two.'

Bea heard Mel's sharp intake of breath behind her, knowing instinctively her sister was seconds from exploding with indignation. 'Mel, why don't you go through to the kitchen and pour us both a drink,' Bea suggested, turning back to face Simon, his beautiful face contorted with spite. 'This won't take long.'

Mel did as she was asked and stomped down the hallway towards the kitchen.

Bea narrowed her eyes at Simon. 'I suppose you're here about your letter?' Bea pulled out a crumpled tissue she found in the jacket pocket, and spat on it before rubbing it against the lipstick on her cheek. 'I can't believe you want half of this house. You've always hated it here and you know Aunt Annabel left it to me.'

'Yes, she wanted to make sure you were looked after,' he said, repeating her aunt's often said words. 'It's not my fault your father has a scheming wife, or that your mother died. But the fact remains that your aunt died when we were still married.' He lowered his face closer to hers. She could almost taste his minty breath. 'Technically, we still are. And as such, the house is considered a matrimonial asset, and I, as your husband, am legally entitled to half of its value.'

The heat of her fury towards him almost gave her heartburn. How could he be so heartless to push her into selling Aunt Annabel's house? 'Legally maybe, not morally though.' She recalled his letter. 'And what exactly did you mean by D-Day?'

Simon smiled, looking satisfied with himself. 'I thought that was rather clever, didn't you?' Bea glared at him. 'Suit yourself. D-Day, Debt Day. Get it?'

Bea closed her eyes slowly, willing him to disappear. 'Right. Very funny.'

'I thought so. I don't want you forgetting the date.'

'I'm hardly likely to do that, am I?' She'd had enough. 'What did you want?'

'I've settled in to the apartment with Claire. Maybe if we hadn't moved in to live with your aunt our relationship might not have fallen apart so rapidly...' he mused, then shrugged. 'Anyway, I thought I'd collect one or two things I forgot to take with me when you threw me out.' He straightened a picture on the wall before staring at it. 'This is mine, I believe,' he added, lifting the depiction of a bloody hunting scene Bea had always hated off the hook.

She took a deep breath and mentally braced herself. 'Take the painting, Simon, and while you're at it take yourself out of my house, and don't bang on the door demanding to be let in like that again.' Bea went to open the door.

'Well, the door was locked.' Simon put his hand out to stop her. 'When the hell did you change the locks, anyway?'

Was he insane? 'As soon as you left. When do you think?' she asked, stunned by his ridiculous question.

'You've changed, Beatrice,' Simon said, lowering his voice. 'You used to be kind and decent.'

Bea took a deep breath to steady her voice, stunned at his sheer nerve. 'Really? I thought I still was.' She concentrated on remaining calm, unable to believe they were covering the same old ground yet again. 'Don't forget, it was *you* who moved on, not me, so I don't know why you're always so offended by everything I do.'

'Maybe if you were in a relationship too, you'd understand how I feel about Claire. Anyway, you know as well as I do that the only reason I left was because your interfering aunt made such a fuss and wound you up.' He considered his next words and glared at her down his aquiline nose, the same nose she had not so long ago found very attractive, but now wanted desperately to hit, hard. 'I'd still be living here with you if she hadn't interfered.'

'You mean if she hadn't caught you with Claire. Don't you think I might have discovered your girlfriend was pregnant at some point?' She heard the catch in her voice and could have bitten her tongue. She narrowed her eyes. 'Aunt Annabel found you practically having sex in Claire's car. She had every right to be upset with you.'

'Look, I am sorry about the baby. I know how that must hurt you.' He went to put a hand on her shoulder, but Bea stepped back before he could reach her. Simon shrugged and looked over her shoulder at the run-down hallway. 'Why can't you stop trying to punish me for being happy? The trouble with you is you spent far too much time with that old woman. Annabel might have been your godmother, and I understand how she took over when your mum died, but she's gone now. You need to stop hanging on to this heap of rubble. Then we can both move on.'

Bea didn't want to give him the satisfaction of seeing her lose her temper, or even worse, get upset. Her life had not worked out as she had planned and it hurt like hell, but she wasn't going to let him know how she felt. She clasped her hands together. 'I've already moved on, Simon, regardless of what you choose to believe.'

'Whatever you say.' He laughed, glancing at his latest Cartier watch. 'I couldn't care less, but I do want to know when you intend paying me my share of this mausoleum?'

Bea wondered if he was simply trying to punish her for not forgiving him for his affair when he'd asked her to. She felt the familiar nervous tingle expanding in her stomach. 'Simon, I don't know why you insist I buy you out of this place. You're a lawyer. You earn far more than I ever will and didn't need any extra money to buy your new apartment. The house was left to me, not you. Why don't we stop arguing and get this matter sorted, then we can have our decree absolute and neither of us have to bother with the other again.'

Simon groaned. 'Yes, well, are you going to get a mortgage to pay me what I'm owed, or am I going to take you to court to get an order for the damn money?'

Bea hesitated. She didn't have the money to fight him through the courts and he knew it. 'Simon, it's almost impossible to get a mortgage now, you know that as well as anyone. I'm going to need a little more time.'

'Time to find a way out of paying me, you mean.'

'No. I need to come up with a solution and you bullying me won't make it happen any sooner.'

'My lawyer explained everything in his letter to you. You have a year and a day from the date your aunt died, which will be when probate is concluded. That's May 10th next year. I think that's more than enough time to find a mortgage. You're the one insisting on keeping this crumbling 1920's dump, but Claire's given up work now she's pregnant and has decided she doesn't want to return when the baby's born. I need to get my finances sorted once and for all. We're going to get married as soon as the divorce is finalised and that can't happen until we've sorted the finances, so I'm not giving you any longer than I have to.'

'I'm not selling my house.' Bea clenched her fists.

He leant towards her, his eyes like steely flints. 'Be realistic, it's a mess.' He flung his arms wide, as if to encompass the cold hallway.

'That's my problem,' she said, knowing Aunt Annabel's legacy had been her magnificent garden with its endless species of plants she'd brought back over the decades from her travels.

Simon stepped back and made a point of looking her up and down for a final time. Shaking his head slowly, he sniggered before turning his back on her and marched outside towards his gleaming BMW.

Bea slammed the heavy oak door as hard as she could, realising too late it was not a good idea as a smattering of plaster cascaded like icing sugar on to the worn slate floor next to her.

She slumped down onto the bishop's seat. It wasn't in keeping with the period of the property, but Bea had bought it at her first auction with her godmother when she was sixteen. The cool, familiar grain in the wood soothed her. It was all very well, this bravado, Bea mused, but how was she going to afford to sort out the house?

'Drink,' Mel insisted, handing her a double gin and tonic, and settling down next to her. 'That man is such a moron. It's bad enough he did the dirty on you, let alone he still feels he has control over every aspect of your life. He must earn so much more than you, too.'

Bea shrugged miserably. 'Unfortunately, he does.' She took a mouthful of the refreshing liquid, and swallowed gratefully. 'Can you imagine he thought he could still use his key to get in?'

They sat silently in the hallway as her temper gradually subsided. Glancing at her newly French-manicured nails as they cupped the glass, she noticed for the first time the groove on her finger where her wedding ring used to be was finally fading. Soon there would be no trace of it at all. No trace of the Beatrice Porter of old. 'Mel, I'm not sure I can face going out,' she admitted. 'I look a mess and—'

'And nothing,' Mel interrupted standing up in front of her. 'It's my engagement party.' She held out her hands, displaying the brilliant diamond solitaire. 'When was the last time you were invited to celebrate something at Elizabeth Castle? You're not going to miss a second of it. It's not often we get out there and I want tonight to be special. You're my sister — well, half-sister — and you're going to enjoy yourself, whether you like it or not.'

Bea couldn't help laughing. 'Poor Grant, he doesn't have a clue what he's let himself in for, does he?'

'No.' Mel nudged her sister and smiled conspiratorially. 'He doesn't, and you're not going to tell him, either.'

* * *

Bea stepped off the castle ferry that had taken them to the tiny island in the bay, wishing she'd thought to wear more sensible heels. She gazed up at the turrets from the small docking area, amused that Mel had chosen somewhere so romantic to hold her engagement party. Following the signpost inside to the party area, Bea spotted Shani and Paul by the bar. No surprise there then, Bea smiled, amused to see her two closest friends deep in conversation. How they ever stopped talking long enough to fit in their jobs giving classes at the largest gym complex in town, she couldn't imagine.

'Hi, you two,' she said hugging them both. She looked down at Paul's blond head. 'These weren't the best idea,' she said, showing off her heels. 'I don't know why I thought they would be.'

'Only Mel could insist we all travel somewhere you have to get to by boat,' Shani said. 'I was hoping it'd be a little cooler in a castle, but these rooms are still hot.'

Bea nodded. She'd thought the same thing. She fanned her face with her bag. 'I love your hair, Shan.'

'If she has it any shorter everyone will assume she's had it shaved off completely.' Paul laughed. 'Shan, without that girly face you could be mistaken for a bloke. Tall, no boobs, no hair.'

Shani laughed and elbowed him in the ribs. 'Don't start with me! We might be flatmates, but you know I'm tougher than you'll ever be.'

'You two act like an old married couple sometimes,' Bea said, wincing at Paul's horrified expression.

'What a horrible thought.' He shuddered. 'Anyway, even if I was interested in women I can't imagine she'd be my type.'

Bea shook her head, so used to their banter and constant bickering. 'If people didn't know you two were so fond of each other they might be concerned by the way you converse.' She pulled a face at Shani, so tall in her own heels that she towered over them both.

'You're looking gorgeous,' Shani said. 'I can't believe you're actually out tonight.'

Bea nodded to where Mel was chatting to a group of her friends. 'Didn't have much choice, did I? I wasn't sure I would be much fun tonight after Simon's appearance at the house earlier.'

Paul narrowed his dark blue eyes. 'Bea, sweetheart, tonight is a Simon-free zone.' He put an arm around her protectively. 'It's Mel's night, and however annoying she may be, we're not going to let that spiteful prat ruin your fun.' He paused. 'Bloody hell, it's a little warm in here, isn't it?'

'Agreed,' Bea smiled, feeling better already. 'We're going to have a great evening.' She glanced around the grand room full of her sister's guests. 'Have Dad and Joyce arrived yet?'

'Can't have done, we haven't heard a drumroll announcing her entrance.' Paul grimaced. 'I don't know how your dad copes with the two of them in that house. Poor man must be a saint.'

'Look, there they are. Oh my God, Joyce's hair looks like a mutation of Margaret Thatcher's hairdo and a dollop of candyfloss.' Shani giggled and shook her head.

'She does the mother-of-the-bride bit to perfection, doesn't she?' Paul said. Bea and Shani laughed. 'Behave yourself, girls. Now, on to lighter matters. Have we all seen the ring?' He clapped his hands together. 'Assuming we have, what do we all think? Shani, you first.'

Shani mulled the question over for a second or two. 'It's pretty spectacular, that's all I know. It must have cost him a fortune.'

At the other side of the room Grant held up a glass and tapped it with a pen, calling for everyone's attention. 'Melanie and I,' Grant said, stepping nervously from one foot to the other, 'would like to thank you all for coming and sharing our celebrations with us on this steamy July evening.' Mel giggled and Bea ignored Paul's dig to her ribs. 'We've chosen our dream date and so that there are no excuses, we're going to let you all know exactly when our big day will be.' He winked at Mel. 'So, I want you all to keep Liberation Day free!'

'What did he say?' Shani hissed, her arched black eyebrows knitting together in confusion. Bea could hardly form the words. 'They're setting her wedding date for the 9th of May?'

Bea's heart pounded so much at the prospect, that she thought the others would hear it. 'It seems so,' she said, swallowing the lump in her throat.

'But that'll be the first anniversary of your Aunt Annabel's death.' Shani folded her tanned arms across her chest. 'Little bitch.'

Bea took a deep breath and slowly exhaled. She caught her stepmother's triumphant expression across the room as she dabbed her tear-filled eyes with a perfectly ironed, lace handkerchief and determined not to let Joyce see how upset this news had made her.

'Joyce is such a cow,' Paul said, a little too loudly for Bea's liking. 'I bet she's done it on purpose.'

Shani put her arm around Bea's shoulders not hearing what else, if anything, Grant was saying. It was enough that she would have to face that dreadful day at all without having to look happy at her half-sister's wedding.

'Right, come on – I'm getting too irritated to carry on just standing here.' Paul cupped his ear. 'Do you hear that?' he asked, grabbing Shani's hand as the speech finished and the first strains of 'You're the One That I Want' began filling the room. 'Come along girls, let's give it loads.'

Bea let them go to the dance floor and shook her head when they waved for her to join them. The room was far too hot. Bea needed some air and, relieved to have a quiet moment, picked up her bag and gingerly crossed the room and out through the open sliding doors, trying her best not to wobble. She wondered if it were the heels that were unbalancing her, or the overly polished parquet flooring that was the problem. She touched the cool granite castle wall before walking up to the metal railings and leaning against them, gazing across the bay where yachts moved gently in the calm sea. Bea sighed.

'You're not thinking of jumping, are you?' a baritone voice asked from the other side of the Canary palm next to her. 'Bit of a drastic way to make your escape, don't you think?'

Bea would recognise that brusque tone anywhere. She leaned precariously over the balcony in a vain attempt to peer around the tree. 'Fancy seeing you again so soon, Mrs Potter.' He touched her shoulder lightly from behind.

Bea swung round, embarrassed to have been caught looking the wrong way, grabbed at the palm frond to move it away from her face and slipped on the floor, landing with a heavy slap on her bum. 'Ouch.'

'Sorry.' He tried to stifle his laughter. 'I didn't mean to give you a fright. Here.' He held his hand out for her to take. 'Let me help you up.'

She closed her eyes momentarily, wishing he would disappear, and then looked up into those sparkly blue eyes as he waited patiently for her to take his hand. 'Thank you,' she mumbled, her heels not gripping the ground enough to let her stand up.

Luke bent down. 'Put your arms around my neck,' he said, barely hiding a smile.

Unable to see any other way she'd manage to stand without taking off the damn shoes, she reached up and took hold of him. Their faces millimetres apart, she breathed in the heady scent of his citrusy aftershave. Tingles shot to various parts of her anatomy she didn't want to think about right now, and as Luke placed her carefully back onto her feet, he stood upright and smiled. 'I hope you're not too sore.'

She could barely breathe as she looked up at him, so different now with his hair cut slightly shorter and his beard trimmed. Bea rubbed her bottom to sooth the bruising pain. There was something very appealing about him, despite how he enjoyed her small humiliation, and she knew without a doubt that the self-assured Adonis in front of her was the very last man on Earth she should allow herself to fall for.

3

SCORCHING HOT

Luke had to try hard not to let Bea see how amused he'd been by her confusion. Her eyes were the deepest jade he'd ever seen. They were so pretty, despite being narrowed in irritation, as she appeared to be stuck for words.

'My name's Beatrice.' She stepped forward, waving away the palm frond.

'Beatrix Potter,' he mused slowly, unable to help teasing her for a little longer.

The green eyes narrowed even further. 'No, it's Beatrice with a 'c' and Porter with an 'r' and I'll be changing my surname back to Philips first thing next week,' she said, straightening her short skirt and pulling her shoulders back so that she reached her full height of, he estimated, about five feet four without those heels.

'It's not such a bad name... it could be worse,' said Luke, feeling a little guilty for annoying her so much.

'That's easy for you to say. The worst thing is everyone assumes they're the first person to think of that joke.'

He tried to look a little serious. 'Annoying, to say the least, I should imagine.' He watched in silence as she studied his face, wondering if he should explain the bump in his nose was down to a particularly nasty rugby tackle several years earlier. If she wasn't so defensive, he would find it hard to resist kissing those pouting lips right now.

'When Mel gave me your business details,' she said, bringing him back to the present, 'she explained you were a friend of Grant's, though I've never heard him mention you before.'

Luke shrugged. 'School pals.' He didn't add that Grant was the one to break his nose so painfully. 'I only recently met up with him again and he invited me tonight.' He wished her eyes weren't quite so hypnotising. She was managing to stir up feelings he hadn't experienced since, well, since he'd decided that trusting people was a mug's game. 'I was going to make my excuses... I'm not sure this really is my thing,' he admitted, pleased to note she gave a momentary look of, what was it? Surprise? Disappointment? Stop it, he told himself, don't let her get under your skin. Pretty she may be, and there's something a little too intriguing about her. 'I'm glad I came now, though,' he admitted, immediately wondering why he'd said it out loud when he hadn't intended doing so.

She flushed slightly, the colour enhancing her prettiness. He'd bet she had no idea how lovely she looked. 'They're getting married on Liberation Day, too. That must have taken some arranging, don't you think?'

'Probably,' Bea said eventually. Luke frowned. Had he somehow managed to say the wrong thing? 'That'll be something of an ordeal to arrange,' Bea added. 'Although my stepmother will no doubt be delighted at the prospect. She's been dying for the excuse to arrange a wedding for ages.'

'I thought you were sisters? Although to be honest you're so fair and Mel's very dark, you are very different to look at.' He wished he could stop talking nonsense – she'd think he was nuts.

'My mum died when I was four. Joyce was my dad's secretary and they got married a few months later.'

He wasn't sure what to say to such honesty, noticing for the first time the deep sadness in this beautiful girl's eyes. His problems had been different to hers, but he saw she knew what it was like to be hurt, betrayed. Luke wasn't sure what to say next. 'That must have been a little strange for you to come to terms with?'

Bea shrugged. 'I don't remember it very well, if I'm honest. They sent me to stay with my godmother when they left for their honeymoon, and soon after that Joyce became pregnant with Mel. I loved living at The Brae and it suited Dad and Joyce for me to be where I was happiest, and so that's where I pretty much grew up.'

'Was your aunt your mum's sister then?' he asked, wanting to make the most of her openness. He had the feeling she didn't often speak so readily about her past. She seemed a little detached as she spoke, as if she was recalling something.

Bea nodded. 'If I'm honest, Aunt Annabel is the only mother I truly remember.'

'You must miss her very much?' He couldn't help asking such an obvious question, and the dark green pools of sadness in her eyes when she nodded made him want to take her in his arms and comfort her. He was about to change the subject when someone called her name from the doorway.

'Bea, there you are.'

Luke turned to see who had made her face light up so instantaneously, and watched as a blond man, about the same height as Bea, entered the room.

'Sorry, sweets, I didn't realise you had company,' he said, looking Luke up and down before smiling. Luke glanced at Bea waving her friend over to join them.

'Paul,' she said. 'Come and meet Luke. He's a friend of Grant's.'

Luke could feel Bea watching them as he shook Paul's hand.

When Paul didn't speak and gawped silently up at him, Luke wondered if maybe they wanted to talk in private. He turned to Bea and smiled. 'Maybe I'll catch you later,' he said. 'Pleasure to meet you, Paul,' he added, shaking Paul's hand once more before walking away. He glanced over his shoulder at her talking animatedly to her friend, before returning to the party. She might be beautiful, but where did this compulsion to look after her come from? She seemed perfectly capable of taking care of herself. Luke sighed. He had enough to focus on with his own near bankruptcy and problems with Chris. He regretted ever meeting the man, let alone agreeing to set up their building business together. Never mind, tonight wasn't the time for regrets. He forced a smile and went back to join Grant to congratulate him on his forthcoming wedding.

* * *

'Well, you're a dark horse,' Paul teased Bea once they had re-joined Shani. 'Fancy keeping such a magnificent specimen all to yourself!'

'He is drop-dead gorgeous, and so tall.' Shani sighed. 'How come I've never come across Luke Thornton before?'

'Do you know him?' Bea asked, unable to hide her interest.

'No, but I've seen his picture in the *Jersey Gazette* a few times. Something to do with a court case, I think. He's very ambitious, and a bit of a ladies' man, or so I'm told. Mind you, looking at him it's hardly surprising.' She winked at Bea. 'Good for you.'

'Good for me, nothing.' Bea frowned and rubbed her bottom again. Later she'd have to find the arnica cream she'd bought last year to put on the bruising. 'I slipped over on these bloody shoes and he had to help me up. It was so embarrassing. If Paul had come to the conversation a little later, he'd have probably heard us discussing the work his men will be doing on my house. I just hope Luke gives me a fair price, that's all.'

'Maybe I could offer to help out?' Paul teased, pursing his lips.

'I can't see you sanding down walls or being any good with a paintbrush,' Bea laughed.

'How do you know? I could be brilliant at it. Why don't I come along one day?'

'What, and embarrass me? I don't think so. He's a friend of Grant's, and I have a feeling he's doing him the favour rather than me.' She looked at the two disappointed faces in front of her. 'I doubt he'll be the one actually doing the work at The Brae, anyway – it'll more than likely be the two other guys who came to the house with him.'

'Er, excuse me,' interrupted Mel, from behind Shani. 'Grant said you were chatting to Luke... are you grateful to me now for giving you his number?'

'Never mind that.' Bea glared at her sister, happy to finally be able to confront her out of earshot from the other guests. 'Why are you getting married on Liberation Day? You know that day is going to be horrific for me.'

'It's not all about you, you know.' Mel ran her hands over her shiny black bob.

'It is a little insensitive though, Mel,' Shani said.

'More than a little, if you ask me,' Paul snapped.

Mel stood with her hands on her hips and looked at each of them in turn. 'The entire island has a holiday on Liberation Day and there are flags decorating many of the houses. I don't see why I can't make the most of those decorations, good moods and fun to hold my wedding.'

'But what about Bea?' Shani asked, resting a hand on Bea's shoulder.

'For pity's sake, surely it's a good thing to change the day from one of sad memories to one of celebration?'

Bea sighed. She'd like to think so, but it was too soon. 'Maybe in a year or two, but not for Annabel's first anniversary, Mel.'

'You're just being selfish, as usual. It's always got to be about you, hasn't it? Mum said you'd react like this.'

Paul glared at Mel and stepped forward. 'Leave it,' Bea said. She didn't need a full-scale row at this party. She took his arm and for a moment Bea thought Mel was about to slap him. 'Now isn't the time for this conversation.'

'Too bloody right it isn't. I'm sure you'll all excuse me,' Mel snapped. 'I think it's time I return to my friendlier guests.' She leant towards Bea. 'Once you've got over your sulking about my wedding date, remind me to talk to you about taking an injunction out against Simon. He can't be allowed to keep coming to your house and abusing you like he has been doing.'

Bea took a deep breath. She couldn't decide if Mel was really as unfeeling as she made out, or if it was down to her mother's influence about the wedding.

'She really doesn't get it, does she?' Paul said, as soon as Mel had walked away.

'She's so odd. One minute she's giving you what for about the wedding date, the next she wants to help you against Simon. I think I'm the one that doesn't get it, Paul,' Shani said, bemused by the exchange. 'She does love being a legal assistant though, doesn't she?' Shani turned to face Bea. Thinking for a moment, she asked. 'So, what has Simon been up to this time?'

Bea shook her head 'No, we're not going to talk about him, and I don't want you two getting involved in my rows with Mel. We've always been like this, so it's bound to be worse with the wedding coming up. Those things always cause friction within families.'

'Especially yours, it seems,' Paul said, still red in the face with irritation. 'If her mother wasn't so desperate to push Mel forward in your dad's affections, there wouldn't be this problem between you both. You get along perfectly well when Joyce isn't pushing Mel to do things.'

Bea had to agree with him. She wasn't sure if it was because her mum had died so suddenly in that car crash that she'd become this mythical figure to them all. She recalled asking Aunt Annabel about it a few times years before and she'd always maintained that her father never stopped loving Bea's mum, and just because he'd married his secretary so soon after didn't mean that he'd forgotten her. Bea supposed she was right.

'Getting back to more interesting topics.' Paul indicated to where Luke was talking to a group consisting mainly of fluttery-eyed females.

Bea looked over at him. Luke seemed to sense he had an audience, and turned his head to look straight into Bea's eyes. Paul sighed. Then, just before she managed to tear her gaze away from him, he turned back to his friends and continued with his conversation.

'He really is hot,' Shani groaned. 'Powerful looking, which is always preferable when you're as tall as me.'

'Shame he's not interested in you then, isn't it?' Paul teased, clutching his shoulder where she slapped him. 'Ouch.'

'Paul wasn't kidding, though – you're a lucky girl.'

'Will you both stop it,' Bea whispered. 'We're not teenagers any more, and he's only being polite. I'm a prospective client of his, nothing more. To be honest, I won't be able to use him for much of the work because I've hardly got any money to spare for it. Anyway, I hate to disappoint you both, but I'm going on a date with Tom, probably next Saturday night, though he's got a lot on at the moment, so maybe some time after that.'

There was a heavy silence. Bea wished one of them would speak.

'Tom? Tom Brakespear?' Paul walked over to a nearby sofa and slumped down, patting the seats either side of him. 'Sit, spill, I want to know everything. Wasn't he that beautiful boy from Jersey whose heart you broke when you dumped him to go out with Simon? The one you went to uni with?'

'He is.' Bea nodded, relieved to have so successfully drawn their attention away from Luke and remembering how amused her father had been that the boy she'd gone out with at university was also from Jersey.

'Where's he been all these years, then?' Shani asked sitting down next to them.

'London mainly, I believe. He moved back home to Jersey a couple of years ago with his wife and two kids, but he's getting divorced. Oddly enough his job is administering trust companies like me, and he's my new line manager at work.' Bea enjoyed their wide-eyed surprise at her news.

'He's the new boss you were wondering about the other week?'

Bea nodded. 'I couldn't believe it when he was introduced to us all on Monday.'

'Won't that be a little awkward?' Paul asked thoughtfully. 'After all, you didn't part on great terms.'

'He seems fine.' Bea shrugged. Meeting Tom again had been far easier than she'd ever hoped it would be.

'Are you sure it's a good idea to go out with him, though?' Shani picked up her drink, stared at it for a moment and placed it back down on the table without drinking from the glass.

'He asked me, and I couldn't think of a reason to turn him down. I thought you both liked Tom, and let's face it, you two have been desperate for me to go out with someone. You should be relieved.'

'We, um, we are,' Shani said unconvincingly. 'But surely, if you have the chance of going out with someone new and exciting, like Luke, then why bother with Tom?'

'Tom has asked me and Luke hasn't. And it may not have occurred to you, but I can't imagine I'd appeal to Luke in that way.'

'Why not?' they asked in unison.

'Mel reckons he has enough on his plate right now.' She checked Luke wasn't within earshot and leant forward, lowering her voice. 'And looking at him, you can see why. He's obviously a popular guy, and busy with his business.'

'I'd rugby tackle him to the ground if he came to my house,' Shani said.

Bea laughed. 'You probably would too, but I can't really see me literally flinging myself at a bloke. Anyway, it's not a real date with Tom,' Bea changed the subject. 'We're only going out for a meal to catch up.'

'It'll do you good and should take your mind off Simon and that house for a bit. You're far too young to have been left with all these responsibilities,' Paul mumbled, taking a sip of his drink and gazing longingly in Luke's direction.

'Aunt Annabel expected to be here for years yet,' Bea said sadly. 'She was only seventy.'

'Yes, well I'm glad you're going out with Tom. Is he still hot?' Shani asked, nudging Bea.

'He hasn't changed much. In fact, I think he's better looking now. Not so much boy band, more rock band.' Bea laughed as she pictured Tom in a leather jacket and jeans, his hair all ruffled.

'Rocker in a grey suit,' Shani teased. 'He was too immaculate to ever be in any band, apart from maybe a sixties crooner. At least you know him, and knowing you you'll want someone you feel relaxed with, at least to start off with.'

Bea smiled. 'We'll see. He might have changed, but he used to be good fun and didn't spend all our dates preening in front of other women, like Simon seems to do now. I have to admit I'm looking forward to Saturday.'

* * *

Bea slowly opened her eyes after an unsettling night dreaming that she had found a secret passage behind her wardrobe where she might find the mysterious legacy her aunt had left her.

It was another sweltering day. She stretched, relishing the heat, then remembering her aunt's plants in the greenhouse threw back the bedsheet and stood up. Staring at the antique wardrobe standing an inch or so away from the wall, it was obvious there were no hidden entrances behind it. She'd better go and water the plants before the temperature rose too much and the heat burnt their leaves. Bea pulled back the curtains and opened the window a little wider, staring out at the garden and wishing her aunt had given her a hint or clue as to what the Jersey Kiss could be. Pulling on a pair of denim shorts and a bikini top, she went downstairs.

As she stepped back into the kitchen to slip on her bunny slippers, someone rapped at the heavy doorknocker.

'Oh, hi.' She was surprised to see Luke standing on her doorstep on a Sunday morning, wishing she'd thought to brush her cloud-like bed hair.

'I hope I didn't disturb you,' he asked, eyes twinkling, taking in her fluffy pink slippers.

She felt her cheeks heat up as she followed his gaze down to the floppy pink rabbit ears she secretly loved. 'A fun birthday present from Paul.'

He shook his head. 'I know its Sunday, but I was on my way to my boat and thought I'd quickly check exactly what work you still want doing.'

'But I thought I told you?' Bea said, wondering if she'd missed anything.

'You did.' He glanced up at the plasterwork. 'But it's a big job, and your sister hinted about a few issues with your ex-husband and this place.'

Bea clenched her teeth together in irritation. Why didn't Mel mind her business? 'I'll pay your bills, if that's what you're worried about.'

Luke frowned. 'No, of course not. I just didn't want to put added pressure on you with building work, if you weren't sure you wanted it done.'

'I don't know exactly what you've heard, but if I change my mind about your men coming here, I'll tell you. Okay?' It was too hot to be so angry, Bea decided. She hurriedly tied her hair into a ponytail.

'Yes. I'm sorry I upset you, it wasn't intentional.'

She watched as he looked around the large hallway with its wide staircase that wound around the walls to the first floor, and then to the original black-and-white tiles on the expanse of floor. 'Look, I'm sorry if I was rude,' Bea said, aware she wasn't being very welcoming. 'I'm not a morning person, as you've probably noticed.' She stepped back. 'Please, come in.' She led him down the passage at the back of the hallway towards the kitchen. 'Would you like a coffee?'

Bea made them both a drink.

'You looked like you were having a lot of fun at the party.' Luke leant against the kitchen table, appearing more relaxed than Bea felt.

'Yes, I had a good time,' she said, the embarrassment of her fall making her toes curl. As Bea passed the mug to him, his fingers grazed her hand lightly, shooting tiny electric currents throughout her entire body. 'I'm not usually that clumsy.'

'I think they'd polished the floor a little too highly,' he said. Bea wasn't so sure, but smiled, hoping that was what he'd thought. 'I'm looking forward to putting this place in order,' Luke continued. 'It's a beautiful twenties home and still has so much character left. You're very lucky to own it.' He held the hot china mug in between his large hands. 'It's a big house for just one person. Wouldn't you prefer something a bit smaller?'

Bea shrugged. 'I would if this place didn't hold so many memories for me. It's more of a home to me than anywhere else.'

'It has a certain charm; I can see why you want to restore it.' Luke looked directly into her eyes. 'I couldn't help noticing the beautiful gardens as I drove up.'

Bea nodded. 'It is pretty amazing. My godmother planted the orchard herself when she first moved here years ago. She sourced so many different plants and trees from her travels over the years. It's why I'd hate to move so much. All my memories are here – the important ones, that is – and I can't take her garden with me if I have to move.'

'There aren't many people your age who are into gardening like you are.' He sipped his coffee.

Bea enjoyed his questions. It helped her to think of things that usually only upset her, since Aunt Annabel had died. 'Maybe not, but it's a way of life for me. I can't imagine not spending time out there. My aunt adored her garden. She put years of her expertise as a garden designer into lovingly restoring it back to how the original owners had planned it, adding her own special extras as she went, of course.'

'She wasn't so interested in the house,' Luke smiled. 'Did she live here long?'

'Decades. It was bought for her by her second husband, Antonio. He was an Argentinian polo player. They loved each other very much, although she couldn't have children, which broke her heart. He bought her this house and encouraged her in her love of gardening.'

'He died, too?'

'Years ago, and they'd only been married a few years. It was very sad for her. Then my mother died, my father remarried and after a few years they sent me off to boarding school. I was really home-sick, so my aunt insisted I came home to Jersey and pretty much took me on. I think it helped her to come to terms with the loss of the two most important people in her life. Well, that's what my dad seems to think, and I have to agree with him.'

They stood in silence for a few minutes. Bea wondered why she'd been so open with this man about such personal and still painful issues. What was it about him? she wondered.

'Is that a walled kitchen garden through there?' he asked, peering over her shoulder to the wooden French windows halfway along the kitchen wall.

'That's my favourite place of all. I'll show you, if you like?' When he nodded, she got up and walked over to push them open, the creaky wooden doors reminding her of another job to add to her to-do list. 'These will definitely collapse on me one of these days,' she said, not joking.

The heat of the morning sun warmed her face even further and she breathed in the sweet scent of rosemary. 'My herbs,' she pointed. 'The vegetables are along there – all organic, of course – and the smaller fruit trees along that wall. Over there's my aunt's greenhouse,' she said, wondering why she had bothered stating the obvious to him. 'My greenhouse,' she corrected herself.

He surveyed the area, eyebrows raised in what she presumed was appreciation. 'Impressive,' he said. 'And you look after all this by yourself?' Bea shrugged. 'I wouldn't think you'd have the time, what with holding down a job and doing up the house.'

'I'm not able to spend as much time as I'd like here, but I catch up on the most urgent things at the weekends. I'm dreading the winter when it'll get dark so much earlier. I hate the short days.'

'Maybe, but you've got more than enough to do inside this place to keep you going until the spring,' he said. 'You're very lucky having a home with such character.'

'I know,' she agreed, ridiculously thrilled he seemed to like the place so much. 'I just wish I still had Annabel around to enjoy everything with. She loved this place so much. I'm determined to bring it back to its former glory, even if I end up having to sell in the end.'

'Why would you sell it?' He picked up a small trowel she'd left on one of the brick pathways and placed it on the rickety metal table in the corner of the small patio. 'Is this what your sister meant when she referred to problems with your ex-husband?'

Bea nodded. 'I might not have a choice about selling. My ex-husband wants me to buy him out, but I'm not sure I'll be able to raise enough money.'

Luke looked up from the raised vegetable border and frowned. 'That would be a pity. I hope you can sort something out.'

'Me too.' She picked up her dented metal watering can and filled it at the tap, showering the bases of her plants. 'How about you, where do you live?'

'If you saw where I lived, you'd never believe I was in the building trade,' he laughed. 'It's a disgrace.'

'Why?' She straightened up, not sure why she was surprised. 'Surely you have all the know-how and contacts to do any work you need?'

'True, but I don't seem to have the time,' he admitted. He pushed his fringe back from his tanned face. 'I've got so much work lined up, and...' he hesitated. 'I'm a bit snowed under, which is why I'm calling in on a Sunday.'

So that was why he decided to visit her at such an irregular time. 'Where do you live?'

'Near St Catherine's Woods.' He smiled thoughtfully. 'It's only a small granite cottage, but it's in a leafy area, quite quirky from the outside, and almost uninhabitable. So I'm living on a boat for the time being.'

Bea could picture him on a boat and liked the idea. 'Sounds fun. I don't know how you manage to fit all your belongings into a boat though?' she asked, making him laugh.

'Probably because I don't have that many things to store. A few shoes and no handbags.'

Bea liked the sound of his laugh. He seemed so carefree for once, and it suited him. Resisting a strong urge to lean forward and kiss him, she turned away and picked up their mugs to take them back inside.

4

AUGUST – SOWING THE SEED

'It's so hot out here,' complained Paul, fanning his face with an old notepad as Bea silently sowed tiny seeds into compost-filled trays in the small greenhouse. 'Do you have to do that now?'

'Stop moaning. You know I do. Why don't you go and wait for me in the house?' She looked over at him and smiled. 'Anyone would think you were going somewhere special in that outfit.'

'What, this old thing?' He winked, holding his arms out and turning around for her. 'I thought you'd like it.'

She loved his baby blue T-shirt, but it wasn't exactly the right clothing for a dusty greenhouse. 'You know I can't wait to hear all about your visitor, and you'll only forget the time like you always do out here, and then I won't end up hearing the more interesting details,' he moaned. He stepped outside and continued fanning himself. 'Hurry up, before I melt out here.'

'I told you, there isn't anything to tell. So be quiet and let me get on with this.'

'I thought we could go out for a quiet lunch, somewhere away from paint pots and peat bags.'

'Sorry, I can't,' Bea said, trying to concentrate as best she could on placing just one seed into each of the tiny sections of the plastic container. 'Anyway, where's Shani today? I didn't think she had any classes on a Sunday.'

'Out with this new bloke of hers, Harry-someone-or-other. Besotted, she is. I offered to join them, but she told me to bugger off.'

'I don't blame her,' Bea said, throwing him a washed ice-lolly stick and biro. 'Here, write "Beetroot" on that for me, would you? Then you can come with me to buy paint for the house.' Paul grimaced. 'Choosing paint can be fun, you know?' Bea laughed. 'Although, I can see by your expression that you wouldn't be interested in helping me with the prep work I need to do on the bathroom and box room tonight then?'

'No, I wouldn't,' he said. 'I've got a good bottle of red waiting for me back at the flat and it's going to need my attention far more than your decorating.'

* * *

Returning home after a long day at work, Bea almost fell through her front door. She managed not to drop the shopping bags weighing her down, and kicked the door closed behind her with the heel of her court shoe. She noticed a large white envelope in the wire basket attached to the back of the door and put the bags down on the floor, resting them against the wall. Taking a deep breath, Bea ripped open the envelope. Luke's quotation was lower than she had feared and suspected he was being a bit too charitable for his own good. After reading it through several times and debating for a little longer, she knew her conscience shouldn't let her accept the amount. She picked up the phone to give him a call. 'Luke, hi, it's Bea.'

'Bea,' he said. 'You've received my quotation, then?'

'Yes, thank you, and I'd like to accept it. Although, I'm sure it's more reasonable than it probably should be.'

'Not at all. How soon can you have all the prep work done?' He was more business-like than she had expected. She felt a little foolish for being so casual on the phone in the first place.

'Um, well, your men can start on the bathroom as soon as they like.' She quickly tried to estimate how long it would take her to do the work needed on the box room. 'I can concentrate on the others in my free time. I'll make sure I'm finished for whenever your men are ready to start work on them.'

'Great, I'll have two men there tomorrow. Will eight o'clock be ok?'

'Perfect. Thank you.' She hurriedly rang off with the distinct feeling she had been dismissed. Bea stared at the phone for a moment. When she caught sight of the rickety banister, she was reminded of a pair of fiercely blue eyes and the hairs on the back of her neck instantly stood up. Whether this was from some sort of lust or embarrassment, she couldn't tell – she'd lost count of the years that had passed since her last real 'first date'. Dating was something in her hazy past, like her onesie and sneaker wedges. Maybe it should just be left there.

Bea carried her shopping bags into the kitchen and unpacked everything before going to fetch her hammer and chisel-like tool to begin removing the ugly chocolate-coloured tiles from the house bathroom. She found it hard to imagine her godmother ever thinking they were tasteful. With one wall finished, Bea brushed the dust from her hair and took a shower. 'I must be clinically insane to attempt to do all this.'

* * *

Two men in a white van arrived at exactly eight o'clock the next morning. They followed Bea as she led them out to the disused stables at the back of the house. 'You'll find the bathroom suites in there,' she said. 'Sorry about the mess. I'll get around to clearing all the junk out one of these days.'

'No problem, love,' the older of the two men assured her. 'You leave us to it. Luke has explained everything.'

'It's looking great,' she told Luke when he came to check the work later on, relieved that she'd showered and changed in to her favourite summer dress and sandals. 'I didn't expect for them to work on a Saturday, too.'

He stared at her for a few seconds. 'They're good blokes and both happy for the overtime. You need to get the house sorted and I thought it best if they came today, to get as much done as possible.'

'Thank you. Would you like a coffee, or something cold?'

'Coffee for me, thanks.' He followed her down the stairs and through to the cool kitchen.

Luke tilted his head down to her level and kissed her, causing Bea's mind to go blank.

'Sorry, I probably shouldn't have done that,' he apologised, looking anything but sorry. 'You look so pretty with your hair up and those loose blonde strands over your cheeks.'

Bea attempted to tuck some of the hair behind her ears. 'My ex-husband always thought I looked better in suits and high heels,' she said, unable to think straight at this unexpected turn of events.

'Then he's a fool.' He leant forward and kissed her once again. This time Bea responded instinctively.

'I come bearing gifts,' Shani shouted from the hallway. 'I thought you could do with some chocolate digestives. We'll put them in the fri...'

Shocked, Bea stiffened and stepped back. Luke walked to the other side of the kitchen as Shani entered the room.

'Hello, there.' Shani widened her eyes and pulled a face at Bea. 'I didn't realise you had company.' She strode purposefully into the kitchen. Dropping the Saturday papers onto the worn pine table and kicking off her flip-flops as she sat, she crossed one long leg over the other. Shani glanced from Luke and back to Bea, raising an eyebrow at Bea. She held out the packet of biscuits. 'These need to go in the fridge.'

Bea turned to Luke. 'You remember Shani from the party, don't you?'

Luke smiled and nodded. 'Of course.'

'Phew, it's hot.' Shani's lips drew back into a wide smile as she arched an eyebrow.

Bea thought her friend was enjoying their obvious discomfort a little too enthusiastically. '*Shani.*'

'Well, it is,' she argued. 'It must be getting on for twenty-nine degrees out there.' She turned so Luke couldn't see her and winked at Bea. 'You look pretty today.'

'She does, doesn't she?' he said quietly, glancing at his watch, barely able to hide the hint of a smile. 'I'd better be off.' He placed his mug on the draining board. 'See you on Monday, Bea.' He nodded politely at Shani. 'Nice to see you again.' For once, Bea noted, Shani didn't come out with a quick retort. 'Don't worry,' he told Bea, as she went to follow him, 'I'll see myself out.'

They listened to his footsteps until they heard the front door close heavily behind him.

'Oh. My. God.' Shani squeezed Bea's arm, hurting her in her excitement. 'He's so...' Shani sighed. 'Well, big and impressive, and if you think you can convince me there's nothing going on then you don't know me at all. The atmosphere was electric when I came in.'

Bea turned to wash up the used mugs. 'He kissed me.' She almost breathed the words and touched her lips with her fingertips, unable to believe what had just happened.

'Alle-bloody-lujah,' cheered Shani. 'And before you start to justify this to yourself, I'm relieved that maybe now you'll begin to see yourself as the gorgeous girl you are. You need to get back some of the self-esteem you had pre-Simon.'

'He's the opposite of Simon, which is probably why I find him so attractive, but I don't think what happened meant anything to him. I think it was a spur of the moment impulse.'

'We'll see.' Shani's voice interrupted her thoughts. She picked up her jacket. 'Never mind biscuits, I'm taking you to the Bunker for a cup of tea and some of their delicious carrot cake.'

'Okay, but I need to go to St Brelade's beach afterwards.'

'To the polo? I'd have thought you'd want to stay well away. Memories and all that.'

Bea had to agree; it was the last place she'd choose to be today. 'I'm not going by choice, but I received a phone call from one of the committee members reminding me that Aunt Annabel is one of the sponsors of the event. She donated a trophy and someone else has to present it on the day.'

'Ah, I did wonder why you were wearing a dress and those gorgeous sandals.' Shani walked over and gave her a hug. 'I'm sorry. I don't suppose you can turn it down?'

'Not really.'

* * *

As they walked up to the converted WWII bunker, built during the occupation on St Aubin's beachfront, Bea couldn't help thinking how pleased she was to get out of the house. She'd been dreading going to the polo, but now at least she could keep her mind off it a little until it was time to go to the match. Shani went to the counter to give their order and Bea sat down at a table near the window that had, during the Occupation, been the space where a large gun faced out towards the channel, guarding the Nazi-occupied island from attack.

'You all right?' Shani asked, sitting down opposite Bea. 'I'll come with you this afternoon.'

'Thanks, I didn't think you'd miss an opportunity for staring at tight bums in jodhpurs.'

Shani laughed. 'Cheeky cow. You're right though, it'll perk up my mood no end.' She smiled at Bea. 'It's still very soon, you know. You mustn't expect too much of yourself. Losing Annabel is like losing a parent for you.'

'It is. I was remembering how she used to bring me here after school sometimes.'

Shani placed a hand on Bea's arm. 'I know it's hard for you losing her, but I'm sure once you sort out this problem with Simon you'll feel a little more settled.'

'You're right. When I can talk to Mel without wanting to argue with her, I need to find out more about her suggestion of taking out an injunction. And as far as Luke is concerned, I'm not even going to let myself think about how gorgeous he is. I'd rather be alone than with someone who's going to end up breaking my heart. I might only be thirty, but I've got more responsibility than expected, and I can't afford to go out to clubs with the rest of you all the time.'

'Well, whatever you say,' Shani added, as the waitress placed their plates of food down in front of them, 'I think it's going to be very interesting having him coming to your house each day. I can't wait to see how it all turns out after that kiss.'

'Just eat your cake.' Bea pushed a fork towards her friend and shook her head.

Shani dug her fork into her cake and took a mouthful. Bea did the same, surprised when Shani grimaced and pushed her plate away. 'What's wrong with it? You love this cake.'

'Nothing.' She forced a laugh. 'I just don't feel like it for some reason.'

'Is everything okay with you and Harry?'

Shani nodded. 'Yes, he's great. I adore him.'

'So why do you look so miserable whenever you think no one's watching?'

Shani narrowed her eyes at Bea. 'You don't miss much, do you?'

'Well?'

'Nothing. Eat yours and then we'd better get to the polo match. You can't be late if you're presenting a trophy, then you've got your date with Tom to look forward to.'

Bea popped a forkful of cake into her mouth and studied her friend. 'You're sure everything's okay?'

'Yes. Too much sex has probably just turned my brain a little, that's all.'

5

SPRINKLING OF SAND

Bea was glad she'd worn a sleeveless cotton dress and gladiator sandals. The heat was tremendous. She re-tied her ponytail, slid her sunglasses over her eyes and waited for the teams to come out. Grateful to be one of the VIPs for the day, she took a sip of her champagne cocktail and smiled at Shani. 'You glad you came?'

'Hell, yes.' Shani leant in and lowered her voice. 'You didn't tell me we'd be getting free drinks and mixing with the nobs, though.'

'I didn't realise. I only checked the invitation on our way here to make sure we had the correct time.' Bea walked out onto the balcony reserved for the invited guests. 'Bloody hell.'

'What?' Shani looked out to the beach below. 'Luke Thornton. You never mentioned he played polo.'

Bea felt the familiar contraction in her stomach muscles. Aunt Annabel would have approved, she thought, smiling and feeling more cheerful than she had all day. 'I didn't know.'

She watched as the horses and riders moved into their teams and halted in front of the balcony to be introduced. Luke patted his horse's sleek neck. He looked up and his gaze immediately met Bea's. He smiled and gave her a nod.

'He's gorgeous,' Shani whispered, sounding as if she was in pain. 'I thought he had money worries, though? How can he afford polo ponies?'

'I was thinking the same thing,' Bea admitted, raising her glass to him slightly.

Watching the chukkas took Bea back to when she'd been taken to England by her aunt a couple of times. This time though, with the waves lapping the beach behind the marked-off arena and the sand being thrown up by the horses' hooves, it was different.

Luke came on with a different pony for his third chukka and she watched him stroke the grey neck, slowly calming the agitated animal down as best he could. The ball was rolled in and the players went after it. She stifled a scream when one of Luke's opponents bumped into his pony's shoulder a little harder than she thought acceptable, but watched as, unfazed, Luke chased after the ball. They swung their mallets and Luke's connected with the ball first. He scored. A horn sounded, terminating the chukka.

'Yay, he's done it!' screamed Shani, jumping up and down with Bea, both forgetting where they were in their excitement.

Bea shook her hand to get rid of most of the drink she'd spilled on her arm.

'Wow, I didn't know it was such fun to watch. We'll have to come again next year.'

'You're not kidding.' Bea laughed. Maybe it had been the best thing to do, coming here. At least now she could think of polo without feeling miserable. 'Aunt Annabel would have been in her element here.'

'She's not the only one.'

An official came up behind Bea and cleared his throat. 'Mrs Porter, it's time to present the trophy to the winning team.'

Bea handed her drink to Shani and followed the official down the steps to the beach. She waited as they announced the winning team and was handed the heavy trophy just before the team captain's name was called out.

Luke stepped forward and Bea couldn't help smiling up at him. She held out the trophy and congratulated him. Luke held it up in the air and the crowd cheered for their local winners.

'Please step this way for photos.' The photographer from the Gazette arranged them in position, and Bea and Luke smiled and shook hands once more for the camera.

Luke bent down and kissed her on the cheek. 'I didn't expect you to be here, but it was great to see you and your friend up on the balcony.'

Bea couldn't hide her happiness. 'I haven't been to a polo match for a few years, and never one on a beach. I didn't know you played.'

'Shall we get a drink?' Luke handed the trophy over to his teammates and accompanied her back into the hotel. 'They're not my ponies,' he said, pulling a sad face. 'I wish they still were. I had to sell mine when the financial situation with my business became untenable. I couldn't owe people money and keep such a luxury for myself.'

'So, who do they belong to?'

'A friend of my father's. He'd seen me play on them and knew they were good. He made me an offer and I couldn't refuse.'

'So, why didn't he ride them today then?'

As they walked onto the balcony, Luke took two glasses of champagne from a tray held out by a waiter. 'His son was supposed to, but he broke his wrist falling from one of them a week ago and when they asked me to step in, I was only too pleased to do so.'

'You were great,' Shani said, smiling widely. 'Where did you learn to ride like that?'

Luke laughed. 'When I was a kid at my dad's farm in South Africa. It's very popular over there and not such an elite sport as it seems to be in the UK. Would you ladies like to join me tonight?

The team are going out for something to eat first and then on to a club.'

Bea wished she could accept his offer, but felt unable to let Tom down. 'I'd love to, but I'm already doing something, sorry.'

'I'm meeting Harry, so I won't be able to either.'

He shrugged. 'Never mind, maybe next time. I'd better go and catch up with the others.' He kissed Bea on the cheek once more and smiled at Shani. 'Have a lovely evening.'

* * *

Bea couldn't shake off the image of Luke playing polo and wished she was looking forward to an evening with him rather than Tom. She was pleased Tom didn't still hold her decision to leave him for Simon against her.

'You look very glamorous.' Tom said, dabbing at his mouth with his napkin. 'I thought you'd enjoy the view here.'

Bea looked out of the large picture window across to Gorey Castle and the long stretch of Grouville beach beyond. 'It's fabulous. I haven't eaten here for ages. It's good to be back.' Bea sighed heavily. 'I don't think I've eaten so much in years.' She took a sip of her wine. 'I can see now why they have such a good reputation here.'

'I'm glad you've enjoyed it. I used to bring my son and daughter here for the children's lunches on a Sunday, when things were friendlier between me and Vanessa,' he said. 'Now, though, I seem to see them less and less.'

'That's so sad, Tom.' Bea reached out to touch his hand. 'I do hope things get sorted out soon.'

Tom nodded. 'Me too.' He sat quietly for a moment, returning to the present when the waitress asked them if they wanted coffees or liqueurs. Bea nodded. 'Coffee for me, please.'

'Make that two,' he said before looking across at Bea. 'So, who's doing the work on your house?'

'He's someone Mel's fiancé suggested, Luke Thornton. Do you know him?'

'A friend of yours, is he?'

She was a little taken aback by the sudden change in the tone of his voice. 'An acquaintance rather than a friend,' Bea explained, aware she was doing her best to keep her voice light. The waitress arrived with the coffees, and Bea stirred the muddy-coloured liquid unnecessarily. 'He gave me a good price, which is a relief because I don't really have much money available for the work.'

Tom stared into his cup for several seconds.

'What is it?' Bea asked. 'Tell me.'

Tom looked around the room and then moved a little closer to her. 'I shouldn't really confide in you about this, but you're a trust officer, so you'll understand how these things work.' Bea nodded. It niggled a little that Tom was a director already, even though their qualifications were the same and they had been in the business almost the same length of time. 'I look after a couple of companies for Luke's partner.'

Bea tried to steady her breathing. She could sense she wasn't going to like what was coming next. 'Go on,' she whispered.

'They're both under investigation.'

'For money laundering?' she whispered. It changed everything. Damn Tom for telling her this confidential information. Now she was aware Luke was under investigation she would have to watch every word she said to him.

'Sorry, Bea, but I couldn't let you, in your professional capacity, get close to someone who was being investigated. You know that if you let slip that this is going on, you could get a maximum sentence of five years in prison, and any criminal record will make a big difference to your career.'

'I'm aware of my duties, thank you, Tom. Tipping off is one of the worst offences I could be caught doing.' She sighed. 'And if you hadn't told me, then I wouldn't have known, or been in the position where I could do so.'

Tom sat back in his chair and folded his arms. 'Ahh, yes, I see what you mean.'

'You shouldn't be discussing your clients with me. This matter is confidential, you know that.'

'Yes.' He took her hands in his. 'But would you prefer I kept it to myself? If he were to discover he was being investigated, you – as an employee of the trust company – would be an obvious suspect to have tipped him off, and we both know how difficult it would be to prove you didn't say anything.'

'True.'

'At the very least you'd probably stand to lose your job.'

And then how would I afford a mortgage for my house? Bea thought. 'What about him working at the house, though?'

'Just try to get him to finish what he's doing as soon as you can. It would be even more suspicious if you suddenly cancelled everything.'

'Do they really think he's capable of money laundering?'

'You know as well as I do that the first thing we're taught in anti-money laundering training is that they don't look a certain way. They can be anyone, from any walk of life. So, who knows?' Tom shrugged. 'He and his partner have made vast amounts of money through real estate and development over the past few years. They made a lot of money very quickly.'

The waitress placed a silver tray on their table with their bill and a couple of dark chocolates. Tom picked up the bill thoughtfully. 'They were school friends and although Luke is probably less likely to be involved in this, the fact that they are partners means he's involved in some way.' He frowned and looked across at her. 'I'm sorry, Bea, but I thought you should know.'

Bea nodded. 'You're right, thanks. It just makes things a little awkward, that's all.' She still wished she hadn't been told. It changed everything.

* * *

'Don't just sit there, pedal. Faster.'

'Shut up, Paul, I'm only here because you wouldn't stop nagging.'

'You haven't been to the gym for over a year now and you can't keep making excuses.'

'I think you'll find I can,' Bea grumbled, deciding that as soon as she was out of Paul's studio she would not be returning.

'So how was the date?' asked Paul, running on a treadmill that looked to Bea as if it belonged on *Star Trek*.

'It wasn't really a date, more like two old friends catching up.'

'Sounds a bit more like a date to me.' He pressed a few buttons and the machine sped up. 'Come on, you, keep going.'

'Bloody hell, Paul, I'm going to die here.'

'You're not. Now pedal.' She sat up for a moment and wiped her sweaty forehead with her T-shirt. 'Do you think there's something odd going on with Shani?'

Paul frowned, but continued running. 'No, what do you mean?'

Bea thought for a moment, then picked up her bottle of water and took a sip. 'I don't know, I thought she was acting a little odd the other day when we went for tea and cake.'

'Nah, she's fine. I'd have noticed if she wasn't.' He shook his head at Bea. 'Stop trying to distract me. You're going to do at least three miles. Get on with it.'

Bea groaned. This was so boring! No wonder she hadn't been to the gym in so long. 'I didn't tell you about my visit to Mr Peters at the bank, did I?' she puffed, resting forward on the handlebars.

'No, but you can tell me without stopping for yet another breather.' Paul winked at her. 'I suppose this is because you received another letter from Simon?' He waved at her to keep pedalling. 'Go on, what did he say?'

'I couldn't really put it off any longer. I explained everything to him and he asked to see my credit card statements and gave me an application form to complete. He was lovely,' Bea said, thinking back to the man she'd met the day before.

'What happens next?'

She shrugged. 'He's going to check out my figures. He doesn't think it'll be good news for the entire amount Simon wants.'

'Why not? You earn a decent wage, surely?'

'Not that good, obviously.' Bea stopped pedalling again. 'He's sending out an estate agent to value the house and they'll be able to make a more informed decision after that. I should know later this week, hopefully. At least then I'll have a better idea about what I'm dealing with.'

'Good for you. I'm sure it'll be good news. And if it isn't you'll just have to try at another bank.'

'I have,' admitted Bea. 'This is the third bank I've contacted. I did the other two online and spoke to someone, but they weren't positive either. Mr Peters knew my aunt and I've banked with them since I was a teenager, when Aunt Annabel opened an account with them for me. I only looked at the online sites to see what I could expect. I didn't think it was going to be so difficult. It's not as if I owe money all over the place.'

Paul stopped his running machine and went over to sit at a torturous-looking contraption in the corner. 'Did he remember you?'

Bea nodded. 'He did. I was going to ask him if he recalled her mentioning anything about A Jersey Kiss, but he started chatting about Aunt Annabel and how they'd known each other since primary school, then he went off on a tandem and I stopped listening.'

Paul let the handle he'd been pulling on revert to its original position and stared at her thoughtfully, before bending over, laughing hysterically. He wiped his eyes before laughing again.

'What?' Bea frowned.

'I presume you meant 'tangent'.'

'Sorry?'

'Never mind,' he said, starting his workout again and shaking his head. 'You carry on.'

'I don't think he works full-time any more. He's probably near to retirement age if he's known my aunt for so long, and it seems fairly difficult to get an appointment with him, but I think he's my best bet to get the mortgage secured.'

Bea took a few deep breaths to try and slow her panting. She couldn't wait for her session with Paul to finish. It was one thing doing this exercise lark for fun, but another entirely when she had so much decorating work she should be doing during any free time. 'That's it,' she said climbing off the bike. 'I'm off for a shower and then home.'

The following lunchtime, Bea raced home with her shopping. She struggled into the house with three overflowing shopping bags and dumped them on the kitchen worktop.

'You should have asked me to help you carry those,' Luke said, poking his head around the kitchen door. 'You don't usually come home at lunchtime.'

Bea quickly unpacked the frozen vegetables and pushed them

into her fridge freezer. 'No, but today I've got to spend the afternoon with a client on his yacht.'

'Sounds fun.' Luke raised his eyebrows and smiled, catching a tin of soup as it rolled off the side.

'Not really. He's a nice bloke, but I've got so much to do back at the office that I really don't need to take time out to sit and chat. But I registered his boat for him the other day and he isn't often over in Jersey and wanted to treat me to lunch.'

'On his boat?'

'Yup,' she said finishing packing away her food and turning to face him. 'You don't have to look so concerned, I'm a big girl and I'm more than capable of taking care of myself.'

Luke laughed. 'I didn't think you couldn't. You seem pretty feisty for a titch.'

Bea placed her hands on her hips and narrowed her eyes. 'Really? Do you want to see how feisty I can be?' He shook his head. 'Anyway, Tom will be coming along.'

'Tom Brakespear?'

Bea nodded, not letting on she was aware they knew each other. 'He's the director I report to at work.'

'Right.' Luke nodded thoughtfully. 'Well, I suppose I'd better get on. I don't want you complaining that you're paying us to stand around gossiping.'

'Haha, very funny,' she said, noting the change in atmosphere. 'Coffee?' She wondered if it would be more sensible to terminate his contract with her. Then again, to do such a thing without any obvious reason would make him wonder why she'd changed her mind. She pulled off her black linen jacket, hanging it over the back of a chair. 'I've got time for a quickie before I have to race off, and I'm too thirsty not to have one myself.'

'Please,' he answered, leaning back and half-sitting on the edge of the table, his palms resting on either side of him. 'Are you still sure you want us to get on with the plastering in the hallway?'

She passed him his drink, studying his face to try and spot any hint of criminal behaviour. Idiot, she thought, what would a money launderer look like anyway? You and me, that's what. She thought about her training for her trust exams and how the lecturers had emphasised the fact that it's the people you don't suspect that could be the criminals. It's what made them so hard to spot. 'I'd love to say leave it, but if anyone slams the front door, or even closes it with slightly too much force, plaster rains down on them, and it'll only get worse. So if you can organise to have someone start as soon as possible, I'd be grateful.'

Bea wished she could simply ask him about his business partner and what went wrong, but couldn't risk becoming involved in something that could end up with her losing her home, or even worse, having to move in with her father and stepmother. She shivered.

'You okay?' he asked.

Bea nodded. 'Fine, just a bit stressed that's all.'

'Your ex?'

'Yup, he sends me texts every so often with the D-Day countdown.'

'D-Day? What the hell is that?'

'Debt Day.' She rolled her eyes. 'He's a moron, what can I say?'

'I wish I could do something to help you, Bea. Really.'

She smiled at him. He obviously meant what he was saying. 'Thank you, but I'll think of something. The thought of losing this house because of him is not something I'm going to let happen that easily.'

* * *

'I'll see you two tomorrow,' Bea said to Shani and Paul as she left their flat. She pushed her hands into her bag to find her car keys, catching her nail on an old paperclip at the bottom. 'Damn.' She sucked her finger, groaning when she heard Mel shouting from along the precinct towards her.

'Hey, wait for me!' Bea could hear the click-clack of her sister's heels as she ran along the pavement towards her. 'I know you can hear me.'

Knowing when she had no choice, Bea turned slowly, forcing a smile onto her face. 'Melanie, I'm in a rush to get home... Can't this wait?'

'No. I gather you've been seeing Tom what's-his-name, from years ago? Why didn't you tell me?' She pushed her huge Dior sunglasses up onto her head, holding back her shiny bob.

'It didn't occur to me that you'd be interested.' Bea wondered how long it would take Mel to turn the conversation into one about her wedding. She listened as patiently as she could manage.

'But he's gorgeous. I always liked him.' She seemed lost in memory. 'He reminded me of one of those immaculately suited sixties film stars – without the cigarette, though.'

Bea shook her head and laughed. She doubted Mel remembered Tom at all. 'You hardly met him, so I don't know what you ever found to like about him. Apart from maybe the way he dressed.'

'Rubbish.' Mel frowned, or tried to. Bea stared at her sister's forehead; there wasn't a line on it.

'Have you had Botox?'

'Don't be ridiculous.' Mel waved the notion away with her perfectly manicured hand. 'I'm twenty-five, why would I need anything like that?'

Bea smiled. 'Mel, I was born with more lines on my forehead than you have now. There isn't a single one.'

Mel attempted to raise her eyebrows. Bea tried to hide her amusement. 'Now, I was thinking, if you're seeing Tom, then he'd make a perfect best man for Grant.'

What? 'Grant doesn't even know him.'

'Who cares.' Mel tapped Bea's arm and lowered her voice. 'He'd look perfect for the wedding photos.'

'Never mind his wardrobe,' Shani said, coming out to join them and shooting Mel an irritated glance. 'Sorry, I couldn't help over-hearing your comments.'

'That's because you must have been listening at the door.'

Shani smiled. 'Really, Mel, you should run a shop or a salon. Your interest in grooming and fashion is wasted on a legal assistant.'

'Maybe,' Mel said. 'but I earn far more as a legal assistant, which is why I can afford to buy the clothes I like and pay someone else to do my manicures.'

'Mel is right, though,' Paul sighed, carrying out a tuna melt and taking a bite from it. 'I always found it hard to imagine Tom as a scruffy uni student; he was always so smart whenever I saw him.'

'He wasn't ever scruffy, that's why it's hard to imagine. He was the only immaculate student I remember mixing with, which is probably why I fancied him so much. He always smelt so clean.' Bea laughed at the memory. She couldn't help picturing Luke, not at all smart – scruffy, in fact – but always smelling so heavenly.

'I think we can all understand why Bea would find Tom attrac-tive. Can't we, Shani?' Paul said, nudging Bea. 'Stay with us, love.' Bea could see he was trying to make a point, but wasn't sure why he was determined for Shani to grasp it. 'Let her take some risks in her life. You do,' he added.

Shani narrowed her eyes but ignored him. 'When are you going to ask him all about his situation with his wife—ex, Bea?'

Bea wasn't sure when the conversation had moved on from

Mel's wedding to her dating plans. She recalled Shani admitting a crush she'd had on Tom years before when they'd been dating, and Bea wondered if she still could have any feelings for him. Maybe that was what concerned Paul right now? 'I don't know what all the fuss is about,' Bea said, ignoring her suspicions. 'He told me they've signed the separation papers. And after Simon it feels, um...'

'Safe?' Shani volunteered.

'Yes, I suppose.' Bea nodded, not too sure she liked to admit this point. 'He's easy to be around. I know him and, to be honest, I don't feel like I'm going to fall for him in any way.'

'At least he's not the sort to mess you around,' Mel said, checking her mobile for messages and quickly texting someone. 'He seems very loyal and must have married that Vanessa soon after leaving uni.'

'Which is probably why he took years to return to Jersey. He must have visited his family over here at some point, but I've never bumped into him in all that time. He does seem loyal though,' Bea said. 'And even though she was the one to have the affair, he doesn't sound bitter in any way.'

'Mmm.' Shani shrugged. 'Then he's a bigger man then most would be. I'm not so sure I'd be happy to forgive something like that. You weren't either, Bea.'

'Bea is going to do whatever she decides, so let's not psycho-analyse why she is seeing Tom,' said Paul, before taking another bite of his lunch and staring at Mel. 'Have you had something done to your forehead?'

Mel glared at him. 'No.'

'Anyway,' Shani interrupted, 'if Tom's getting a divorce, then she's nearly an ex-wife. Take note, the emphasis is on the word 'nearly'. Do you want to be loaded down with more baggage, Bea?' Shani continued, obviously not ready to give up just yet. 'You're still sorting things out with Simon. I know you're old friends and all that, but there are loads more blokes out there. Why pick someone who's going through a divorce? Move on before you get too emotionally involved. I mean, why go for him when you can take your pick?'

'Yeah, right,' laughed Mel. 'There's such a wide choice of available, sane, heterosexual men out there just waiting.'

'Don't be so smug.' Shani glowered at her. 'And it's obvious you've had Botox, Mel, so stop trying to deny it.'

'What the hell is your problem, Shani?' Mel asked, dropping her phone back into her bag and pulling the strap up onto her shoulder. 'Bea's more than capable of watching out for herself.'

'I am, and I'm enjoying being single for a change. Maybe it's a relief being with someone who says something and means it, rather than Simon who always said one thing but was getting up to all sorts behind my back.' Bea was growing tired of their bickering. 'If you must know, I'm seeing Tom this Friday.' She patted Shani's hand. 'This isn't a great romance. We really are just friends. Relax! What can possibly go wrong?'

6

SEPTEMBER – DIGGING FOR THE TRUTH

Bea glanced out of the hall window to see if the taxi had arrived yet and spotted a note on the hallstand that Luke must have left earlier.

Please leave back door open tomorrow morning. Will bring paint samples for you to look at. L

She smiled. His untidy handwriting on the torn piece of paper was similar to others he'd left her over the previous few weeks. Just like the writer, she mused, straight to the point and abrupt. Could this man really be involved with something underhand and illegal?

She heard the taxi's tyres crunching on the gravel outside the front door and, pushing further thoughts of Luke to the back of her mind, she grabbed her jacket and bag.

Arriving at Sammy's Bar, Bea paid the cab driver and walked in. She glanced around the noisy room but couldn't see Tom, so bought herself a vodka and tonic and took a seat at a small table with a clear view of the entrance. Tapping the table with her newly painted fingernails, Bea surreptitiously glanced down at her watch for the fifth time. She was contemplating whether to order another drink or leave, when the door opened and in strode Tom.

His eyes twinkled as he smiled at her. 'Hi, gorgeous,' he said, striding across the room dressed in his trademark bespoke suit, his sandy hair combed to one side. 'You look perfect, as usual.' Unable to help grinning back at him, Bea couldn't help notice the admiring stares he was getting from other women in the bar.

He leant down and kissed her on both cheeks. 'Good to see you,' he said, settling down in the seat opposite her. 'I'll get us some drinks.'

'Red wine for me, please.' She watched him go to the bar and when he turned to smile at her, she pointed to the ladies' room. Tom nodded.

She washed her hands and touched up her lip-gloss. Hmm, she didn't look too bad, considering she'd been painting for a couple of hours after work. Bea rubbed her thumb across her newly applied nail varnish. She missed having decent nails.

Bea returned to their table and sat.

'I could do with the weather dropping a few degrees,' Tom said, undoing the button on his linen jacket. 'September, and it still feels like mid-summer.'

Bea took a sip of her drink as he looked her up and down. She wanted to ask him about Luke's involvement with the money laundering case, but could see he was about to say something.

Tom leant across to her, and taking her lightly by the wrist, pulled her towards him. She could feel his breath against her ear, and wondered if he was going to kiss her. 'The label from your knickers is hanging out of the top of your trousers,' he whispered, trying unsuccessfully to stifle his laughter.

'Oh,' muttered Bea, quickly tucking the offending label away while furtively glancing around the bar to see if anyone else noticed her faux pas.

'Hey, don't look so embarrassed,' he said. 'I'm sure no one else noticed, but thought you'd like to know.' He winked at her.

'So,' she said, mustering as much dignity as possible. 'How're things going with your separation?'

He looked at his drink, a grimace passing across his previously cheerful face. 'Well, if you're sure you want to know?' She nodded. He leant back and turned his wine glass by the stem for a few seconds. 'As I told you, I found out she was seeing someone else. Had been for about eighteen months.'

'That's awful. How did you find out?' Bea winced at the unfeeling way her question had come out. 'I meant, who told you?'

'I wasn't told exactly. She was meeting up with a guy who I discovered was one of the beneficiaries of one of the bigger trusts I looked after. I've had bi-annual meetings with him over the past five years, and we've always got along well. So, last year, instead of meeting up in the boardroom, he suggested we go out to lunch and discuss everything away from the office.'

Bea was surprised Tom appeared so happy to tell her everything, and wondered if maybe it was because she'd asked him after he'd had a drink. She waited for him to continue.

'Well, you know how it is,' he said. 'Do business, have lunch, knock back a couple of glasses of wine. Him that is, not me,' he explained, raising an eyebrow. 'He started to relax and began telling me about this woman he was seeing.'

'How horrible,' Bea murmured, wishing she had ignored Shani and not been quite so nosy after all.

'Not at first,' he continued quietly. 'He didn't know he was describing my wife. We chatted like old friends and he told me how great she was, and although she had a husband the marriage was all but over. How it was only a bit of harmless fun for both.' He shrugged at the memory. 'I agreed with him on that point, too. It never occurred to me for one second the poor fool we were discussing was me.'

Bea winced. Bloody Shani, now she felt truly intrusive. 'When did you realise?'

'It was at the following lunch, six months later. I asked him how everything was going. He told me, although this time mentioning her first name, and describing her Titian hair. At first I felt a little unsettled, but shrugged off the notion.' He made a loser sign with his thumb and forefinger. 'I thought I was being paranoid. Up until that point, it had never occurred to me Vanessa could ever be unfaithful. Then, when he said how he looked out for her drophead silver Audi, the penny dropped. I mean, let's face it, Jersey is a small enough place and there aren't that many silver Audis, especially ones driven by redheads.'

'What did you do?' Bea remembered exactly how sick she felt when her aunt had sat her down and told her that she'd caught Simon making out with someone in his car.

'Nothing,' he replied, his face expressionless for a moment.

'Nothing? What, nothing at all?' It didn't sound like the Tom she had known all those years ago.

'You married in your early twenties, too – didn't your family and friends warn you that you were rushing things?'

Bea nodded. 'My stepmother must have told me dozens of times that it would end badly with Simon.'

'Anyway, what's the point? It wasn't as if he knew who I was. I mean, think about it – he was a good client of mine, and until then we'd had an excellent business relationship.'

'But he was sleeping with your wife,' she said.

'Exactly, my wife. She was the one being unfaithful. And let's be honest, if you have to get divorced, and to me there is no other option when there's no trust left, I was going to need all the money I could get for legal fees. I didn't need to lose a good client. Well, not just then anyway.'

Bea couldn't think what to say to such a revelation. 'That sounds so calculated,' she said, shocked at his callous admission.

'It does when you say it out loud.'

She put her hand over his. 'How horrible. So what's happening now?'

'Everything's in the hands of the solicitors. We've gone for a year's legal separation, like I explained the other week. She still doesn't know he's my client.'

'Really?'

'He knows. I told him when I left the company and moved to where I am now.' Tom smiled triumphantly. 'It was one hell of a shock to him, too. I can still picture his face. He didn't know what to do with himself.' He squeezed Bea's hand. 'Can we change the subject now?'

'Of course. Sorry.'

Tom looked at the clock above the bar. 'I've booked a table for us at Giuseppe's, if that's ok?'

'Perfect.'

Bea was relieved to get out into the warm evening air. She couldn't remember being out to dinner with someone other than Simon. 'When we were dating we never went to restaurants together.' She laughed.

'No money, which is why I'm enjoying taking you tonight.'

They entered the dimly lit restaurant. Bea looked forward to seeing Giuseppe. 'I used to come here quite a lot with Simon.'

Tom frowned. 'You should have said, I could have booked for us to go somewhere else.'

'Don't be silly, this is great. You can't beat the food.'

Giuseppe welcomed them with open arms. 'Cara, I'm so sorry about you and Mr Porter,' he whispered as he gave her a brief hug.

'He says though that you're very happy now and have both moved on.' Gio looked across to where Tom was now waiting by their table. 'And I can see he was telling the truth. I am pleased. He is a handsome man, no?'

Bea nodded. 'He is, Gio.' Gio pulled back a chair for her and Bea sat down. Gio took their order then departed.

Tom smiled. 'Do you remember we were thrown out of that pub the first summer we were seeing each other, when we got drunk with the drummer from that band?'

'You mean *you* got drunk. I had to get you home afterwards and my aunt panicked when I was late home.'

'I remember, you wanted to take over the world,' he teased. 'You insisted you'd be a millionaire by the time you were twenty-five. What happened?'

Bea sighed. 'Life got in the way. Anyway, what about you? You were supposed to be running your own multi-national business by now.'

He shook his head. 'I know. Disappointing, aren't we?'

'Never mind,' said Bea holding her stomach to ease the pain caused by so much giggling. 'We didn't succeed because our priorities changed. And we've still got loads of time to achieve stuff.'

'True,' he said quietly. 'What do you want to do most?'

'When Aunt Annabel first died, I thought I wanted to continue with her gardening designs, especially the one she was taking to the Chelsea Flower Show this year.' She pictured Annabel with her designs in her shed. 'But although I grew up with her teaching me stuff about gardens, I've got my own garden to keep going and need to find a way to buy out Simon. I don't have a sponsor for the show and to be honest I don't have the expertise to see it through.'

Tom smiled at her. 'You're still grieving over her, Bea. Most of my memories were of your aunt chatting to us while we lay in the sun, or her bullying me to mow her lawn or something. She was a big character and brilliant at her designs. You're doing well enough just trying to keep her home together for her. That's enough for anyone to deal with on their own.'

'Thanks, Tom. It's good to hear you say that.' Bea swallowed the lump in her throat and pushed away a memory of passing bulbs to her aunt as she planted them. She'd always been happiest in her garden. 'I sometimes don't know how I'll manage it. I try and remember the fun bits of my aunt, but I miss her too much to be able to do that very often.'

'You're doing very well. Just hang in there and focus on fighting that lousy ex of yours.'

Gio arrived with their food. 'Ah, this looks delicious,' Tom said as Gio put a plate down in front of each of them.

* * *

'Er, Tom,' Bea said, noticing Giuseppe was cashing up and a waiter was watching them with a tired expression on his face. She waved her hand in front of Tom to get his attention. 'I think we've outstayed our welcome.' She motioned to the empty room. 'We're the last people here.'

'When did that happen?' Tom asked, downing his drink and nodding at Giuseppe for the bill. That paid, he stood up. 'Come on then, let's make a move.'

Taking her by the hand, they said their goodbyes to Giuseppe and his staff and headed outside where Tom flagged down a passing taxi.

He shouted Bea's address into the cab's window, and helped her into the back. 'Bea,' he murmured huskily, sitting down heavily next to her. 'I've had a wonderful time tonight. It's been fun catching up and not having to concentrate on work issues.'

'Tom, I was wondering... while we're not at work, if you'd be able to tell me more about this Luke business. You know,' she mouthed the words 'money laundering' so that the taxi driver couldn't hear her. 'I just can't quite believe he could be involved as you think.' There, she thought, she'd voiced her doubts to him.

Tom took her hand, all humour vanishing from his expression. 'I understand how difficult this must be for you, but he is involved, or at least I suspect he is.' He thought for a moment. 'I know I shouldn't, but come to my office on Monday and I'll show you irrefutable proof that I'm not lying.'

Bea grimaced. She'd ruined their evening by bringing this matter up. 'I wasn't insinuating that you'd lied, Tom, but it seems so unlikely.'

'You know him that well, to believe him incapable of something like this?'

Bea shook her head. 'No, but...'

He put his arm round her and gave her a hug. 'I know, I'm so sorry. It's difficult to be involved in something this distasteful, however you're connected. I do understand your concerns, Bea. You're right to ask me for proof, and on Monday I'll hopefully show you that you can trust me.'

Bea sighed. 'Thank you. You must think me so rude to ask after the lovely evening we've had.'

'Not at all. Once you can see for yourself the seriousness of the situation, it'll help you keep Luke in his place in your mind. It doesn't have to be too difficult – he's carrying out work for you, nothing more. I'll give you a ring in the morning, if that's ok?' he asked, as the taxi moved through the noisy St Helier streets. 'Not too early, I promise. Maybe I could take you kayaking?'

'I'd like that,' she agreed, wishing she felt a little less miserable. 'But not before ten, though. I have to make the most of any lie-ins I can get nowadays.' She didn't mention that she wanted to avoid

Tom bumping into Luke, who she hoped would be gone soon after sorting out the workers' schedule.

The taxi drew up at the front of her house and Bea opened the cab door. 'Thank you for a lovely evening,' she said, kissing him on the cheek and getting out. She watched as he waved and the taxi disappeared into the darkness.

It would be good to see some proof of Tom's allegations against Luke, Bea decided, not wishing to think about how awkward dealing with Luke would be when he came to the house. Bea removed her makeup and was thinking back over her evening, when the phone rang. 'Bloody hell, that was quick.' She laughed. 'He must live really close to get home so quickly.'

Bea slumped back onto the bed and picked up the phone. 'When I said after ten, I meant ten in the morning,' she teased.

'Am I talking to Beatrix Potter?' demanded a controlled, clipped voice, tinged with threat.

Well, it certainly wasn't Tom. 'This is Beatrice Porter, and it's one-thirty in the morning,' she retaliated, irritated by the caller's aggressive tone.

'Never mind the sodding time!' the woman screeched. 'What the hell were you doing with my husband?'

7

BEA STINGS

'She said what?' Shani gasped. Bea had rung her as soon as she'd ended the call with Vanessa.

'You needn't sound so excited about it,' Bea said, annoyed that Vanessa's call had given her such a fright.

'Sorry, you must have been spooked being in that house all by yourself.' Shani lowered her voice. 'You can't do anything about it tonight, so why don't you snuggle up in bed and try to get some sleep? I haven't got any classes first thing tomorrow, so I'll be able to come over to your place after ten. We'll discuss everything then.'

'I want to go to her place and give her hell,' Bea said. 'Her call was so unexpected I didn't have time to think of anything clever to say.'

'You don't know where she lives,' Shani reminded her. 'And anyway, losing your temper with her probably won't solve anything. Let Tom sort his shitty wife out.'

Bea had to agree. Vanessa was Tom's problem, not hers. She settled down for the night, relieved to find she was a little dozy despite everything and put it down to the evening's alcohol consumption. She closed her eyes and let her mind wander until she fell asleep.

* * *

Bea heard Shani's battered Astra backfiring down the driveway as she hurriedly finished dressing the following morning. She pulled on a pair of pink cut-off trousers and ran to open the front door, to be instantly engulfed in a bear hug by Paul. 'Oof.'

'Poor you,' he said, leaning back and studying Bea's face. 'Shani told me what that cow said to you.'

'You've heard, then?' Bea asked, knowing full well Shani would have told him as soon as she had put down the phone. 'Come through.' They followed her down the long passageway into the kitchen.

'It's lovely and cool in here.' Shani shivered. 'We're dying up in our flat. It's too hot in the summer and freezing in the winter. I'm starting to hate it there.'

Bea leant back against the cool metal of the Aga. 'Never mind the weather – I need to talk about last night.'

'I can't believe you're the other woman this time,' Paul teased. 'Not like you at all.'

'Not funny, Paul,' Shani said, joining Bea in front of the Aga. 'Just pour us some water if you haven't got any cans of drink. It's too hot for tea.'

'It's not funny,' agreed Bea, suddenly feeling chilled. 'I don't need this.' She stood from one foot to the next, retying her ponytail. 'I'm the last person who'd want to upset someone's wife. Don't forget, I know how she must feel. I certainly felt like saying the same to Simon's Claire.' That felt odd, she thought. Simon's Claire. It used to be Simon and Bea.

'Sit down,' Shani said. 'Now take a deep breath and tell me exactly what else she said to you.'

Bea did as she was told. 'Tom told me they were legally separated, which is pretty much the same as being divorced. I mean, to be separated you have to sign a legal document stating you're no longer living together, don't you?' She waved her hand at Paul, declining the proffered biscuit barrel in his hand. 'I can't believe he lied to me. It's not as if we're dating, we're supposed to be friends.'

'You don't know he's lied yet.' Paul sprayed her with crumbs, as he munched on a digestive. 'Maybe she's the one telling porkies, or she could have been dipping one time too many into the Merlot.'

Bea took a deep breath to stop her temper from rising. 'She screamed at me like a complete nutter, calling me all sorts of things. I'm not a slag, or — what else did she say? — oh yes, a bitch. Bloody cheek, in the circumstances.'

Shani slammed her hand down on the worktop. 'Will you just tell me what she said? We'll deal with the unfairness of it all later.'

'She had the nerve to threaten to make my life a living hell, if I ever saw him again.' She shuddered at the memory. 'I think she meant it, too. Let's face it, this is a big house to be rattling around in at the best of times, but when someone makes threats in the middle of the night, it takes on a creepiness that I've never noticed before.'

'I can imagine. She probably even looks like something from *The Texas Chain Saw Massacre*,' Shani said, taking a seat at the table, and motioning for Bea to sit in front of her.

'It's all right for you to sit there and joke, but it's me who'll be smacked in the face.'

The doorbell rang. 'Sit down,' Shani said. 'Paul will deal with it.'

'Oh, thanks,' he said, grimacing. 'What if it's the mad woman?'

'You're such a hero, Paul.' Shani took the biscuit tin away from him. 'Baby. I'll go, then.'

'I will,' Bea said.

Shani got up and pushed Bea back into her seat. Bea fell back, wondering how someone so tall and skinny could be so strong. 'Leave this to me.'

Paul leant towards Bea after Shani had marched out of the kitchen. 'She loves being the one to sort everything out. She's the same whenever someone kicks off at the gym. Always has to barge in and give everyone hell.'

'And you just let her, I suppose.' Bea smiled at him, imagining Paul, almost a foot shorter than Shani, letting her take charge of any dramas. Bea strained to hear who was at the door. At first, she couldn't hear anything at all, and wondered what Shani could possibly be doing. She then heard whispers and giggling getting louder as Mel and Shani made their way to join them in the kitchen. 'It's Mel. I've said she can come in because she's brought food with her.'

'Hi, Mel,' Bea said, sensing Shani had given her sister a hurried, abridged version of events. 'Why don't I go and heat these up?'

Bea took the chocolate croissants from her sister. After a busy evening with Tom she'd forgotten she'd invited Paul, Shani and Mel for breakfast, so couldn't expect them to leave her in peace before they'd eaten. Anyway, they were here for her and another drama. When had her orderly, seamless life dissolved into this chaotic mess?

Paul looked up as she returned from the pantry with a coffee percolator. 'Never mind, Blondie, we'll get through this one, too.'

Bea shrugged. 'I know I'm a bit useless, but I'm not totally hopeless,' she said, placing cups and plates on the bleached pine table in front of them then made coffee.

The phone rang. 'Hello?' said Bea, relieved for the distraction.

'Hi, Bea, it's me,' said Tom, his voice cheery. 'Sleep well?'

'As a matter of fact, no,' she admitted, still cross with him for lying to her about being separated from Vanessa.

'Why? What's the matter?' he asked, beginning to sound a little unsure.

'The matter, Tom, is your wife.' She waved the phone at her audience for them to be quiet, so she could hear what he was trying to say. All three were now paying full attention, croissants and coffees paused in mid-air.

'Vanessa?' he asked.

'Who else?'

'I'm coming to yours.' Tom sounded anxious. 'And you're going to tell me everything.'

Bea went to argue, but he'd already slammed down the phone before she'd uttered a single syllable.

She pointed at the phone. 'He's on his way.'

'Great,' cheered Shani. 'Now I get to see what he looks like after all these years.'

'I only remember him vaguely,' said Mel. 'I suppose it's because I was so much younger when you saw him.' She tore off a piece of croissant and dipped it into her coffee before devouring it.

'That's disgusting, Mel. Anyway, I'm surprised you remember him at all.' Bea shook her head.

Paul rid his hands of crumbs. 'He was always hot, though we were only friendly because of you.' He grinned at Bea. 'I bet he's aged badly.'

'He hasn't.' Bea stood up. 'I'm going to take a shower.'

'What?' they cried in unison.

'You don't mind looking like hell in front of us,' laughed Mel. Shani nudged her and shook her head.

'Can you three clear up a bit?'

'What for?' frowned Mel, tearing apart a second croissant.

'My kitchen is a tip. Give it a quick tidy up whilst I'm upstairs, *please*,' she said, walking out of the room.

'She's always like that when she's in a state about something,' mumbled Mel, chewing her breakfast and completely ignoring Bea's request.

'If I had my way,' Shani said, 'he wouldn't get a chance to see inside the house at all.'

'Bugger it, I'm not tidying up for him,' said Mel. 'It's not as if she'll notice.'

'I can still hear you, you know,' called Bea from halfway up the stairs.

She had almost finished drying her hair when she heard the doorbell followed by Mel's flirtatious giggle. So typical of Mel, thought Bea smiling – she didn't take long to forget whose side she was on.

Bea pulled on her oldest jeans and a faded T-shirt that had seen better days and she was ready for action. After all, she decided, they may only be friends and she didn't want to appear to be trying too hard, but she did have her pride. What little there was left of it.

She took a deep, calming breath just before entering the kitchen, and saw Tom standing in front of her friends. She couldn't help thinking of the three wise monkeys as they sat at the table next to each other, studying him in silence. Tom's face was grey, causing his green eyes to appear more intense than they usually did. Bea could tell he was doing his best to appear friendly. As disturbed as she was by the call, she couldn't help feeling sympathy for him, having such an accusatory audience.

'Tom, let's go through to the living room,' she said, sounding less angry than she had on the phone. 'We can talk privately through there.' She narrowed her eyes at the threesome who had purposefully ignored her telepathic pleas to go, staying exactly where they were at her kitchen table.

As soon as they were alone, he took her gently by the shoulders. 'Bea, I'm so sorry. I know how this must look, but I promise you I haven't lied about anything. I've told you pretty much everything there is to know about Vanessa. We do get along well, but it's purely for the children's sake, even though I don't see them nearly as much as I'd like to.'

Much as she had enjoyed Tom's company, she wasn't desperate in any way for a social life. She had had enough of being on the receiving end of lies and dramas. Bea replayed the call between her and Vanessa. She stepped back from him. 'Tom, as much as I've enjoyed your company, I really don't need to be dealing with a psycho right now.' He went to interrupt, but she held up her hand to stop him. 'This is too intense for me. I've got more than enough to be coping with and don't want us to fall out if we must work so closely together. So I think the best thing you can do is concentrate on sorting out whatever issues you two have, once and for all.'

Tom's shoulders stooped. He stared back at her for a moment. 'You're right, of course. It would be selfish to expect you to get involved with me after this.' He leant forward, kissed her lightly on the cheek, then left without saying another word.

Hearing the front door close, the others called Bea back to the kitchen.

'Well?' Mel nudged her on her way to busy herself with the percolator.

'I don't know why you're bothering to ask me; you were all listening, I presume?'

Paul shrugged. 'You know we were. So he's gone, now what?'

'It's a shame,' Bea said finally. 'We had fun the other night and he makes life at Malory's bearable.' How typical there has to be a hiccup somewhere, especially such a major one.

Mel handed out coffees.

'Well, you all said I should give dating a go.' Bea smiled at their serious faces. 'I think I've had my fill of it for now.'

'Right,' said Paul. 'Anyway, I've heard tales about him liking a little flutter.'

'He's a gambler?' Shani widened her eyes.

'That's what I heard.' Paul's eyes glistened as he turned to Bea. 'So whether or not the wife is a problem, you don't need to get involved with someone who is addicted to losing money.'

'You know,' Bea said shaking her head wearily, 'sometimes living on an island can get really tiresome. You know you shouldn't listen to rumours about people, they're usually untrue.' She turned to Mel. 'How are things with Grant and your wedding plans?'

'Oh, all right, I suppose,' she mumbled, in between mouthfuls of croissant. Bea couldn't understand how Mel remained slim, as she never seemed to stop eating, and certainly didn't exercise.

'Only all right?' asked Shani, grimacing at Mel eating. 'Aren't you ever full?'

'You must have bought all the newsagent's wedding magazines, and I know for a fact you've been on the internet scanning wedding planner's websites for ideas,' Paul winked at her.

'I only asked you to check out one woman for me, Paul, and that was supposed to be in confidence.' Mel sighed. 'I've been scanning the glossy magazines too; I need all the help I can get.' She put down her cup and studied her immaculate manicure with satisfaction. 'You know, I only agreed with Mum to hold the wedding in May because I was certain we would easily manage to plan everything in that time, but it's not as simple as I thought.'

Shani and Paul glanced at Bea, but she wasn't in the mood to row with her sister, not today. It was exactly four months since Aunt Annabel had died and eight months and one day until she had to find Simon's money. It seemed like forever ago that she had kissed her aunt's forehead that last time. The 10th of May was coming around a little too quickly for her liking.

Shani motioned for Bea to say something first. She shook her head. Shani glared at her with her best schoolmistress look, then turned her attentions to Mel. 'You know you only have to ask and we'll help however we can.'

Bea stifled a groan; the thought of having to spend more time with her stepmother and wedding plans was almost more than she could contemplate. 'Yes, of course,' she said, relenting with as much good spirit as she could muster.

A smile slid across Mel's mouth. 'Really? I wasn't sure you'd want to still help me given the wedding date. Thanks. Obviously, I'll need to pass everything by my mum first, but then I'll let you all know what you can do for me.'

Paul widened his eyes at Bea. She tried not to smile at him, aware she'd been cornered into helping too. He hurriedly snatched his napkin from his lap and held it up to his mouth to cover his giggling.

Despite being surrounded by her closest friends, Bea suddenly felt very much alone. She stared out of the French doors and decided she needed solitude.

Mel glared at Paul, nudging him hard.

'Ouch. That hurt,' he whined, still laughing, but now frowning in pain at the same time.

'Good. My wedding is no joke,' she pouted. She looked at Bea. 'I know we have our differences, but you'll only have to deal with this wedding and then you won't have to cope with my mum's desperation to make sure I'm seen as number one daughter in Dad's eyes.'

Bea's eyes widened. 'I didn't realise you were so aware of what she does.'

'Yeah,' Paul said. 'We all thought you were a bit switched off where your mother's game-playing was concerned.'

Slamming her palms onto the table, Mel glared at Paul. 'I don't want you to bother if you're only getting involved so you can take the mickey out of me and Mum at every opportunity. It's my wedding, Paul, despite your loyalties to Bea and her obvious annoyance about the date, but this is something that will have to last me forever. Bea has a right to insult my mum; you don't.'

'Mel,' Shani snapped. 'He didn't mean to be rude, but I don't think you see the full extent of how badly Joyce treats Bea.'

Bea stood up. 'That's enough. I'm a big girl now, Shani. Thanks, but I don't need anyone looking after me and I'm perfectly capable of standing up to Joyce, if I feel the need to do so.' She turned her attention to Mel. 'We're happy to help you plan the wedding. I don't like the idea that it's going to be on Liberation Day, but you were aware of that when you set the date. I'm more concerned about everything Dad will be coping with, and if I can make it any easier for him, I will.'

Mel didn't reply for a moment. Bea waited for her to speak. 'Fine. Not exactly the enthusiasm I was hoping for from my own sister, but it's better than nothing. You're probably a little down now that your relationship with Tom has gone down the pan.'

'It was hardly a relationship,' Bea said, standing up and collecting their cups. 'Listen you lot, I've got a lot to catch up with here, if I ever want a weekend out of this house again.'

Mel picked up her bag and slung it over her shoulder, 'And I've got a wedding to plan,' she said, pointedly.

'I was hoping to chill out here for a bit,' Paul moaned.

'You can, if you pick up a paintbrush.'

Shani grabbed her car keys. 'I would, but I need to get off. I've got to try and pin Harry down.'

'Everything all right?' Bea touched Shani's arm lightly 'You're looking a little peaky. Overdoing it at the gym?'

'Hah, I don't think so,' Paul laughed. 'She's off all week.'

Bea raised her eyebrows. 'Why? You never said you'd been unwell. What's the matter?'

'Thanks, Paul,' Shani snapped before looking at Bea. 'I'm fine. It was just a stomach bug.'

'Let me know if you need anything,' Bea said. 'I know I've got my own problems right now, but that doesn't mean I don't want to know everything that's going on with you. We should catch up sometime, just the two of us.'

'That would be nice,' Shani said, hugging her quickly and following Paul out of the room.

8

OCTOBER – BUDDING ROMANCE

Bea ran up to her room and changed into her old tracksuit before heading outside.

'Smell that?' she said to herself. 'That's the scent of the end of summer.' She picked a reddening leaf from a nearby acer. 'Such beautiful colours.' She gazed at the acre of green expanse before her and sighed. 'I'd better get a move on and mow this otherwise it's going to be even more of a jungle.' She was grateful for Tom's recent help in keeping the lawn mown, and remembered teasing Simon about his determination to mow the lawn every week during previous summers, insisting he didn't dare let it get out of control. Now she appreciated what he had meant.

Suddenly unable to face the mowing, Bea went into the kitchen and, after flicking through several dog-eared recipe books, found Aunt Annabel's hand-written note on how to make lemonade. She told herself she wasn't putting off the mowing, simply preparing a thirst-quenching drink for when she'd completed the arduous task.

The lemonade done, she placed the jug carefully into her fridge and went back outside.

'It's not going to cut itself,' she groaned, aware she couldn't justify paying someone for a task she could do herself. 'No time like the present, I suppose,' she said, breaking into a jog towards the old brick stables at the back of the house where she kept the mower.

Maybe her aunt had hidden her mysterious item out here somewhere? She stood on the concrete floor staring up at the rafters and trying to think of any hiding places she might have missed. After a brief and unsuccessful search that only uncovered an ancient chest containing moth-eaten books, she decided to give up looking for the day.

The mower was sitting exactly where Tom had left it three weeks before. Bea stared at it, hands on hips, as she contemplated asking him to come around and do it for her again, but since the incident with Vanessa she'd done her best to be as friendly to him as possible in a professional capacity only. After all, they did still have to work together and there was no point in giving him the idea she may want something more from him, even if it was only to help mow the lawn.

Bea filled the mower with fuel, spilling petrol onto her hand. 'Sod it.' Bea shook her hand and walked back into the kitchen to wash. As she replaced the towel back on the rail, she spotted a piece of folded paper on the floor and bent to pick it up. It was Luke's latest invoice with a note pointing out extra plastering that needed replacing in the back bedroom. It must have fallen onto the floor when she'd opened the door, letting in a draught. She called him.

'Sorry, I only saw your note last night and it was too late to give you a ring.'

'About the plasterwork?'

'Yes,' she said, thinking how sexy his deep voice sounded on the phone. 'I know you're coming to the end of the work now and to be honest I can't afford to do much more. In fact, I'm going to have to...' Bea held the phone away from her ear. Were those voices outside in her driveway? 'Simon?' she whispered, before realising Luke was calling her name. 'Sorry, I was distracted.'

'Is everything all right?'

Bea sighed. 'Yes, I...' It was bloody Simon. What the hell was he doing here, again? She ran over to the French doors and pushed them open wider. 'Hey, what do you think you're doing? Get off my property, now.'

Simon carried on talking to someone she didn't recognise.

'Bea?' Luke shouted, concern in his voice.

'Sorry, Luke, I've got to go.' She ended the call before he was able to answer, furious with Simon.

'And this is my ex-wife.' Simon smiled as if he'd just introduced her as a tiresome teenager.

'Yes, and this is my house,' she said, holding her hand out to the man in a bespoke grey suit. 'And you are?'

'I'm the estate agent your, er, ex-husband contacted for a valuation on this property.' He glanced down at his black leather clipboard and then smiled awkwardly at her.

Bea raised her eyebrows and stared at Simon. 'Why?'

Simon sighed. 'Beatrice, we both know the bank will send someone to value this place in your favour. I'm not an idiot. I remember your aunt talking about Mr Peters, the bank manager who she dealt with for the last two hundred years or whatever. I'm bringing in someone to make sure I don't get cheated out of my share.'

'You bastard. If Mr Peters was so easily influenced I would have raised the money to buy you out by now.'

Simon's triumphant expression made Bea grit her teeth in irritation. 'So, you've been trying to sort out our little problem, then?'

Bea glared at him.

'Good to know. Only seven months until D-Day.' He looked around the garden. 'I'm perfectly entitled to bring in an independent valuer. So, if you don't mind finding something else to do, we'll get on.' He moved towards the house.

'Oh no, you don't.' Bea grabbed Simon's arm. 'You can come inside,' she said to the estate agent. 'You, Simon, can bloody well wait out here.'

She led the agent into her kitchen, trying to remember that it wasn't the poor man's fault Simon had involved him in their problem.

'Don't worry, I'll only be a few minutes.' He forced a smile, making Bea feel slightly guilty at dragging him inside so hurriedly.

'See?' Simon said, tapping his watch at her ten minutes later. 'That didn't take too long, now did it?'

Bea turned her back on them and began walking towards the stables, stopping abruptly when she heard another vehicle coming down her driveway.

'Oh God, here comes the cavalry,' Simon sneered, shaking his head as he pointed at Luke. 'Come on, let's get out of here. Bye, Bea, see you in court.'

She frowned and turned to see Luke striding across the gravel. 'Are you okay?' he asked, ignoring Simon's pained expression as he passed.

Bea's stomach flipped over. He seemed so concerned for her. 'I'm fine, thanks... just another confrontation with my adorable ex-husband.'

'What the hell did you ever see in that man?' Luke said, in the direction of Simon's disappearing car.

Bea shrugged. 'I thought he wanted the same things as me,' she said, wondering if she had ever really known Simon at all. 'And believe it or not he can be great fun.'

'Hmm, maybe he's changed a lot.' He smiled.

Bea laughed. 'Or maybe I've woken up and can finally see the real Simon that he used to hide so well. Would you like a drink?'

'No.' He shook his head, his untidy curls settling in a way that made Bea want to push her fingers into them. 'You hung up so abruptly that I wanted to make sure everything was okay.'

'That's kind, thank you. But I'm fine now he's gone.'

Luke gazed at her. 'While I'm here, I just want to check on something the men mentioned to me about the hallway,' he said, heading into the house.

Bea smiled to herself as she returned to the mower and pushed the heavy machine around the side of the house, across the gravel driveway and onto the lawn.

Red in the face at the exertion, she thought back to Simon telling her how to start it. Pushing forward the bar and holding up the handle, she leant forward, grabbed the handle and gave it a strong tug. Nothing. Bea breathed in, took hold of it once more, and pulled as quickly and as hard as she could. Again, nothing.

Bea gritted her teeth in frustration. Several attempts and two broken fingernails later, she wondered how anyone could manage to hold up the brake bar while at the same leaning forward to yank the end of the rope with enough energy to make the machine burst into life. It was simply impossible. Maybe it was broken.

Bea kicked the mower, achieving nothing more than the satisfaction of inflicting a dent onto its rusting bodywork, and was battling with herself whether to find a hammer to smash the useless machine to bits.

'Having problems?' Luke asked, as he ambled over to her.

Bea could feel her face reddening. So much for independence. 'I can't get this useless thing to work,' she stammered, fully aware the exertion had left her unattractively puce in the face.

He grinned at her. 'Let me have a try.' Luke raked a hand through his messy, wayward hair and stepped over to the mower.

Bea pushed her hands into her pockets and waited to see if he had any better luck with the useless machine.

Luke roughly rolled up the sleeves of his denim shirt, revealing tanned, muscular forearms and started the mower on his first attempt.

'I thought it was broken,' she explained, feeling ridiculous for making such a fuss.

'There's a knack to these things,' he said, shrugging. 'Years of practice as I was growing up certainly helped. Tell you what, why don't I do this for you, and you can make us both one of your excellent coffees?'

'I've got something much more tempting than coffee,' she said, thinking about the lemonade cooling in her fridge. When she noticed Luke's surprise at her comment, she hurriedly changed the subject. 'Do you realise how much lawn there is?' Bea asked. 'It goes up the other side of the driveway too, as well as down past the orchard.'

He raised an eyebrow. 'Tell you what then, I'll do the main lawn areas now, and leave the less obvious areas for another day. How does that sound?'

Bea couldn't believe his offer, but had no intention of turning it down. She loved pottering in gardens, sowing seeds, dead-heading, and even planting, but the prospect of mowing, especially the part where it had to be repeatedly emptied, left her cold. 'Well, if you're certain you don't mind, it would be a great help. Thanks.'

She almost skipped into the house, and when she was sure he couldn't see her from her vantage point behind the dining room window, took a sneaky look at the handsome, bearded man with the untidy hair and deep, mesmerising blue eyes. He was like a bear. A sexy, big bear. It was wonderful to enjoy appreciating his powerful physique more fully for once. She watched his long legs pacing back and forth in straight lines across her wide, overgrown lawn and felt a warm glow inside.

She was relieved Tom's promise to show her the paperwork had been delayed by an unexpected project keeping them apart at work for the last few weeks. She wasn't going to consider Luke guilty until she saw proof that he was. Bea hugged herself. Luke was so different to Simon and Tom; it wasn't like her to be attracted to someone so rugged. She smiled.

Bea calculated it would take him well over an hour to finish his task, enough time for her to sort through her wooden seed box in the potting shed.

'I saw a door open on one of the stables,' he announced from outside the door, what seemed like moments later. She stopped tidying away the spilt compost from the worktop and looked up at his damp chest. 'I presume the mower is kept in there.' Bea nodded.

'Thanks so much for doing that. I've been dreading tackling the mowing for weeks.' She brushed the peat off her hands as he looked around the walled-in garden, wondering what had taken his eye.

'Are those Jersey lilies?' he asked, pointing to a clump of pretty pink flowers with tiny red crosses on their petals.

'No, I'm not sure what they are.' Bea pointed to the larger pink lilies nearby. 'Those are Jersey lilies, *amaryllis belladonna*. My godmother always thought the Guernsey lilies were prettier; they're smaller, daintier.'

'I like those first ones, they're unusual. Would you like me to take a picture of them and ask my uncle if he knows what they are? He's a horticulturalist, or something like that.'

'If you like, thanks.' He took a picture using his mobile. 'I suppose I should know what each of these plants are called if I'm going to look after them properly. Do you want to come in the house to freshen up a bit?'

Luke followed her to the house and she watched as he bent down to remove his boots. He washed his hands and face at the sink and Bea handed him a towel to dry himself before fetching the lemonade from the fridge. She wasn't sure if she was disappointed or relieved that he chose not to remove his top. He sat opposite her, leaning his bare forearms on the bleached pine of the table. Bea had to force herself not to stare at the golden hairs covering his skin.

'I'll come and do the rest of your mowing another day, if that's ok?'

'Only if you're sure you don't mind. I was hoping to employ a gardening firm to come and sort it all out, but I can't afford to.'

'Well, it's one hell of a garden to look after.' He didn't take his eyes off her as he spoke, and Bea was unable to tear her gaze away from him.

'Luke, as well as the garden, I also want you to know how grateful I am for the work your men have done here,' she said. 'Their standard is so high, and I've heard horror stories about workers beginning a job and disappearing halfway through, sometimes for months.'

'I know what you mean,' he nodded. 'It's a pet hate of mine, which is why we don't take on work unless we know we can complete it without messing clients about.' He sat back and stared at her for a while. 'On the phone you were going to tell me something about the work, but you didn't actually say what it was.'

'I'm not sure how much more I can afford to do here. I'll do as much as I can, and I owe it to my aunt to keep her garden perfect.' She was unsure how to continue with the conversation. 'Lemonade?' she asked, indicating the crystal jug in the middle of the table. 'I thought you might appreciate this more than coffee after all your hard work.'

'Looks good.' He took a sip of the cool drink, the bitterness making his eyes blink.

Bea stifled a giggle. 'Mmm, I think this batch is probably a little tart, but it's the coldest drink I have, unless you'd rather have water. Or there's coffee, of course.'

He cleared his throat, shaking his head slowly and wincing. He smiled. 'No, this is fine,' he said, his voice raspy. 'It takes me back to my misspent youth.' He crossed his legs at the ankles, stretching his long legs out under the table and grazing her ankle.

Bea didn't move away from his touch. 'Hardly very misspent, if you were drinking lemonade,' she teased.

'It was what we added to it that was naughty.' He raised an eyebrow.

'What was it? Gin? Vodka?' she asked, enjoying the banter.

Luke laughed. 'Granny's cherry brandy.'

Bea grimaced. 'Gross. I bet you only did that once.'

He nodded, watching her silently for a moment or two. 'Now that the mowing's done and we're both free agents, why don't we make the most of this great weather and take a trip to the Écréhous islands?'

'In your boat, you mean?' Bea hadn't expected this, but what was stopping her? He waited for her to answer.

'We could take our lunch there, make the most of what's left of the day. I think we could both do with some time off, don't you?'

Bea was sorely tempted, despite knowing she should keep her distance from him. Sod the investigation, she thought, it was only lunch. 'Why not? I've never been to the islands before, and who knows when I'll get an offer like this again?' she said. She'd just have to be careful not to say anything that could raise his suspicions and alert him about the investigation.

Luke stood up. 'Great. The sea should be calm and now that most of the holidaymakers have left, we might even be the only ones there.'

'Sounds perfect,' she admitted, liking the prospect even more than expected. She tucked a stray strand of hair behind her ear self-consciously. 'I've always wanted to go there.'

'Good,' said Luke. 'Then it makes our trip even more fun.'

* * *

As they approached St Catherine's Bay, Luke pointed out the window towards the Channel.

'Look,' he said. 'Over there, the Écréhous.'

Bea peered out of the window and saw the islands, appearing nothing more than a cluster of rocks poking up out of the sea about halfway between Jersey and the coast of France. 'People don't actually live there, do they?' she wondered.

Luke shook his head. 'No, but several of the islanders own huts on the main islands, and you can rent one of them, The Old Customs House, from the Parish of St Martin.'

Bea couldn't wait to get out there. She wasn't sure if she was more excited about going on his boat or seeing these intriguing little islands for the first time.

He parked the car in front of a café. 'Just popping in to get our lunch. I won't be long.'

Bea breathed in the warm, salty air and watched as Luke went in to talk to the owner. After a few minutes Luke emerged, hands full, and jumped into the car.

'Lobster and champagne,' he said, smiling, as they set off again.

Once Luke had showered and changed and they'd cast off, it took Bea a little while before she got used to the movement of his beautiful wooden boat. She relaxed against the open door to the wheelhouse. Gazing up at the high mast, she wondered how often he hoisted the sails, or if it was easier to use the engine to get anywhere.

'Engine,' he said, smiling.

Bea narrowed her eyes, wondering if she'd spoken her question out loud. 'What?'

'You were thinking about whether I use wind or diesel to get from place to place on this beauty of mine.'

Bea laughed. 'Yes, I was. Why don't you use the sails though?'

'I do, when I'm further out to sea.' He looked across at the breakwater and Bea followed his gaze, watching St Catherine's receding away from them.

'I really should come here more often,' she said, breathing deeply and closing her eyes in the sun.

'St Catherine's, or my boat?' Luke teased, as he steered the boat.

'St Catherine's,' she said, eyes shut but aware he was watching her.

'Well, I'll just have to make sure you enjoy your trip enough for you to want to come again, shan't I?'

'Yes,' she said. 'This is bliss. Do you ever see dolphins?'

'We do, especially when the sea is warmer. They swim by the boats, and you see them quite a lot from the café.'

Bea leant back, resting on her elbows, and watched Luke, so comfortable with his boat as if it were a part of him. She ran her fingers along the varnished handrail. 'It's so classical,' she said. 'You must have to spend a lot of time working on all this wood.'

He shrugged. 'I love beautifully crafted things and this boat is a bit of an obsession of mine.'

'So, you're in no rush to finish the restoration of your cottage, then?'

Luke laughed. 'No, which is just as well.'

'Why?'

'I might be selling it sooner than I'd thought.' Before Bea could question him further, he pointed back to Jersey's shoreline, at the rich green trees and tiny coves, then across to the Normandy coast. 'Perfect, don't you think?'

Bea nodded, suspecting he had opened up to her more than he'd intended. 'I really don't make the most of living on this island, you know.'

'Most people don't,' Luke said. 'I think life gets so busy sometimes we forget to enjoy everything we have around us.'

She felt the engines slowing down and saw the little group of islands nearby. 'They're so pretty,' she said. 'Like something in a picture book.'

'Not so inviting in the winter, and damn frightening during a storm,' Luke said, dropping the anchor and moving their bags of food and drink from the galley into the dingy at the back of the boat. 'Here, let me help you.'

She took his cool hand and tentatively stepped down into the small boat. 'Thanks,' she said, holding on tightly until she was safely seated.

Luke showed her around the small islands, and Bea couldn't get over the tiny, one-room huts, used mainly by fishermen and more recently by the lucky locals who owned one of them. She peered into another window. 'Why doesn't anyone live here?' she asked.

'No fresh water supply,' Luke said, leading her over to a small cove and laying out a blanket for them to sit on as he took out their lunch. 'Holidaymakers have been coming to stay here since Victorian times.'

'Can't say I blame them.' She took a plastic plate with the freshly cooked lobster and a dollop of yellowy mayonnaise from his hands. 'This is heavenly,' she said, unable to remember anything more perfect. 'Thank you for bringing me here.'

Luke smiled at her. 'My pleasure, I'm glad you're enjoying yourself.'

After a few minutes, Luke said, 'Tom.'

'What?' Why did he want to know about Tom, Bea wondered?

'I think I saw him here a couple of months ago.' Luke didn't look at her, but thoughtfully took a drink from his bottle of water.

Bea shook her head. 'I doubt it; Tom hates the sea.'

Luke stopped eating and looked at her. 'Does he have two children?'

Bea nodded, wishing he'd drop the subject. 'He does, they're quite small.'

'Then I'm sure it was him. I thought I'd seen him somewhere before when I saw you both at your house that evening. I'm sure it was here, although I can't be certain because I was in the boat at the time and he was onshore.'

'I think you must be mistaken. I can't see him coming here. He once told me about nearly drowning at Green Island when he was small, so he's very wary of the sea. I know he doesn't like boats. It can't have been him.'

Luke didn't look too convinced. 'You're probably right. How's that lobster?'

'Delicious,' said Bea, feeling better now he'd changed the subject.

They finished their lunch in silence and Bea relished being with him in such a tranquil place, with nothing but birds and the sound of the waves breaking against the rocks to disturb them. After tidying up, Luke helped her to her feet. 'Fancy seeing more of the islands?' he asked.

Bea nodded. His dark blue eyes, shining with a carefree enthusiasm she didn't often get to see, made her want to take his face in her hands and kiss him. As if he'd heard her thoughts, he abruptly stopped walking, turned and took her in his arms. Pulling her closer, he kissed her, his cool lips hard against hers. Bea forgot everything and was lost in the moment.

Then, gently letting go of her, he sighed. 'You're so beautiful,' he said, before taking her hand once more and leading her across the sandy beach.

Bea felt like she'd been hugged on the inside somehow. As he told her about the old Abbey on the little island of Maitre, and how the French had invaded twice in the nineties, she found she couldn't quite concentrate because of the touch of his firm hand around hers.

'I remember my dad ranting about that,' she laughed. 'I'm glad they didn't get them back though.'

Luke looked surprised. 'They'd have a fight on their hands if they really tried to.'

'Typical Jersey boys,' she giggled. 'So patriotic about your island.'

Luke helped her back into the dingy and passed over the bags containing the remnants of their lunch. 'And why not? It's worth fighting for, don't you think?'

She wasn't sure if there was more to what he was saying, so decided to simply nod her agreement.

Back on the mainland, Luke drove her home, entertaining her all the way with anecdotes about island life.

Not wanting her perfect day to end, Bea asked Luke if he wanted to come in for a drink. She finished her second glass of wine and looked up at his tanned face. 'I've had such a lovely day today,' she said. 'It was like being on holiday.' She felt heady and more alive than she had in years, and couldn't help noting Luke's muscles. 'I don't suppose you ever need to go to the gym, do you?'

Luke laughed. 'Never have the time. I'd rather get my exercise outside in the fresh air than in some sweaty gym.'

Bea thought how different he was to Simon and Tom, who worked out at the gym religiously. She realised she hadn't heard what he was saying and wasn't sure how to answer. 'Um, yes?' she offered hopefully.

He laughed, 'You haven't been listening to a word I've said, have you?'

'No,' she stammered, her face reddening. 'Sorry, I was in a world of my own.'

'Somewhere enjoyable, I hope.'

If only he knew, thought Bea, trying not to smile. 'It was very enjoyable.'

Luke, glass of wine in hand, sipped it slowly as he watched her over the rim. 'I like spending time with you, Bea.'

'Shall we move into the drawing room?' suggested Bea, unsure how to reply. It was so long since she had felt such an attraction for anyone and was a little lost for words. 'It's getting rather chilly and I can light the fire in there.' She didn't like to add how she'd prepared the fire earlier expecting to be spending a quiet evening alone with a good book and a glass or two of rosé.

'Of course.' Luke carried their drinks and followed her into the vast, cream room, settling down on the sofa as she lit the fire.

Bea took her place at the opposite end to him. Dragging a cushion onto her lap, she drew her legs up underneath her.

'Why do you do that?' he asked, passing over her glass.

'Do what?'

'Feel awkward when someone compliments you?'

'Well, how do you think I should reply?'

He moved towards her, gently taking the cushion from her hands and tossing it over to the opposite chair. Then, moving closer, he put one hand behind her head and kissed her.

Bea's heart almost stopped. The pressure from his firm lips and the feel of his tongue gently exploring her mouth caused her senses, already hazy from alcohol and long-suppressed lust, to go completely haywire.

One minute, there were light, delicate kisses on her face, neck, throat; the next, urgent discarding of clothes as he kissed her lips, his hands moving deliciously over her skin. Bea sighed as Luke laid her down gently onto the Persian rug in front of the fire. He kissed her before lowering his head to her breasts, sending exquisite shards of ecstasy through her entire body.

'You're so perfect,' he whispered hoarsely, a hand caressing her thighs, moving slowly upwards between her legs. Just when she thought she couldn't take any more, Luke finally entered her. Bea clasped him to her as they moved, her pleasure increasing until she climaxed seconds before he did. Luke groaned, holding her tightly, as Bea felt her body exploding into a million, tiny pieces.

9

NOT A BED OF ROSES

The next morning, Bea woke to the sound of heavy rain battering against her bedroom window. Wearily opening one eye, she took a tentative look towards the chink of grey light beaming through her bedroom curtains. Her head felt fuzzy, and her mouth was parched. Reaching over to her bedside table, she patted around aimlessly until she found the ever-present bottle of water. She took a sip trying to wake up.

As Bea leant forward to sit up, her foot skimmed a warm leg. Someone murmured behind her. Her eyes snapped open, sending a shooting sensation burning through her dehydrated brain. Turning slowly, her gaze fell on Luke, asleep on his back, muscular arms bent above his head, his tousled dark hair framing his handsome face, looking peaceful and content. Bea's heart contracted, and more than anything she wanted to kiss him again.

Taking the opportunity to survey the hairs on his chest, she managed to retain enough self-control not to push her fingers through it. He was even more beautiful when he was sleeping. The rest of the time he appeared to be concentrating, on what she wasn't sure, but hoped it was his partner creating many financial difficulties and not his own involvement in them. She pushed away the thought.

The sheet only covered him from the waist down, but Bea could tell he was naked underneath. For many years she'd only ever shared her bed with Simon and couldn't help gazing on this perfect specimen, completely relaxed, as if he was perfectly at home. She felt different with him, somehow, wanted him more desperately than she could recall wanting any other man. Her intense attraction to him unnerved her. So unlike Simon or Tom, the only other men she'd ever slept with; they'd made her feel beautiful and cared for, and had always wanted to please her, but never like Luke had done. She hugged herself at the memory of making love with him.

She pulled the sheet up around her as Tom's words about Luke being investigated seeped into her mind. Losing Aunt Annabel was hard enough, and being betrayed by Simon was a different kind of cruelty, but to let herself fall in love with this man when she'd been warned about his financial problems was careless.

'Damn,' she murmured, wishing yet again that Tom had thought to keep his information to himself. She needed to distance herself from Luke, however much she felt the urge to be with him. She tried to get more comfortable, but moving her legs woke him up.

'Morning,' he murmured, his voice croaky, as he stretched. He smiled up at her then narrowed his eyes. 'What's the matter? Didn't sleep well? Hangover, I suppose. I'm feeling rather heavy-headed too.'

'Luke?' she whispered awkwardly.

'What is it, sweetheart?' He pushed himself up on his elbow, his expression gradually changed to one of concern. 'What's wrong?'

'We had sex.'

He smiled. 'Yes, we did.'

'And?'

'And, it was wonderful,' he replied, placing his hands behind his head.

This felt too perfect, too dreamlike. Why hadn't she refused to go with him on his boat? She wasn't an idiot and knew what she could and couldn't say. Bea couldn't help smiling as she looked down at him.

Luke gently pulled her down onto him, kissing her. Bea melted into him, relishing the feel of his mouth on hers pushing away unwanted thoughts.

His hand moved down towards her bottom. The shrill ring of his mobile startled her. 'Ignore it,' he whispered.

The ringing continued.

Eventually, with the mood broken, Bea pushed away from him. 'You'd better answer it. Maybe it's something important.'

'I'm sure it can wait.'

Bea wondered why he was so determined not to answer the call. 'I'll go and take a quick shower, leave you to it,' she said, handing him his mobile.

She got out of bed and with a quick glance back could see he was frowning at the screen. He smiled at her, probably waiting for her to leave the room. Bea went into the bathroom and closed the door behind her. She could hear his voice though the door. He sounded irritated. She stepped into the shower and stood under the spray of water and soaped her body. Something was wrong... or was she just being overly sensitive? Maybe Simon's deceit had coloured her perception of how others lived their lives.

Showered, Bea found Luke standing in her kitchen wearing only his faded blue jeans. 'Feeling better?' he asked, passing her a mug of steaming black coffee and kissing her lightly on the neck, making her shiver. 'Mind if I take a quick shower?'

Bea's heart pounded as she watched him walk out of the room. His toned arms, back and tousled hair making her wish they were back in bed. 'Go ahead.' He was delicious and so opposite to everything Simon had been. It was such a relief.

The phone rang. Bea answered it after a couple of rings. 'Hi, Shani,' she said. 'I can't really talk now. Can I give you a call later?'

'Yes, of course, but let me quickly tell you about that hunky builder of yours.'

Bea groaned, not wanting to hear anything negative. 'You're such a gossip. Go on, what tittle-tattle have you learned at the gym this time?'

'Did you know he lives with a model? Legs up to her armpits, so I heard. They've been together on and off for years.'

Bea's legs seemed to lose some of their strength. She quickly pulled out a chair and slumped down onto it. 'What?' she whispered. 'Are you sure?'

'Damn right. They were seen together only the day before yesterday. She lives on his boat with him. Lucky cow.'

Bea felt as if Shani had slapped her. Hard.

'Bea? Are you there?'

'Yes,' she murmured. Hearing Luke's footsteps on the landing as he walked towards the stairs, she took a deep breath and tried to clear her mind. 'I have to go, Shan. I'll call you later.' Bea ended the call without waiting to hear Shani's answer. She took a sip of her coffee, ready to confront Luke.

'That's better,' he said, taking her in his arms and going to kiss her, his damp hair sticking up at all angles. Bea shivered at his touch, hardly able to look at his tanned face. She now knew he could never be hers, not in the way she would like him to be. She let him hold her for a second longer, not wishing for the moment to end. The pain of knowing how perfect it felt to be made love to by Luke only compounded her misery to learn he belonged to someone else, and she was probably nothing more than another conquest.

She pushed him away. Luke frowned. 'What's the matter?'

'This can't happen again,' she insisted, staring at the steam rising from her cup and ignoring his confused but gentle expression.

'What do you mean?' He frowned, water dripping onto his face from his wet hair.

Bea struggled to find her voice. She had to look away from him. She wanted to be with him, but she could not ignore he had a girlfriend. Wasn't the threat of the investigation against him enough to put her off, she mused? I'm so stupid, she decided, aware that by being with him she might be putting into action something that could result in her losing her home. Annabel's house. No, she owed too much to her aunt and her trust in her to let that happen, despite how much she was attracted to Luke.

A black look shadowed his face. 'If you don't want it to happen again, then it won't.'

Bea moved away. She'd hurt his feelings and didn't want him to get the wrong idea. 'You have a girlfriend.'

He raised his eyebrows. 'You knew that when we slept together last night?'

'No. Shani phoned a few minutes ago and told me.'

He shook his head slowly. 'It's not like that.'

'Okay, then,' Bea said, determined to know the extent of his relationship with this woman. 'Just answer me this. Do you live together?'

He smiled and folded his arms. 'She stays on my boat sometimes, but that doesn't mean...' He shook his head. 'Bea, we're just friends.'

Bea swallowed the lump forming in her throat. 'Have you ever slept with her?' She didn't want to know the answer, but wasn't going to be made to look a fool yet again by some man, however gorgeous he might be. 'Well?' she asked, when he didn't answer immediately.

Luke sighed. 'Yes.'

Bea stepped back and leant against the sideboard. 'So, she lives with you and you've slept together, but you're just friends. Sorry, Luke, we're not looking for the same things, obviously,' she said. 'I'm going through a divorce and however it may look to you, I don't go in for one-night stands.'

He walked up to her and stood so close she could smell the soapy scent of his skin. 'Bea, look at me.' He lifted her chin, but Bea snapped her head away from his touch. After a moment's hesitation, he spoke. 'I don't know what you think I'm looking for, and I can see that the situation with Leilani sounds a little odd, but you must believe me when I tell you that there really isn't more to our relationship than friendship now.'

'Now?' Bea couldn't hide her anger towards him. 'I think it's best you leave.'

Luke stared at her for a moment. She could see he was upset, or was it annoyance with her for being so — what was it Simon called her? — oh yes, naive. Well, naive or not, she wasn't going to put up with being second best again.

'You've obviously made your mind up about me already, so I'll let you get on. Goodbye, Bea,' he said, leaning forward and kissing her on her cheek. 'I'm sorry it had to end this way.'

Me too, thought Bea, letting him see his own way out.

* * *

'I can't believe he has a live-in girlfriend,' Bea admitted to Shani on the phone the following day after work. With her voice lowered, she gave a vague outline of what she'd said to Luke.

'How could you have known? Bastard. If nothing else though, it'll do you good, getting a taste of a new man. Out with the old, and in with the new, I say. So it's not the end of the world, is it?'

That's a matter of opinion, thought Bea miserably, trying to push away the memory of her night with Luke. 'I feel so stupid.' She wished she'd never taken his number from Mel. She'd been doing so well before that. Her house might have been crumbling, but she'd slowly been learning to cope without Annabel, and her anger towards Simon had helped her deal with Luke's betrayal. Now, it all seemed so raw once again. 'He wasn't happy when we argued about it.'

'Are you surprised?'

'No,' Bea said miserably. 'He's probably relieved to have had a lucky escape from the mad divorcee.'

'Relax,' Shani said. 'He had fun that night too, don't forget. You shouldn't be so hard on yourself. You're young, free and single. You've been betrayed by your louse of an ex-husband. You deserve a bit of spice in your life. Sleeping with a guy doesn't have to mean you need to be in a full-blown relationship with him. This isn't the dark ages, you know.'

Shani was right. 'Yes, look at you and Harry. How is he, by the way? I still haven't met him,' Bea said.

Shani groaned. 'He's driving me nuts.'

'Why?' Bea couldn't help smiling. Shani was always so in charge of her men; she only wished she was as tough.

'Nothing much, just a little disagreement we're having.'

Bea could tell something wasn't quite right. 'You're always so in control of your relationships. You are okay, aren't you?'

Shani sighed. 'When have you known me not to be? Tell you what, I'm booked up for a few extra classes this evening, but I'll give you a call tomorrow. If you're not busy, we can take a walk on the beach.'

The thought appealed to Bea. If only she could discuss what Tom had told her, but she'd signed a confidentiality agreement when she joined Malory's and couldn't divulge any information about a client, even if it was about Luke. 'Lovely, and Shani?'

'Yes?'

'Why don't you bring Harry along sometime? It would be good to get to know the man in your life. It feels weird not knowing him at all. A bit too mysterious, if you ask me.'

'Bea?'

'Yes?' Bea replied hopefully.

'Shut the hell up. You and Paul will meet him when I'm good and ready, and not before.'

Bea laughed. She knew when she was beaten, and hung up feeling sure Shani was behaving a little too secretly. Then again, thought Bea, I'm probably being over-anxious about everything. Shani was tough and never had a problem admitting if something was wrong in her life – and then, mused Bea, sorting it out without needing anyone's approval or assistance.

* * *

Shani and Bea drove straight to L'Etacq.

'So, Shan, how are things going with Harry?'

'You're not going to let this drop, are you?' Bea smiled and shook her head. 'Not so good. In fact, I haven't heard from him for about a month.' She kicked a lump of sand with the toe of her worn, white trainer.

'A month? Why?'

'No idea,' Shani said, looking away from Bea.

Something wasn't right. 'Are you okay? You would tell me if there was something wrong, wouldn't you?'

'Yes. Now stop going on. When have you known me to have a problem I couldn't cope with?'

Bea couldn't think of one solitary occasion. 'True. Maybe it's just me.'

'It is, now shut up.'

Bea picked up a piece of pale green glass, frosted by the sand and tide, and brushed the dried sand from it before dropping it again. 'Did I tell you the bank manager has called me in for another meeting?'

'No, when?'

'Next week. I'm hoping Simon's estate agent did a decent enough valuation so that I'll be able to get the full loan, but I'm not feeling all that confident.'

'What will you do if you don't get enough money?'

Bea shivered and breathed in the fresh, sea air. 'I've had sleepless nights over this, Shan. If I don't come up with the money, then I'm going to have to sell the house. He's entitled to half.'

'But that's unfair. Annabel loathed him ever since she caught him with Claire, and she left the house to you, not him.'

'I know, it seems unfair to me too, but I inherited it while we were still together so he considers it a matrimonial asset.'

'But you've signed separation papers now.'

'Yes, after Aunt Annabel had died, not before. So, if I do sell,' she continued, nauseous at the thought of an unsatisfactory outcome, 'I suppose I'll have to move in with Dad and Joyce until I sort something out.'

'You'd go mad living with that old bag.' Shani grimaced. 'You always hated being in the same house with her, even when you were small.'

'I think she found it harder having me there. It messed up their little family unit somehow, which is why Dad agreed to let me spend most of my childhood with Aunt Annabel.'

'I don't know why they ever made you go back home again.'

Bea had spent many miserable nights wishing they hadn't. 'Me neither, and it never lasted very long, but I suppose it would have looked bad at her charity lunches if her husband's dead first wife's daughter was sent to live somewhere else.'

'Despite his inability to stand up to Joyce, your dad does love you. Don't forget that.'

Bea smiled. 'I know he does. He's just too under her thumb to be able to show it. Poor man has spent most of his life doing things he doesn't want to so that she'll be kept in a good mood.'

Shani shook her head. 'It's a shame that Joyce always stirred you and Mel up. You're always so competitive towards each other.' Bea nodded. 'Do you think that's why she chose Liberation Day to hold her wedding?'

Bea didn't doubt it for a second. 'More than likely. The date's set now, so I have to deal with it.' She didn't add that she also had to try and find a way to get through the day without falling apart. 'I've no idea what she was thinking.'

Shani folded the front of her jacket over her stomach. 'I can't believe we all ever liked Simon.'

Bea smiled. 'I know. It makes me wonder if I can really trust my judgement in people,' she said, thinking again about Luke. 'I'm not sure if he fooled everyone with his charm, or if we're all – me in particular – simply gullible. Getting back to Harry though, you do know if you need any help you can come to me.' Bea stroked Shani's arm. 'However, I do think if Harry won't speak to you, then maybe you should go to his surgery. He'll have to talk to you then.'

'Don't worry, I will.' Shani said. 'How I ended up sleeping with a dentist, I'll never know. Tell me all about you and that delicious man you slept with the other night.'

Bea cringed. 'What's there to say? I thought we had something special, but obviously I was the only one who felt that way. But I want to know more about Harry.'

Shani groaned. 'He's a little older than me, interesting to talk to and fun – especially when he comes to boxercise – but I'm not sure how I really feel about him right now.'

'Okay, I know when you've had enough interrogation for one day.' Bea nudged her. 'It's getting cold out here so let's go.'

10

NOVEMBER – DISHING THE DIRT

Bea hadn't seen Luke since they had spent the night together two weeks ago. She tried to push the whole episode further to the back of her mind, as she made a few notes in one of the meeting rooms at work. She couldn't help feeling slightly deflated, even though she had been the one to tell him to leave. Surely if he felt anything for her at all, he could have contacted her by now, even on some pretext?

Her mobile rang. Bea scrambled for it in her pocket, aware she should have it on silent in the office. She quickly answered it.

'Hi, where are you?' Tom asked. Bea tried not to let her disappointment show. 'I've called your extension and walked by your desk. I couldn't see you anywhere. I need to chat to you about a couple of things, if that's all right?'

Bea tucked the phone between her ear and shoulder, continuing to scribble her notes. 'Talk away; I'm just putting together a few details for a client. I've come into Room Three to get a bit of peace.'

'I'd rather we speak out of work?'

She thought he sounded quite unsure of himself. It wasn't like him at all. 'I can meet you outside in about half an hour; we could get a coffee and have a chat.' Bea didn't know why Tom couldn't simply make time to talk to her at the office. Maybe, she mused, he wanted to keep their friendship away from prying eyes. She'd heard enough gossip at Malory's to not want her private life being the next morsel passed around.

* * *

'So, Tom,' she said, finding him outside the coffee shop. He handed her a latte and went to kiss her on the cheek.

'I thought we could take a stroll along the promenade over-looking the marina.'

'Sounds good to me,' Bea said, happy to be outside. 'How are things?'

'I wanted to let you know Vanessa and I spoke about what happened, and you can rest assured it won't happen again. She understands how rude it was for her to phone you like she did.'

'That's a relief, I suppose,' she said, not sure why he was bringing this up so long after the call.

'I was also wondering if you and your friends would like to join me at the opening of The Dark Side?'

'The what?' Bea frowned, taking a sip of her milky drink.

'The Dark Side,' he explained. 'It's a new nightclub. The opening night is next weekend. If you're free, I was hoping you might want to come along?'

It sounded like fun, but she wasn't sure. Then again, it wasn't as if she had anything else in her diary for the foreseeable future. Bea knew she could do with letting her hair down, and somewhere new and exciting sounded tempting and fun. She hesitated. 'I'll speak to the others,' she said after a moment, 'and get back to you. I'm sure neither of them will want to turn down an offer of an opening night anywhere.'

'It's great to see you again.'

'Tom, you can see me most days at work.' It was good to see him too, she realised. How did he manage to look so immaculate when the wind was so strong? She suppressed a smile, pushing away the thought of how much hairspray he must use to keep his hair in place.

'I've got something to show you,' he said, opening an attachment on his phone. 'I have to be careful at work and these files are confidential, so I thought I'd take a photo.'

Bea waited silently, not wanting to see the proof of Luke's guilt. Tom handed her the mobile. Bea's mood plummeted when she read the report from the financial commission confirming her worst fears – Luke was under investigation, and she knew as well as Tom that there had to be enough evidence to warrant investigating his finances. Her hand began to shake so she quickly returned Tom's phone. 'So, it's true,' she said, wishing more than anything that he hadn't shown it to her.

She took a deep breath and began walking. Walking down here always relaxes me, she thought, but not this time.

'You didn't think I'd lied, did you?' Tom came up beside her, concern obvious on his face.

Bea realised what she'd done. It wasn't Tom's fault Luke wasn't the man she'd hoped him to be. Like Simon, she'd read him wrong. When would she learn, she wondered, holding tightly onto her cup. 'Sorry, no. I suppose I was hoping you'd been wrong.'

'I'm not. I'm sorry, I know you're upset.' Without any notice he gave her a bear hug, holding her so tightly it almost took the air from her lungs. 'Thanks for agreeing to meet me today,' he said over her shoulder. 'It's been a relief to clear the air.'

Confused by his reaction, Bea waited a second or two before

gently pushing him away. 'Tom, you do realise I'm only agreeing to go to the club as a friend, don't you? If you're going to get the wrong idea, then I'm going to have to turn down your invitation.'

He shook his head, looking hurt. 'Not at all. You've made your feelings clear and I understand where you're coming from. I want us to be friends, too. We've known each other for so many years it would be a shame not to spend some time together outside that air-conditioned breezeblock we call an office.'

'We'll see. I'm not going to get in the middle of whatever odd situation you and Vanessa have between you. I'll give you a call about the club, but knowing Shani and Paul, they'll be only too happy for an excuse to go out and party.'

Tom went to kiss her on the cheek, stopping before actually doing so and raised an eyebrow. 'Sorry, force of habit,' he said. 'I'd better get on, I'm meeting a client in ten minutes in Colomberie.'

She watched him go, wondering if maybe she was doing the wrong thing accepting his invitation. Then again, she didn't really have any reason to be anti-social. She looked up, coming eye to eye with Luke as he drove past. Her stomach lurched and she pushed away the memory of those lips pressing down hard on hers. Bea recalled the image Tom had shown her, unable to force a smile as Luke nodded to acknowledge her before driving on.

Bea drove into town to meet Tom, Shani, Mel and Grant at The Dark Side. Paul turned up a few minutes later with Guy, a French chef he had met the previous month.

'He wanted to make sure they had some sort of a future together before introducing him, or so he says,' Mel whispered from the corner of her mouth as she eyed Guy up and down. 'They look cute together, don't you think?'

'He's hot,' Shani murmured, as they stared at the tall, brooding Frenchman. 'Don't you just love that accent? How Paul's managed to keep him a secret I'm not sure. Mind you, I've been so involved with my own stuff I probably wouldn't have noticed if he'd moved him into the flat.'

'He might have done,' Bea laughed. 'I think their looks complement each other, the tall, dark Frenchman and the shorter, blond Jersey boy. They do seem happy.' It was the first time Bea had seen Paul with anyone since his long-term partner had broken his heart by leaving him to return to Canada five years before.

Mel took Grant's hand in hers. 'Come on, let's go and find other people to talk to.'

Bea looked around the darkened room with its purple lighting and mirrored dance floor. She was relieved she'd worn trousers and not a dress. 'Love's young dream,' Bea murmured to Shani, wishing she didn't feel just a touch of envy at her stepsister's happiness.

'Love's young drips, if you ask me.' Shani rolled her eyes, smiling at Paul as he and Guy came up to them.

'Don't take any notice of her.' Paul joined them. 'She's jealous.'

'Oh bugger off.' Shani shook her head emphatically. 'You wouldn't get me being all soppy like that in public. Shouldn't you be getting the drinks in? It must be your round by now.'

'No problem, your ladyship.' He patted his pocket. 'Plenty in here to spend tonight, but you can come and help me carry them.' He flounced off towards the chrome bar at the other end of the cavernous room, taking Guy by the hand, a wide smile on his cheeky face.

Tom laughed as he watched Shani striding after Paul, her long toned legs on display in the shortest skirt that barely covered her knickers. 'I'm beginning to think you're surrounded by mad people.'

Bea secretly agreed. She held up her hands and nodded. 'I

know. And what's more, these are my closest friends, so there's no hope for me. Guy seems fun though, don't you agree?'

Bea watched as Shani, bored with waiting at the crowded bar, swayed her hips onto the dance floor and waved her arms in the air, lost in the music. Paul followed and mimicked her, leaving Guy to buy the drinks.

'It's like something from one of those documentaries on 1970's discos in New York,' Tom joked. 'Except these two haven't quite mastered the moves.' As he took a gulp from his drink someone caught Tom's eye on the other side of the room. He nodded at them.

Bea couldn't see who it was over the mêlée of people, then noticed Shani gesturing frantically in her direction. She scanned the bustling nightclub, unable to see what all the fuss was about.

Tom leant closer to Bea. 'Look at—' he started, before a hand landed heavily on his back. Tom turned around mid-sentence and, his shoulders tensing, he forced a smile. 'Luke,' he shouted, over the noise. 'How are you?'

Bea frowned. She hadn't expected to see him here.

'You know Bea, of course,' Tom said, sliding his arm around her shoulders. Bea shrugged him off.

Luke's mouth twitched. He nodded at Tom. Was that contempt she spotted on his face? He caught Bea's eye and his expression softened slightly. Luke found the power of speech first. 'Of course,' he answered, his deep blue eyes boring into hers. 'You haven't met Leilani yet.'

Bea noticed movement next to him. Her heart plummeted when she saw one of his arms was casually slung around a tall, tanned brunette, who she couldn't help noticing was wearing the same scarlet stilettos she and Shani had lusted over in the latest edition of *Vogue*. Bea didn't think she'd ever met anyone this glamorous and impossibly beautiful before. No wonder Luke was seeing her; Leilani was utterly gorgeous.

She looked down at Bea and smiled. 'Hi, I'm pleased to meet you,' she said, before turning her attention to Tom, who, Bea couldn't help noticing, was dumbstruck at the vision in front of him.

'This is Tom and Beatrice,' Luke said, his smile showing off his white teeth. His beard appeared to be clipped, little more than designer stubble. They made a breathtaking couple, and Bea wanted to cry. She swallowed the lump in her throat, determined to appear unfazed.

'God, they even have matching teeth,' Shani whispered from behind her.

'What a typically English name,' Leilani drawled sexily.

Bea's insides had contracted so much they hurt, and try as she might she couldn't help sneaking another peek at Luke's face. He didn't seem as happy as she'd expected, although his lips drew back into a smile when he caught her looking at him. Tom gazed appreciatively at Leilani's impossibly pert bosom, which was almost at his eye level. Bea couldn't imagine where Luke had found Leilani. She had certainly never seen her in Jersey before.

'Nice to meet you, Leilani,' Tom stammered. As both men turned their attention to her, Bea knew in no uncertain terms that she could never hope to compete with this impressive Amazonian.

'Lukey has been showing me round the countryside you have here on Jersey. Everything is so quaint. I must admit to being a city girl at heart, though. As far as I can see, you either turn left or right when you go for a drive on this little island,' she giggled. 'And you still end up back in the same place one hour later. There's not much space here to escape to, is there?'

'We say *in* Jersey,' Shani said pointedly. 'Not *on* Jersey.' She leant towards Bea. 'Lukey?' Shani murmured a little too loudly. Luke glanced at her having obviously heard her comment and Bea couldn't tell if he was annoyed or simply amused.

'Manhattan is more my thing,' Leilani continued, oblivious to Shani's sarcasm. Bea suspected Leilani was used to dealing with jealous females. She couldn't help being amused by Shani's instant dislike of Leilani, though; it made her feel much better.

'You're on holiday, then?' Tom asked, not appearing at all bothered by her insulting comments about his place of birth.

'Yes.'

'How long are you planning on staying in Jersey?' Bea asked, feeling happier at this news.

'I haven't decided yet. I suppose I'll be here for as long as Lukey wants me to be.' She stroked the tight, hard bottom that Bea sadly remembered only too well. She stiffened at the memory. Bea cleared her throat. Leilani pouted at Luke. He replied by giving her a slow smile that was so sexy even Shani gawped.

'What is it that you do?' Tom asked, unable to take his eyes off her.

'I'm a model,' she announced, smiling at him as if to prove her point. 'On runways mostly, but I specialise in stockings and lingerie.' She pointed one foot forward and raised her immaculately waxed eyebrows.

'Well, it was nice seeing you again,' Luke said. He glanced at Bea. Taking Leilani's hand, he added, 'We'll catch up with you all later. Have a fun evening.' He led her away across the dance floor.

'It was lovely to meet with you,' Leilani added over her shoulder at Bea. She oozed sex appeal, and Bea doubted she had ever felt as thoroughly self-satisfied as Leilani seemed. Bea wanted to dislike her, but apart from her proximity to Luke and her perfect looks she couldn't honestly do so. What little confidence she had managed to muster before leaving the house had completely vanished. And, as for Lukey, well, Bea decided, Leilani could keep him.

'Wow,' Shani said. 'He is so hot.' I know, thought Bea. 'But Lukey?' said Shani once again. 'Eugh.'

'I think all the sex they're having has turned his brain to mush.' Bea grimaced at the thought.

'He could turn my brain to mush any day.' Shani glanced away from Luke's receding back and noticed Bea watching, hands on her hips. 'Oops, sorry.'

Bea shrugged. 'No, you're right. He's gorgeous, although I thought that performance was a little staged, didn't you?'

'That smile wasn't.'

'Ladies,' Tom said, reminding Bea that he was still there. 'Can I get you both a drink?'

Bea pulled a face at Shani and turned to him. 'Yes, please.'

Bea watched as Luke and Leilani moved away, horrified when he looked back over his shoulder and caught her. She stared at him transfixed, mortified when Leilani noticed him looking. She immediately pulled him closer to her, winking at Bea. 'Come on, big boy, let's have some fun,' she said, kissing his neck. Luke took her hand away from his buttock and led her to the bar, where he said something to her for a few seconds before turning to the barman.

'Well,' Mel said later, when the girls visited the ladies' room. 'It didn't take him long to get over you, did it? Typical man.'

Bea could have killed Shani. She must have told Mel what had happened between them and now her sister would never let her forget it. She regretted being so open, and stupid.

'Two entirely different things,' Bea assured her through the locked door, grateful for the time to gather her thoughts. 'It was a friendly meal, nothing more.'

'He kissed you.'

'So?' Bea felt instantly bad for suspecting Shani of gossiping behind her back.

'Er, you had sex?' Mel said, rather more loudly than Bea would have liked.

'Thanks, Shani,' Bea called to the next cubicle. So she *had* told Mel about their conversation.

'Sorree.'

'So what? Now he has a proper girlfriend.' Despite her bravado, Bea felt thoroughly fed up, and she struggled to zip up her tight trousers before exiting the cubicle.

'Melanie,' interrupted Shani pointedly. 'None of us are in a position to criticise Bea's choices. You've had your problems with Grant, and look at me with Harry.'

'Harry who?' Mel said sarcastically. 'I don't think any of us have been allowed to meet him yet, but I suppose you're right,' Mel said, reapplying her crimson red lipstick. 'Though Bea, he can't have been that hurt by you being so weird towards him. After all, he took no time to replace you. And you must admit, he looked happy with Leilani. At least you don't have to feel guilty about anything.'

'I wasn't,' Bea said, brushing her hair and wishing it was straight and shiny like Mel's, rather than curly and a little wild.

'I just don't understand, that's all,' Mel added, her expression one of concern. 'You don't jump into bed with guys, so you must really fancy him.'

Bea shrugged, trying to make light of her reactions to Luke. 'What's your point, Mel?' Bea asked, bored with her sister's interest in her non-existent love life.

Mel narrowed her eyes. 'I don't understand why you'd sleep with him, even if he's a little rugged and messy-looking, and then give him the brush-off?'

Bea groaned. She was too embarrassed to tell Mel about discovering that Luke had a girlfriend after they'd slept together, and couldn't divulge the information Tom had given her about the suspected money laundering, but her sister was a legal assistant and knew how these things worked. She considered her words carefully. She wanted to prove to herself that her instincts weren't completely rubbish. Maybe if she could find out more about Luke's alleged money laundering activities then at least she might feel a little less foolish for not seeing through him.

'Tom told me something about him and as much as I may like him, I stand to lose my professional integrity, not to mention my freedom, if I allow some sort of closeness to develop between us. Sleeping with him was just a one-off. A moment of weakness I mustn't allow happen again.' She watched Mel trying to make sense of what she'd just told her. 'At least for the time being.'

Her sister wasn't stupid and would be able to put together various scenarios that could link Tom's, Luke's and her own business connections. At least she hoped she could. She waited for a moment.

'Ahh.' Mel raised her eyebrows as it dawned on her. 'I think I understand your predicament, and if it's what I think it is then it's definitely better that you keep your distance from someone who could be involved in… *washing*.'

Bea nodded miserably. 'I know.' She put her hairbrush back in her bag and clipped it closed. Life stank sometimes.

Shani shook her head, frowning. 'I have no idea what the hell you're both prattling on about, but if that's the case then am I to take it that Tom did a good thing by tipping Bea off about Luke?'

Bea caught Mel's eye and pulled a face at Shani's unintentional use of one of the two words they'd made a point to exclude from their conversation. 'You could say that,' she said, as they left the loo and returned to the others.

She was soothed by the sight of Paul grimacing as he relayed an amusing anecdote to Tom, who was laughing loudly. Guy watched Paul, his black eyes glistening with adoration. Noticing Bea walk up to him, Tom smiled at her. 'You all right?'

'Fine, thanks. Shani had some gossip for us. You know how it is.' She was determined to relax and enjoy her evening out. At least she didn't have to worry about Tom causing her emotions to go into meltdown. She studied his sea green eyes as he bent his head towards Paul to catch the punchline of a joke and noticed Luke out of the corner of her eye as he leant against the bar, his back to Leilani. He didn't seem bothered that his girlfriend was flirting with the barman right in front of him. When Bea looked back at Luke she saw him staring directly at her with an intensity that confused her. She saw Mel had noticed too, so glanced quickly at Tom who was listening to Paul and Shani, debating which bands played the best music.

Mel gently took Bea's hand, and in a rare moment of sisterly affection gave it a light squeeze. 'We'll talk tomorrow. I'll have a think, see if I can maybe find out more about the case against him. Try and switch off until then.'

Bea sighed. Somehow this was more painful and heart-breaking than finding out Simon had been unfaithful to her. It seemed ridiculous, but true. She'd been drawn to Luke and it concerned her that her instincts could be so wrong. What an emotional mess, and this time she had no one else to blame.

11

NEVER ENOUGH THYME

Luke watched Bea leave the nightclub with Tom. He couldn't miss her reaction to Leilani, and knew she'd assumed they were sleeping together. There was more to her emotional distance towards him than his relationship with Leilani, surely? Bea was an independent woman, a professional who didn't need validation through whatever man she was seeing, but he should have insisted she listen to him about Leilani. Then again, if she'd told him the same story, would he have been willing to believe nothing was going on? He doubted it. He wasn't going to let her believe that he was moping around after her, especially now she was spending time with Tom Brakespear again. What the hell was going on between them?

'Honey, are you sure you don't want to invite me onto your boat for a nightcap?' Leilani raised an eyebrow. 'It's closer than my hotel.'

He shook his head. 'No, I think you should go back to your room.'

'You never used to be so reluctant to sleep with me.'

Luke laughed. 'We used to be in a relationship.'

'It's that Beatrix girl, isn't it? Something's happened between you.'

Luke shook his head. 'It's Beatrice, and it's not your business what, if anything, has gone on between us.'

'Lukey,' she teased, pouting. 'Come on, you know you want to.'

'Stop it.' He tried to sound stern, but it didn't work; she knew him too well. 'We both know you're only here for a few months, and whatever happened between us finished long ago.'

'You were my first love.' She smiled, tilting her head to one side and flicking her long hair behind her shoulder. 'We could still make it work.'

Luke couldn't help thinking back to when everything seemed so much clearer. He'd thought himself in love with Leilani, and probably had been; after all, she was good fun as well as very beautiful. But he had more pressing matters to consider now. His business was in a mess, and despite his better judgement he knew he had strong feelings for Bea.

'What?' Leilani asked, resting a hand on his thigh. 'You're not thinking of changing your mind, are you?'

'No, I'm not.' He laughed, removing her hand. 'Right, you can sleep in one of the cabins tonight if you like.'

Leilani groaned. 'I've never had anyone play as hard to get as you, and I don't like it.'

'Too bad. Now, where will you be sleeping? I'm shattered and must get up early, so I need to get you settled.'

'I'll sleep in the other cabin, then. If you're sure you can't be persuaded. It's just a shame you won't be in there with me.'

'You'll be fine, stop sulking.' Amused at her persistence, he thought of his younger self. He would never have turned down such an appealing offer.

* * *

With enormous relief, Bea arrived home. She couldn't wait to shower and somehow wash away the memory of seeing Luke with Leilani at the club. She began removing her makeup and did her best to push away thoughts creeping into her aching brain. However, as much as she tried, she couldn't help thinking about her being in this room with him that night.

She had little choice but to admit that while she may have strong feelings for Luke, he was having the time of his life with someone else. Worse still, someone like Leilani.

Bea sat down heavily on the edge of her bed. Her life had been mapped out since she was a teenager. She'd always planned on living in her own home with a supportive husband and two children. She tried not to get upset as the memory of her miscarriage seeped into her mind. Her child would have been starting nursery school about now. She pictured her aunt sewing name labels into endless pieces of Bea's own uniform, and had always imagined doing the same for her own little boy or girl. It hurt to know she'd missed out on something so life-enhancing. Children might not have come along, but she had thought Simon to be *the one* when they married. They had this house, even if he resented her aunt being here with them. It hadn't occurred to her that her life would ever change so drastically.

'No wonder I'm making such a mess of it all,' she groaned. 'I never saw this coming.'

The following morning, bored by her self-pity, Bea went through to the small room her aunt had used as a study and sat down in front of the untidy desk. She rested her palm on the scarred wooden surface and sighed. If only she could solve the puzzle of the Jersey Kiss. It must be something important if her aunt had included it in her will. Maybe there'd be reference to it in her aunt's papers? She pulled open the middle drawer and lifted out the mass of papers, sifting through one invoice after another.

Nothing referencing a mysterious item in there, she thought, frustrated by her unsuccessful search.

Checking the back of the drawer, her fingers touched something. Bea took out several small envelopes she vaguely recognised. She read the childish scrawl on the front of each one and breathed in the faint scent of her aunt's perfume. Reading one of the letters she'd sent to her aunt from boarding school, Bea was instantly transported back to the misery she'd experienced being away from everything familiar to her.

She carefully replaced the invoices and letters and checked the other drawers. Nothing. Wondering if her aunt had maybe filed something away about the legacy, she spent the following two hours carefully working her way through the dusty lever arch files on the bookcase.

Bea had scoured every inch of the study, but apart from her old letters and a few heartfelt ones from Antonio, she'd found only paperwork relating to the garden. She remembered standing in here with her aunt many times over the years, with Annabel proudly showing her designs that she'd won prizes for at flower shows. She'd even discovered several of her school photos and a certificate for coming second in a painting competition, but nothing that could possibly relate to the Jersey Kiss.

In the garden, Bea pushed an orange plastic wheelbarrow half-filled with weeds and dead wood. As she walked to the compost heap, she concluded that she was perfectly happy without a man in her life. She just needed not to lose this house.

Paul had a partner and Shani would no doubt work things out with Harry – or find someone to take his place. She needed to persuade Mr Peters at their meeting that she deserved the loan, buy Simon out of his share of The Brae and take back some sort of control of her life. The thought cheered her up.

A couple of hours later, Bea had worked her way through

several flower beds, noticing that she needed to plant more thyme for next year. Never enough thyme, she mused. She'd cleared her head a little and worked through her dilemma about the men in her life. She showered and changed, tying her damp hair up in a scrunchie, and then padded through to the kitchen in her worn bunny slippers to make a desperately needed mug of coffee and read through the papers. It helped to immerse herself in other people's chaos as she skimmed the gossip columns.

'It's only us,' Mel shouted from the hallway. 'The front door was unlocked, so we've invited ourselves in.' Bea's heart sank several levels; she knew that tone. It was her sister's organising over-the-top-cheerful one. Not what you needed at any time, but especially not on a rare chill-out day. Had she forgotten their conversation the previous night?

'Through here,' Bea answered, willing herself to sound welcoming.

'Hi, hon,' said Shani, pulling a face from behind Mel's back. 'Mel and I were talking about the wedding and I just knew you would hate to be left out.'

Cow, mouthed Bea, unable to help smiling at her 'disloyal' friend. Shani winked back slyly, as Mel busied herself making a cup of herbal tea.

'Right, listen to me, ladies,' started Mel. 'I've had an idea.' Bea suppressed an anguished groan. 'I didn't initially want to have any bridesmaids, but I think I'd like to have them now. I don't want to have to choose between my friends – you know how sensitive people can be – so I thought you two would be perfect. My sister, who everyone will expect, and you, Shani. You're both so opposite to look at and different to me, we'll look great in the photos. Isn't it perfect?'

Bea shot a rabbit-caught-in-headlights glance at Shani, who gave her a knowing look.

'Well? What do you think?' Mel asked excitedly, arms held out. 'Think of all the fun we can have. Getting dressed together, our hair and make-up, manicures. What could be more fun?'

Struggling for an acceptable answer, Bea racked her brains. 'Um, yes,' she answered lamely. 'Although...'

'Although?' Mel's lengthy French-polished extensions tapped a rapid chorus on the pine table.

The embryo of an idea was rattling around Bea's addled brain and she forced herself to pursue it. She knew she had to make her excuses now, or go along with the horrible bridesmaid idea for the next few months. If she didn't come up with a suitable alternative, photos of her and Shani in peach crinoline dresses or some other hideous creation would forever haunt them. 'What about Grant's nieces?'

'Who?' Mel asked, eyes lighting up.

'His sister's twins,' agreed Shani, immediately making the most of Bea's brilliant idea, relief flowing across her face. 'Yes, your soon-to-be nieces, you must think of them at a time like this. They'll be devastated not to be included in your special day.'

Bea nodded enthusiastically, knowing the little girls would probably be delighted, and even if they weren't, thought Bea, there are times when adults must pull rank, and this was one of them.

'What about them? I presumed you would be having them, to be honest,' enthused Bea, running with the idea now that Mel hadn't immediately rejected it. 'They can walk ahead of you down the aisle, scattering rose petals from a tiny wicker basket, or something.'

Mel looked suspiciously from one to the other and thought through the suggestion. 'What, as well as you two, or instead of?'

'I think two are probably enough, so just the little ones.'

Mel thought about it briefly and Bea had to hold back a sigh of relief when her sister's face slowly broke into a broad grin. 'Of course, why didn't I think of it? It's a great way to score points with his mum.' She clapped her hands together gleefully. 'Clever girl.'

'That's what Shani and I are here for, to help you plan your day as perfectly as possible.' Bea smiled, enormously relieved that her idea had been so eagerly accepted.

'But what about you two?' Mel added, her face filled with concern. 'What will you do on the day if you're not going to be my bridesmaids?'

Shani folded her arms across her chest. 'I can help with organising the setting up of the marquee or whatever else you may need me to do.'

'Yes, are you still going to have it at your mum and dad's? You're more than welcome to have it here if you want, you know?' offered Bea, crossing her fingers behind her back.

'Thanks, but this is your house, where you and your aunt have memories. My childhood was spent at home with Mum and Dad, and anyway Dad's already drawn up a plan of the layout and matting leading from the driveway to the inside.'

Bea remembered how hurt her aunt was at Simon's insistence that they hold their wedding reception at a hotel instead of in The Brea's garden. She'd never forgiven herself for giving in to him on that. 'Whatever you want; it's your day, after all.'

'Great idea,' Shani said oblivious to the tension. 'I've always envied you being able to walk from the end of your parent's garden straight onto the beach.'

Mel smiled. 'To make the most of the view there'll be one of those marquees with windows all along the side of the sea view. And he said that if the weather is good they'll roll up the side so we're almost holding the reception in the garden.'

Bea said thoughtfully, 'I can arrange flowers and the table settings can be put together from the plants here. Or I can do something different.'

'You can both start by helping compile a list of who to invite. I'm scared of missing someone. I must make sure I don't forget anyone who might buy one of the expensive items I intend to have on my wedding lists.' Noticing Shani's frown, she added pointedly, 'There will be cheaper items, too for the tighter guests.'

'How rude,' Shani teased. 'Just don't forget any great aunt Ethel, or you'll never be forgiven.'

'I do have one problem,' frowned Mel.

'What?' Shani asked.

'Not what, but whom.'

'Well, whom then?'

'I need to invite Luke and Leilani,' she said tentatively, looking from one to the other.

'What? Why?' Shani argued, ignoring Bea's frantic mouthing to shut up as she didn't need another interrogation from Mel.

'I have to, he's an old friend of Grant's.'

'Take no notice,' Bea interrupted. 'Of course you must invite him.'

'And I'll invite Tom for you, although I've no idea who can accompany you, Shani. After all, Paul's now with Guy and Harry never seems to be around, so you'll be by yourself once again. I could try and find another of Grant's friends to act as escort for you, if you'd like?'

'Don't you dare.' Shani glared down at Mel from her lofty height.

'Surely Harry will be coming with you?' Bea asked. 'And I'm sure Tom will want to come, so he can be my plus one.' She'd rather Tom be her partner than some stranger Mel might find.

'I didn't think you two were dating again?'

'We're not,' Bea said. 'We do work together though, and if you want me to have a partner I'm sure he'll step in. I'm not bothered either way.'

Shani crossed her eyes and pulled a face, making Bea giggle. Bea knew the arrangements could only get more complicated and that there would be further rows between now and the big day. She needed to keep these chats with Mel as light as possible to be able to face them.

'Well, if you two aren't going to be my bridesmaids, and I'm to only have the twins, then I think I'll ask Leilani to be my chief bridesmaid,' Mel suggested. 'I think I need to add a little extra touch of glamour to the occasion, don't you?'

There was a sharp intake of breath from Shani. 'Are you completely mad? You can't ask her.'

'Why not? She'd look fantastic and could watch over the twins.'

'Don't be so ridiculous, she probably hates kids.'

Bea rolled her eyes. 'Whether she does or she doesn't like kids, she's a model, Mel, not a nanny.'

'I know that.'

A thought occurred to Bea. 'You might be pretty, Mel, but would you really want a professional model walking down the aisle with you? What if she upstages you on your big day?'

'Which she bloody well will,' Shani insisted, glaring across the table in disbelief.

Mel sniggered. 'Honestly, you two are so easy to wind up sometimes.'

Bea and Shani shook their heads at each other. 'Is this going to take much longer?' Bea asked, forgetting her plan to keep things light.

Mel looked at her watch. 'I'm going home to change. I'm meeting Grant later, so I'll leave you two in peace. Oh, and Bea, I haven't forgotten what we discussed last night. I'll get back to you as soon as I find out any info.'

Bea thanked her and saw her out, relieved to have peace restored once again. 'She can be so exhausting at times,' she said to

Shani later, as they sat quietly together in the snug watching an episode of her favourite soap opera.

'I've been thinking,' Shani said. 'If you need help paying off that mortgage.'

'The one I haven't got yet?'

Shani nodded. 'Yes, that one. Well, I thought I could move in here with you and pay you rent?'

Bea was confused by her friend's offer. 'I'd love that, but what about Paul? Wouldn't he miss you?'

'I doubt it. He seems to be spending most of his time at Guy's flat at the moment, so he'd probably be relieved.'

Bea loved the idea. 'It'll be just like when we were kids at boarding school.' But even though the extra money from Shani was better than nothing, it still wouldn't be nearly enough to help sort out her finances.

'I can't believe how miserly Simon is being with you.'

'I think it's probably because I'm insisting on keeping this house and going against his wishes,' Bea said, staring at the dancing flames in the nearby fire. 'But I've had enough of doing what he dictates, and this time, I'm going to do whatever I can to keep my house, whether Simon likes the idea or not.'

12

DECEMBER – TWISTED VINES

Simon arrived at the house a few days later. Bea had just ended a call with the bank, arranging a meeting in the new year with Mr Peters to discuss her mortgage application, but her relief at having a definite appointment was short-lived. She stood on her doorstep, glowering at Simon as he removed an envelope from his briefcase and handed it to her. 'I'm running out of patience with this nonsense, Bea. I know you've tried at a couple of banks, but you'll just have to rethink things or agree to sell this dump. Why you even care about this garden now Annabel is dead, I've no idea. You don't even know that much about gardening.'

'I wouldn't expect you to understand.'

He went to place a hand on her shoulder, but she stepped back. His hand fell. 'I didn't mean for all this to happen, you know?'

Bea folded her arms, creasing the envelope in her hand. 'No?'

'Of course not. If your aunt hadn't said anything about seeing me with Claire that night, then we'd probably still be together.'

'So it's her fault? That's rubbish, Simon, and you know it.'

He marched to his car and turned to her before getting inside. 'Fine, but we don't have to be angry with each other all the time.'

She took a deep breath. 'We wouldn't be if you weren't so dead set on forcing me to sell this house.' Without waiting for his reply, she went back into the house, slamming the front door.

She tore open the envelope and unfolded his letter with shaking hands.

Claire's due date is only a month away now and I need money to buy the furniture we need to complete the apartment before then. I think I've been more than fair with you, Beatrice. The sooner this matter is finalised the sooner we can both move on with our lives. Simon.

'Moron,' she shouted, as a thin layer of plaster dust fell onto the paper. It was time to contact Mel and ask her to sort out the injunction. She wouldn't put up with his unwanted visits any more. She phoned Mel and told her to go ahead and draft something. Enough was enough.

'It's about time,' Mel said. 'Don't hold back from sending it to him, either. He needs to be put in his place.'

Bea agreed.

That evening she sat in the drawing room, carefully turning the tatty pages of her aunt's notebooks trying to absorb some of her gardening tips and work out if the sketches inside related to any of the plants she recognised. It was only five months until D-Day and she still had no idea what she was going to do.

The phone rang. Bea thought about ignoring it, but when the shrill ringing continued she got up and answered it. 'Hello?' Bea said, trying not to show her irritation at being disturbed.

'Hi,' said Tom. 'Sorry to bother you, but I was wondering if I could pop round for a chat this evening.' She didn't answer. 'If that's not a problem, I mean?'

She wasn't in the mood to see anyone after Simon's appearance, but it wasn't Tom's fault she'd chosen to marry the idiot. 'All right, Tom, if you want,' she relented.

'Great. I'll see you within the hour.'

'Look, I'm not in the best frame of mind, and if it's all right with you I was looking forward to an early night.'

'Why, what's the matter?'

'Nothing new, I'm afraid.' She couldn't be bothered repeating what had happened with Simon.

'Bea, I can tell you're worried about something. Is there anything I can do?'

'Thanks, Tom, but there isn't,' she said miserably, sitting back down again and taking up her cup of coffee before reconsidering and relating her earlier conversation with Simon. 'I just have to deal with it. It's tough, but life stinks sometimes. I can do without further legal fees though and will have to delay some of the work on the house, yet again, to pay for it, but I can't have him coming here whenever the mood takes him.'

Tom sighed. 'Sorry, Bea, I can imagine how you must feel. I'll leave you to your early night, but if there's anything I can do, promise you'll ring me.'

'I will,' she said. 'I'll speak to you soon.'

After he had ended the call, Bea wondered what he'd wanted to talk about that couldn't be discussed at the office. It mustn't have been that important, or he would have insisted on coming round, she decided. She looked over to the corner of the room where her aunt always placed the Christmas tree, sad that it just didn't feel like Christmas this year.

She picked up the notebooks again and pulled her legs up onto the settee to get comfortable. If only she could block out the rest of the world and be left alone with her memories. She closed her eyes and rested her head against one of the worn velvet cushions. Shutting out everything was so tempting. She snuggled up and let her mind wander back to happier days when she and Simon had had so many plans. Aunt Annabel singing tunelessly in the potting shed pushed the image of her and Simon away, and Bea couldn't help smiling. Her aunt looked up at her standing at the doorway. 'There you are, darling,' she said. 'Be a good girl and stop wallowing. Go and fight for what you want.'

Bea opened her eyes and sat up. Glancing around the room to check her aunt wasn't somewhere near, she rubbed her eyes. 'She's right, I need to get a grip and stop feeling so miserable.'

* * *

Over supper at Shani and Paul's flat the following evening, Bea pondered how they managed to work together and live in such a small space rarely falling out.

The attic flat, originally Paul's and his previous boyfriend David's, was bright and inviting. The small lounge somehow appeared bigger, with a two-seater cream settee and matching armchair taking up the floor space and a plain oak sideboard along one wall. She couldn't imagine how Paul managed to cook in the tiny kitchenette. It didn't seem much larger than most wardrobes. Paul pushed back the veil of tiny, coloured glass beads hanging from the doorframe and handed Bea a glass of wine.

'I feel bad living in such a big empty house when you two have to share everything here.' Bea could understand why Luke had been so surprised to discover she lived in The Brae alone with all those empty rooms.

'You can always take her ladyship here to live with you,' Paul said.

Shani looked at Bea thoughtfully. Bea could tell she was desperate to tell Paul about the offer of moving in. Neither of them wanted to upset him, though. Shani pulled a face at Paul. 'Thanks,' she said. 'I thought you loved flat sharing with me.'

'I do, but your untidiness drives me nuts. I've never met such a messy woman. Did you know, Bea, she sleeps in an old 1930's bed her grandmother passed down to her, and every time she brings some poor unfortunate bloke home I have to wear ear plugs, it squeaks so much.'

Bea spluttered and nearly spat out her drink. 'Charming.'

'Cheers, Paul.' Shani glared at him. 'We can't all be neurotic about keeping everything neat.'

'A little bit of discretion wouldn't go amiss,' he teased. 'Supper's ready and waiting.' Paul handed Shani a glass of sparkling water. 'Grab a plate and help yourself.' He indicated various tubs of Thai food.

'You're not drinking, Shan?' Bea frowned. She'd never known Shani to turn down alcohol before. 'You're not pregnant, are you?'

Paul and Bea laughed at Shani's horror-struck expression. 'No, I'm not. My stomach is a little delicate,' she said, glaring at them both. 'Not that it's any of your business.'

'All right, calm down.' Paul handed Bea a plate of food. 'Get this down your neck.'

'It smells great,' Bea murmured, forcing herself not to rush the delicious food.

'This is so tasty,' Shani said, her mouth half full. 'I haven't eaten anything this good in ages.'

Bea made the most of every mouthful. For someone with a dodgy tummy Shani was certainly bolting down her food. 'You don't seem to be off your food,' Bea said. 'Only alcohol.'

Shani pursed her lips. 'My stomach has been a little sensitive, so I'm trying out a sort of detox. It's something new, and if it works I'll tell you two about it, okay?.'

'Fine. No need to get snappy.' Paul filled his plate with more food. 'What's happened recently with you then, Bea? Shani was reminiscing about that day you took her to watch Luke Thornton playing beach polo.'

'I wasn't there for that reason,' Bea argued.

Shani waved her fork in the air. 'I can't forget how amazing that polo match was though. Don't you think it was pretty intense?'

Bea nodded, enjoying the image of Luke galloping across the beach. 'It was. I'm going to go next year, if they hold it again.'

'Yes,' Paul scowled. 'I still haven't forgiven you two for not including me. You're both so selfish sometimes.'

'Sorry, we won't forget you next time,' she promised. 'Anyway, this year, hasn't been all fun.' Bea told them about her visit from Simon and then about Tom.

'Well, you both know he's not my cup of tea,' Paul said, sipping from his glass.

'Which one?' Shani asked.

'Either, both, neither,' Paul said.

'Why?' Bea looked at him. 'I know Simon is a waste of space, but what's wrong with Tom?'

'Nothing I can put my finger on, but I can't help feeling he isn't all he seems.'

Bea laughed. 'That's ridiculous, there's nothing suspicious about Tom.' She didn't mention she hadn't been so quick to believe his tales about Luke and the investigation until she saw his proof. 'He was quite sweet when I last spoke to him. So what's wrong with him?'

'Nothing,' Shani said, cleaning up some food from the floor. 'Just ignore him, I think Tom was lovely to apologise and be so sympathetic about that creep, Simon. Paul?'

'Okay, it was the right thing to do, I suppose,' he grudgingly relented. 'What the hell is that?' he asked, hearing the 1812 Overture warble from Bea's handbag.

'My new ringtone. It's Tom,' she said, turning away from her inquisitive friends. After several minutes she ended the call and dropped her mobile back into her bag.

Paul raised his eyebrows. 'What did he want?'

'You're never going to believe this, but his assistant has been signed off work for three weeks after an appendix operation and he's booked me to accompany him to New York for five days.'

They looked at her. Paul opened his eyes wide. 'You're going on holiday with him? That's a little unexpected, isn't it?'

Bea shook her head. 'It's for work. He's always travelling to meet clients. I've gone to London once or twice in the last few years, but never further than that.' She squealed with excitement. 'I can't believe I'm going to New York in a couple of weeks.'

'Lucky cow. I wish I was going away,' said Shani. 'The break will do you good though, and you might find you hit it off. If nothing else, you'll be away from Simon and his bullying for a bit.'

'Sounds good, I suppose,' Paul said, refilling their glasses. 'He must be earning decent money if they send him to the States to visit clients. I hope you get to do some sightseeing.'

'Me too.' Bea laughed, picturing visits to the Empire State building and Central Park. 'I'm so excited, I can't wait.'

'You both must be on decent salaries if you work in trust?' Paul added, interrupting her thoughts. 'Surely you can afford to take out a smallish mortgage for The Brae to pay for the work that needs doing?'

Bea shook her head. 'I wish. My job sounds more important than it is. Only directors and senior managers earn good salaries in my line of work. They're the ones who sign things off. I'd need to pass my professional exams to reach a higher salary and I've got too much on to be able to focus on those for the time being.' She didn't add that the thought of doing them gave her a headache.

'Blimey,' Shani grimaced. 'I always thought you were way up there with the big money.'

Bea scoffed. 'I wish that was true, but it's Simon who earns a decent wage. Which is why, despite what he said in his letter, I know he doesn't need to be chasing me to pay him back. This trip with Tom will be funded by his client. There'll be a reason we must hold the meetings in New York, but he's giving me a great opportunity by taking me.'

She thought of the empty house. 'Look, I know you're spending a lot of time at Guy's flat, Paul, but I was thinking that if you wanted to, you could both move into the house and look after it for me while I'm away.'

Paul and Shani looked at each other and then back at Bea, and without exchanging thoughts on the matter both nodded in agreement. 'I'd be happy to. Guy works long hours, so when he's working I can enjoy the house with Shani.'

'Yes, it suits me,' Shani agreed looking very happy at the prospect.

'You go and have a great trip and leave the house to us,' Paul said. 'Although by the time you return we may have become so used to living there that we'll invoke squatter's rights.'

'I don't think we have them here in Jersey, but as long as you take care of the house for me, you can stay as long as you like,' she said, liking the thought.

'It's going to be strange though, surely,' Shani added. 'Going away with Tom to New York?'

'I know, that occurred to me too,' Bea admitted. 'I'm sure it'll be fine. It's only business.'

* * *

'New York?' Luke knew he sounded idiotic repeating Grant's words, but he couldn't help himself. 'With that jerk?'

Grant shrugged and nodded. 'That's what Mel said. Only for a few days, though. I'm sure it means nothing. I think it's got something to do with work.'

Luke tried to remain calm. He clenched and unclenched a fist.

'I wouldn't have told you if I'd thought you'd be this upset. Since when have you been interested in what Bea gets up to, anyhow?' Grant checked to see Mel was out of earshot. 'I would have thought you had more than enough going on with Leilani. She looks a bit of a handful.'

Luke could see how ridiculous he must seem to his friend. Time to backtrack, he decided. 'I'm not interested in what Bea does, or who with. I just need to speak to her about a few jobs that she put off. I can't very well do that if she's on the other side of the Atlantic, now can I?'

Grant raised an eyebrow. 'Really?'

He could tell he hadn't convinced his friend. 'The work's nearly done, and I need to get my men onto another site. Time is money, and all that,' he added, hoping his friend believed him.

Grant seemed to accept this explanation. 'Right... of course it is. How's the court case going with that ex-partner of yours, any news?'

'Nothing.' Luke felt the usual knotting in his stomach as the anger towards Chris kicked in. 'It's been three years and I've explored every avenue trying to recoup my money, but it doesn't look like I'm going to get anywhere. Serves me right for putting so much trust in him, I guess. I was a fool.'

'Don't beat yourself up. We were friends from teenagers, so why would you suspect he'd be capable of embezzlement? Anyway, you can make it again. You've certainly got the brains and bloody-minded determination to do it,' said Grant, patting him on the back. 'You're clever, Luke. Making money comes easily to you.'

Luke shook his head. Somehow his unpleasant experience had dampened down his enthusiasm and ambition. Knowing everything could simply vanish overnight took away some of the excitement growing his business had once held for him. 'It's the principle that drives me nuts. How could I be such a lousy judge of character?' He sighed. 'What the hell was I thinking, to have trusted him with everything like I did?'

'I know, mate. But you're just going to have to move on, and the sooner you do it, the better for you it'll be.'

Luke knew Grant was talking sense, but couldn't help thinking there was something about Tom Brakespear that reminded him very much of his ex-partner. An underlying slyness he couldn't ignore. And whether Bea could see through him or not, Luke wasn't going to let some slimeball hurt her. She was far too special for that, even if her lack of feelings for him continued to sting. He pulled out a nautical map and started marking a route.

'Is this Leilani's?' Grant held up a tiny pair of cut off denim shorts on the galley seat. Luke nodded. 'You're a lucky sod. I mean, I love Mel, of course I do, but she's so bossy I'm a bit nervous she's going to morph into her mother as soon as we're married.'

Luke laughed and snatched back the shorts, throwing them into the small cabin Leilani sometimes slept in. 'She's always leaving her gear around the place, and before you get any ideas, we're not sleeping together.'

Grant laughed. 'Pull the other one.'

'We're not.' Why was it so difficult for people to believe? 'She's fun and loves winding people up, but she's only here for a couple of months for a break before she decides which job offer she accepts.'

Grant shook his head. 'And you believe that, do you?'

'Yes. Now, let me check this map or tomorrow you'll have to get the ferry to St Malo like everyone else.'

13

CROSSING THE POND

'Helloooo?' Paul announced his arrival at The Brae on the day Bea was to leave for America. He dragged a massive holdall behind him up the wide oak staircase.

'Up here,' Shani called.

'Why do you never lock that front door?' Paul asked. 'Anyone could walk in.'

'Anyone just did,' Shani giggled.

'I'll pretend I didn't hear,' Paul said, amused. 'I've brought everything I should need. Is it safe to come in or will I be traumatised by all your big pants?' he asked, outside Bea's bedroom door.

'Shut up and get in here,' Shani shouted from inside Bea's clothes-strewn bedroom. 'She doesn't have any big pants, not that I've ever seen, anyway.' Shani lowered her voice. 'She's doing well, though it was touch and go for a bit.'

'You can't change your mind.' He squeezed Bea's shoulder as he checked his reflection in the dressing-table mirror.

Bea shrugged. 'I know, but I'm a little nervous about going.'

'You're okay with Tom, don't worry about it.'

'It's not Tom that bothers me, it's how I'm going to manage at the meetings.'

'Stop doubting yourself. You'll be brilliant.'

'Yes, I'm being a wimp,' she said feeling a little better. 'You do know Guy is more than welcome to stay here, too?'

Paul nodded. 'Thanks, I'll tell him.'

'How's it going, still blissfully happy?'

'Parfait.' He clapped his hands together. 'He's wonderful. Not all men are selfish sods, apparently.'

Shani pouted. 'Only the ones I fall for, or so it seems.' She turned to Bea. 'Paul came with me the other night when I went to see Harry at his surgery.'

Paul pulled a face. 'I take it by that expression,' Bea said, 'that it didn't go down too well.'

'Nope.' She shuddered.

'I think it's over between them.' Paul stroked Shani's arm. 'Poor love. You do really have the hots for him, too.'

'I'm so sorry. Maybe he's just had something on his mind. He'll probably be fine in a few days.' Bea hoped she was right. Shani looked so sad and must like him a lot, Bea decided.

'He'll have something on his mind if he doesn't already,' Shani said, before closing the lid of Bea's case and zipping it up. 'There, I told you it'd all fit.'

'What do you mean by that?' Bea asked sensing there was more.

Shani shook her head. 'Nothing. It was just a throwaway comment.'

Bea wasn't convinced. Shani would tell her if there was anything worrying her, but only when she was ready. She hoped she didn't take too long about it. She gave Paul a questioning look.

He shrugged. 'I've already asked her and she's strangely reluctant to confide in me too.' He turned his attention to Shani. 'Aren't you?'

Shani scowled from one to the other. 'No. I haven't told you anything because there's nothing interesting to tell. Can we please stop talking about me?'

'If you insist.'

Bea was relieved they'd agreed to house sit for her time away. Shani and Paul knew where everything was kept, so there hadn't been too much to go through with them. At least, Bea thought, Shani would be able to have a trial run living in the house and could make sure she liked it. Then, if she changed her mind, she wouldn't have to go through the difficulty of breaking the news about moving to Paul.

* * *

'I'm going to be making us healthy meals each day,' Paul announced, as they finished their baguettes, Camembert and red wine bought from the market earlier in the day. 'I won't know myself having an entire kitchen to play in, even if it is a horror from the seventies.'

'Rude.' Bea sighed. 'If I ever get the money to update my kitchen I will, but until then orange Formica will have to do.'

'Shame. I know your kitchen is ancient, but compared to our two-ringed hovel, it's almost state-of-the-art. I can't wait to cook in it. By the way, which rooms do you want us to sleep in?'

'I've made up a bed in the other room overlooking the walled garden and put clean linen on my bed, so it's up to you two which you prefer. Make yourselves at home and have a great time, just don't forget to water the plants.'

'I'm sleeping in your room,' Paul said. 'We're going to have a brilliant time with all this space.'

Paul and Shani grinned at each other with barely suppressed excitement. They looked to Bea like a couple of teenagers being allowed to stay at home for the first time while their parents went away on holiday. 'You're welcome to use my car, too,' she said. 'It's old and battered, so I won't notice a few extra dings.' Her blue Mazda had seen better days, and was her pride and joy when Simon had bought it for her. Since then it had seen a lot of action, mainly due to her lack of concentration, and had already been treated to a few re-sprays.

'Shani, please speak to Harry.'

She nodded. 'I'll try. I've left him a couple of messages at work, but he hasn't called me back yet.'

'Well, don't worry about it.' Bea patted her arm gently. 'You can only do your best. If you don't hear from him, then we'll think of some other plan after my holiday.'

The doorbell rang and they let Tom in. Bea hugged her two friends as he took her small suitcase. She slung her bag over her shoulder and paused, looking at her friends. 'Well, here goes,' she said, walking out the door towards Tom's car.

'Go on.' Shani pushed her out. 'Make the most of the peace.'

Tom leant over to Bea as she settled herself in the front seat of his BMW. 'I can't wait to show you New York.'

Bea didn't even try to hide her excitement. 'I can't wait to get there. Bye, you two,' she said out of the window, waving frantically, 'And be careful.'

'Yes, now bugger off!' Paul shouted blowing her a kiss.

* * *

Bea was determined not to worry about Shani's problems with Harry during the trip. As the plane descended towards JFK airport, she gazed in awe over the water below. She was relieved she'd slept through the flight and couldn't wait to visit the places she'd dreamt about for so long.

After a brief panic that Tom had lost his suitcase, they were collected and driven through the busy Manhattan streets, like corridors through the shiny skyscrapers.

Bea had to hold back her excitement as an enormous red fire truck hurtled past them. Seeing firefighters kitted up, serious expressions on their faces, was even more exciting than she'd imagined. She watched in awe as they barely slowed to manoeuvre through the throng of yellow cabs and cars. The loud blast from their horn alerted their presence to any driver that hadn't already noticed them. Bea thought back to all the movies she'd seen growing up featuring these romantic heroes.

After a short while, their driver pulled over. 'Wow, you never said we were staying at The Plaza,' she squealed, stepping out of the car and seeing the exquisite glass canopy above them before peering through the entrance to the opulence inside. 'This is beyond anything I'd expected,' she gasped, already in holiday mode, determined to make the most of her trip.

'Thank heavens for that.' He glanced over at her, taking their suitcases. 'I wanted to book somewhere you'd enjoy, so you'd forget about everything at home. We're going to have a wonderful time. We have four meetings, but I've scheduled them to run as closely together as I dared to give us some time to see the sights.'

Bea nodded, noticing how thoughtful he'd been. The vitality of the energetic city was infectious, and her nerves subsided a little. 'This is amazing,' she said. 'It's even better than I'd ever hoped it would be.'

Tom laughed. 'You wait until you see inside,' he said. 'I wanted to book us in here because I know how you love old movies. We don't have the best rooms, I'm afraid. I can only push the budget so far.'

'I wouldn't mind sleeping in a store room here.' Bea thought of Cary Grant sitting in the bar in *North by Northwest* and of course the final scene in *Bride Wars* with Anne Hathaway and Kate Hudson that had been filmed in the hotel's Palm Court. 'I can't wait to have a proper look around.'

She followed him inside. It was as if time had stood still. 'This is incredible,' she breathed, feeling like a child on Christmas morning.

'Our rooms are this way,' Tom said once they'd checked in, leading her to the lifts.

In her room, Bea checked her laptop was charged and said, 'Give me half an hour to unpack, then I'll meet you in the lobby. I'll just have a quick look at my emails.'

He looked a little disappointed, but quietly left and headed to his own room.

She thought it only right that she remind him they were here for business. Tom knew how she felt and she refused to feel guilty for keeping their relationship platonic. She wasn't about to rush into bed with anyone, especially after her mistake with Luke. Damn, why did she keep thinking about him? She hurriedly unpacked and freshened up, before quickly checking for new emails ahead of meeting Tom.

He was sitting under the huge ornate clock, mobile against his ear in intense conversation. At her approach he ended the call, slipping the phone into his jacket.

'Looking gorgeous as ever,' he said, taking her hand and kissing her cheek. 'Come along, lovely lady, there's little time to show you this magnificent city. I don't want to waste a moment.' He led her out onto the noisy streets. 'We can grab something to eat at a deli.'

Bea gasped as they stepped outside onto the pavement. She still couldn't believe she was in New York, and it was even bigger and more impressive than she imagined.

'So,' said Tom interrupting her thoughts. 'Where to?'

Bea shook her head and laughed. 'I've no idea.'

'I was thinking we could wander down to Grand Central Station, then on to the Chrysler Building and maybe make our way down towards Battery Park, if we have any energy left.'

'I'd like that,' Bea said, feeling the need to see something that would give her hope things would turn out right in the end.

'At some point we could take a boat over to Ellis Island. What do you think?'

Bea nodded. 'Sounds perfect.' Tom's excitement almost matched her own and she was more than happy to be led wherever he thought best.

* * *

Even the diners they ate their meals in were like something out of a Hollywood movie. 'Did you notice the rear car lights in each booth?' she asked him as they walked back to their hotel later that evening, exhausted, but relaxed and happy.

'I know.' He nodded. 'Everything, right down to the light switches in the gents seemed to be from the fifties.'

'Good food, too,' Bea said. She'd been thrown by the magnificence of it all, and the only downside had been the calls and texts Tom had received. 'Tom,' she said, unable to help from asking. 'Why are you getting so many calls? I would've thought they'd be monitoring your workload back at the office, like mine. Is something the matter?'

He shook his head. 'No, nothing at all.' Despite her assurance, Bea noticed he looked unnerved and that his previously buoyant mood seemed to be deflating.

'It's not a problem,' she said, wishing to alleviate his defensiveness. 'I was a little worried something might be wrong.'

Tom immediately stopped walking, taking her by surprise.

'Leave it, Bea,' he snapped. 'It's a few calls, nothing for you to be concerned about.'

She didn't like his tone, but thought better of arguing with him. After all, it was thanks to him that she was on this enjoyable trip. It wasn't the calls that bothered her, she mused, so much as his reaction when she had commented on them. 'Whatever,' she said. 'I didn't mean to pry.'

The following day, after a morning of back-to-back client meetings, she persuaded Tom to leave the paperwork and go with her to the Top of the Rock at the Rockefeller Centre. 'Look at the view,' she said, pointing out across Manhattan, past the magnificent Empire State Building from so many films from her childhood, and over to the East and Hudson Rivers, the sunlight glistening gold and yellow above them. She took a couple of photos to show Paul and Shani.

'I can't believe you've persuaded me to come up seventy floors, never mind that I'm outside. I'm terrified of heights.'

'You're doing very well. Try not to think about it,' she said, taking his hand and leading him over to the other side before he could start to panic. 'Look over there, isn't that stunning?' she asked, as they gazed out over the rectangle of green in the middle of the city. 'Isn't Central Park incredible? All that green in the middle of this amazing city!'

'Damn,' Tom said, pushing his hand into his pocket and withdrawing his mobile. 'This phone never stops.'

'Don't answer it, then.' Bea's initial relief at the sound of his phone receiving a text was instantly replaced by irritation. She knew he would have to read it. She was preparing to say something when her own phone pinged. She locked eyes with Tom. Bea didn't know who looked more astonished. She turned away from his amused expression to check the message.

'Luke?' she said instantly, immediately regretting it.

'What does *he* want?' Tom snapped.

'He's asked me to call him as soon as possible,' she said, unhappy with his question. 'It must be important.'

'Funny that,' Tom said, the sarcasm obvious in his voice.

'Tom, this is the first time Luke has contacted me, so he's bound to have a good reason.'

'Fine, ignore me. I just worry about you getting involved with him, especially since you know what he's involved in. You should distance yourself from him as much as you can,' Tom said, texting a reply on his own phone.

'I haven't forgotten what you told me,' she said, wishing she could. It wasn't Tom's fault Luke was being investigated, she thought, feeling a little mean for being so annoyed with him. She made the call.

'Luke,' she said, walking to the other side of the open space to put some distance between her and Tom. She checked her watch and quickly made a calculation. 'I've just realised it's ten thirty at night there,' She said, certain now that there must be something the matter for him to call her that late.

'Now don't panic, Bea,' he said, his calm, deep voice causing her stomach to lurch over. 'It's nothing we can't deal with.'

'What isn't?'

'You have a burst pipe in the main bathroom.'

'What?' she said, trying not to panic at the extra cost. 'How?'

'The pipes are pretty worn in places. After all,' he added, 'the house is nearly a hundred years old, these things happen.'

'Not on my budget they don't,' she said, trying her best to sound light-hearted.

'Don't worry about the cost.'

'That's easy for you to say,' she said, swallowing the lump forming in her throat. She knew she shouldn't have gone away, not when she still had to try and somehow finalise things with Simon.

'Bea?' he said, his voice calm.

'Yes?' She took a calming breath, unable to help her heart pounding at the thought of having to find the money for another large invoice.

'You mustn't worry about it. I can sort this out. I'm just calling to ask if it's okay to do some exploratory work on your plumbing while you're away? We don't want this happening again. It's a good thing Shani and Paul noticed the problem quickly. If it had happened while they were at work, it could have ended up being very costly, and you don't want water damage after you've finished your renovations.'

'I don't want them at all,' she said. She tried to work out how she could possibly pay for this. She hadn't even considered any plumbing work and was at the limit of her budget already.

'You're worrying,' he said, his tone gentle. 'Don't. It's fine, really.'

Bea glanced over at Tom. He'd finished his call and was making his way over to her, a fixed expression on his face.

'Bea?' Luke's voice interrupted her thoughts. She trusted him when he said not to worry, which made knowing about his business activities even more upsetting. She wished she was back in Jersey and could see for herself what had happened. 'Bea, speak to me.'

Tom had almost reached her. She could tell he was in a bad mood and now was no time to have Luke on the line. 'Sorry, yes. Do whatever you have to. And Luke?' she added. 'Thanks for sorting this out for me.'

* * *

Luke stared at his phone. She couldn't wait to hang up, no doubt to carry on enjoying her trip with that creep. He picked up his can of lager and took a mouthful, leaning back against the pillow on his bunk, the rhythmic rocking of the boat failing to soothe his frustration.

'Tom Brakespear,' he said, almost spitting out the words. He couldn't help distrusting that man. How had that jerk ended up in New York with Bea?

He picked up his phone and scrolled down to The Brae's number.

Shani answered after two rings. 'Did you speak to her?' she asked. 'I hope you didn't scare her. I don't want her trying to race back here thinking we can't sort it. If anyone deserves a break right now, it's Bea.'

Luke felt better hearing Shani's dogged determination to look out for her friend. 'I assured her it was fine. She agreed I could do whatever's needed, so I'll come over tomorrow, turn the water back on and start checking the other pipes.'

Shani sighed loudly. 'Brilliant, thanks. I hope you didn't mind me phoning, but I didn't know who else to call, and Bea would have done the same.'

Hearing her words made him feel a little better. It cheered him to think of Bea turning to him in a crisis. 'No problem. Now don't worry and I'll see you in the morning.'

'Luke?'

'Shani?'

'Tom's not the problem between you two, you know? She probably feels a little guilty.'

Confused by her comment, Luke pushed himself up onto one elbow. 'What do you mean?'

Shani groaned. 'Forget I said anything. Night,' she said, abruptly ending the call.

'Shani?' What had she meant by guilty? His mood instantly evaporated.

Almost immediately his phone rang. 'Shani, what does Bea feel guilty about?'

'Shani?' Leilani asked, making him curse for answering so quickly. 'Isn't she Bea's podgy friend?'

'Don't be nasty.'

Leilani groaned. 'Why were you asking about Beatrice being guilty of something?' she asked, obviously having no intention of being fobbed off.

'Never mind that,' he said. 'Why are you phoning so late?'

'I was wondering if you needed a little company tonight?' she suggested, her voice softening. 'It's so boring here.'

Luke laughed. As spiteful as Leilani might be sometimes, her diva-like behaviour amused him. She didn't care if people disliked her, though he much preferred her when she was being generous and funny. 'You're staying in a five-star hotel, and they're treating you like royalty.'

'So, can I come over?' she asked, ignoring his comment.

'No. I'm tired and have to be up early for work. I'll come over and see you after I've finished tomorrow. Maybe we could go for dinner somewhere. You choose, if you like?'

'I don't like,' she said. He could picture her pouting in irritation.

''Night, Leilani,' he said. 'Sweet dreams.'

* * *

Bea drafted the minutes from their meetings and completed as much of the directors' report as she could. She wanted to check everything was in order and that she had not forgotten to include details of any of the funds the client had discussed with them. Before sending an email to the Jersey office, she went to query Tom about one of the action points and noticed him ending yet another phone call. There was something about his demeanour that made her suspicious, but what? She knew their client was on a flight to Boston, and was certain they had covered everything in the meetings, so was unable to contain her annoyance. She confronted him on their last evening away during a walk towards Central Park. 'Why so many phone calls?' she asked, keeping her voice as level as possible.

'I explained to you already.' He squeezed her hand lightly before letting it go, as they crossed the road towards the wall of the park.

'Tom.' She stopped walking when they reached the entrance, opposite the Dakota building where John Lennon had been murdered. 'What's going on? If there's a problem, I'd like to know. Maybe I can help.'

'I promise you it's just the odd hiccup at work. Vanessa's phoned once or twice to speak to me about stuff, you know, like the children. Stop worrying unnecessarily. Let's enjoy our last night here.'

They walked on. Bea couldn't banish the niggling doubt in her mind. She wanted to know what he was hiding and assumed it must be something to do with Vanessa, though why he'd hide anything about her she couldn't imagine. Maybe he was still embarrassed about Vanessa's aggressive call to her.

Later, as they returned to the hotel, Tom said 'You were great in the meetings. I knew you would be. Well done, it's not easy dealing with some of these clients.'

'Put in a good word for me at Malory's and make sure my annual review is brilliant, and I'll be happy.'

'I only ever write the truth,' he said. 'Though thankfully in your case, it will be very positive.'

Bea looked at him for a moment and decided to keep her thoughts to herself. Pacified, she smiled up at his concerned face. 'That's good to know.'

* * *

Bea struggled to get comfortable on the return flight to Heathrow, failing to sleep.

'I don't want to go back to the real world,' Tom moaned miserably.

'Nor me,' Bea fibbed. She'd loved every second in New York, and was determined to return, hopefully with Shani or Paul, to show them everything she'd experienced, but she was ready to get back to her house. 'I'm dreading finding out about the burst pipe damage.'

She saw him clench his teeth, no doubt because her comment would remind him of Luke and hoped he didn't start giving her another lecture about being careful.

After their short flight from Heathrow to Jersey, they shared a taxi, each sat in silence lost in their own private thoughts. Tom helped Bea with her bags when they arrived at her house.

'You can tell we're home – the weather's miserable and damp, unlike the cold crispiness we enjoyed in New York,' he said, placing her bags onto the doorstep. 'I'll give you a call later,' he promised, getting back into the cab and waving as it drove off. Bea couldn't help noticing his mobile was already against his ear before the car even reached the turn of her driveway.

14

BARE BRANCHES

'How the devil are you?' Paul bellowed, holding her at arm's length and scrutinising her up and down. 'Was it only sightseeing that's put colour in your cheeks?'

'Yes.' She punched him playfully on the shoulder.

'I'm not sure I believe you, but whatever it is, it's given you a healthy glow.'

'I don't know how,' she groaned. 'I'm exhausted. The jet lag hasn't even hit me yet.'

'Bea,' Luke said from the top of the stairs.

'Hi.' Bea cringed, narrowing her eyes at Paul for not mentioning he was there. 'I'm on my way up to see the damage.'

'By the way, we've kept our eyes open but neither of us came across anything that could be the Jersey Kiss your aunt mentioned in her will.'

'Never mind,' Bea replied. 'It's so frustrating. I wish she'd left me some sort of clue.'

'Me, too.' Paul frowned. 'I hate not knowing things. Right, you'd better go and see to your gorgeous builder while I put the kettle on.' He gave her a quick hug. 'Leave the case, I'll sort it out later.'

Bea ran up the stairs, hoping her flushed face had calmed down by the time she entered the bathroom. 'How's it going?'

Luke put down a wrench and turned to her. 'I hope you didn't panic when I called you?'

Bea didn't want him to feel badly. 'No, I was grateful to you for calling.'

'Fibber,' he smiled, his penetrating gaze causing Bea's stomach to do several somersaults.

Bea tried not to laugh. 'Well, only a little.'

'Sugar?' shouted Paul from the bottom of the stairs. 'I can never remember.'

Bea cocked her head towards the door. 'He's talking to you. He knows I'm sweet enough.'

Luke raised his eyebrows. 'Yes, well, that's a matter of opinion. Two, please,' he called, without taking his eyes off her. 'As you can tell, I'm not very sweet.'

Bea folded her arms, unsure what else to do. 'That's a matter of opinion, too.'

'Teas are on the table,' shouted Paul from the kitchen, causing the moment to pass.

Luke glanced up, but then went back to work on the pipes. 'So, how was your holiday?' he asked, without looking at her.

Bea didn't like the sudden coolness between them. 'It wasn't a holiday. We were there to meet with a couple of clients. But it went well, thanks.' It wasn't any of his business what she did with Tom. Not that he probably gave a damn whether there was anything more between them.

'Coming down?' she asked, moving closer to the door.

Luke followed her to the kitchen. He sat and Bea leant against the familiar warmth of the Aga.

'Can I ask what this Jersey Kiss is that I keep hearing you lot chatting about?'

Bea explained. 'Aunt Annabel left me the house, and something else. Something important enough to mention in her will, but no one – including her lawyer – seems to have a clue what it is. It could be in this room for all I know.' Bea shrugged, wishing again Aunt Annabel had given her some idea where to start looking.

Luke thought for a moment. 'Could it be... a painting maybe, or jewellery?'

Paul sighed. 'You're as useless as we are.'

Bea laughed. 'You're just irritated because you hate mysteries.' She rubbed her face, careful not to smudge what was left of her makeup. 'Talking of mysteries, where's Shani?' She realised she hadn't seen her yet. 'I'm surprised she's not here to hear all my gossip. She's alright, isn't she?'

'She's very all right, actually.' Paul rubbed his hands together gleefully. 'In fact, at this very moment she's with Harry at the hospital having a scan.'

'A scan? Why?' Bea gasped, horrified to think her friend might be ill.

'Don't jump to conclusions. Harry's the one having the scan. Bad back or something, an old rugby injury.' He handed Bea a drink, and took a seat opposite Luke at the table. 'When she didn't hear from him, she went to the surgery to talk to him.'

'And did he speak to her properly this time?' Bea asked, recovering from her shock. Paul nodded. 'Good. I knew she'd been putting on a brave face about him not contacting her.'

'Maybe he had his reasons and was caught up with other things,' Luke suggested.

'Maybe.' Bea supposed he could be right.

'It is a bit odd though,' Paul said thoughtfully. 'Harry phoned as soon as he received the note Shani sent, about wanting to talk. After a brief chat he agreed to let her accompany him to the hospital. Although that sounds like an odd place to talk, if you ask me. Most people would go out for a drink, or walk. I think she's being cagey about him because he's married.'

'But why is he acting oddly? She'll be devastated if he's been lying to her.' Bea felt Luke's gaze on her and wished he wasn't in the room for this conversation. He didn't know her friends, and she didn't want him making assumptions.

Paul rested his chin on his palm. 'She will. She's been much happier since taking control of the situation. I have to say, she's enjoyed all the space here. I think it makes her feel more secure, somehow.'

Bea was tempted to tell Paul about her offer to Shani, but stopped. Shani would want to do that. 'I can't wait to see her. When do you expect her back?'

'Soon.' He checked his watch and nodded. 'I just hope everything went well at the hospital. I don't want her finding anything else to worry about.'

'Same here.' Bea rubbed her hands together. 'It's even colder here than in New York,' she said. 'I'm going to take a day or two to get used to it.'

Shani walked in before Bea could say anything else. She noticed Luke first and smiled. Bea felt a frisson of envy course through her as smiled back. Why didn't she feel as relaxed with him? Probably because despite her best intentions she could feel herself falling in love with him, that's why. The realisation shocked her.

'How did it go?' Paul asked as Shani dropped her heavy handbag onto the floor.

'I think this is my cue to leave,' said Luke, finishing his drink and standing. 'Loads to be getting on with.' Bea watched his retreating back and caught Paul watching her.

Shani folded her arms and shrugged. 'Nothing to tell.'

Bea studied her friend's face trying to work out why her instincts insisted there was more to Shani's situation than she was admitting. Then it dawned on her. How could she have been so blind? 'Shan, that's not entirely true, is it?'

'What do you mean?' Paul looked at Shani suspiciously only for her to ignore him.

'Are you pregnant?' Bea whispered. 'If you're worried about telling me because of my miscarriage, then please don't be. I would always be excited for you.'

Shani looked at her but her expression gave nothing away.

'You're not, are you?' Paul asked, looking from Bea to Shani.

Shani shook her head. 'I don't know where you two get these ideas from. I'm not pregnant, so stop going on at me.'

Bea wasn't sure if she believed her or not, but it was hard to tell just by looking at her. Her boobs didn't seem much bigger, and there was no sign of a baby bump. She glanced at Paul who shrugged. Shani was wearing baggier clothes, but then she often wore loose-fitting outfits. 'As long as you're sure you're okay,' Bea said eventually. 'I'd hate to think you couldn't confide in me.'

'Bea, I'm fine. You've got enough on your plate without imagining problems for me.'

'She's right,' Paul agreed. 'You do have enough going on, and she looks the same as ever to me.' He thought for a moment. 'Something is wrong, though. Is he married? Is that it?'

Shani raised her hands in the air. 'Yes,' she shouted. 'He is married. Happy now?'

'Of course we're not happy.' Bea scowled, annoyed at Shani's tone. 'We're only asking because it's obvious something is wrong.'

'Well, now you know.' Shani looked embarrassed. 'I know, it's awful, but I promise you I believed him when he told me he was divorced.'

Paul scowled. 'The bastard. Will you tell his wife?'

'Of course not. What do you take me for?'

Paul shrugged. 'I can't believe you never said anything. I mean, we live together, and nothing.'

'I know. I'm sorry. I wasn't sure how to tell you.' She turned to Bea. 'Not after what Simon did. Do you hate me, Bea?'

'Don't be ridiculous, of course not. At least you're not pregnant. That would be lousy. For you, I mean.'

Shani sighed. 'I'm not, so there's no need to worry about that.'

'When did you find out he was married?' Paul asked.

'I had my suspicions for a little while but only found out for certain from his business partner yesterday, when I phoned the surgery to arrange a time to meet. They'd had a row. He told me Harry and his wife had been briefly separated. And to make matters worse, he said Harry had done this sort of thing before and one of them had even been careless enough to fall pregnant.'

'What a creep.' Paul scowled. 'Thank God that hasn't happened to you. I'd have to track him down and kill him.'

'Stop being so dramatic,' Bea said. 'You know exactly where to find him.' She rested a hand on Shani's shoulder. 'Don't beat yourself up about it; we're here for you.'

Paul hugged her and Shani began to cry. 'I'm such an idiot.'

'Rubbish,' Bea said, stunned to see her usually tough friend so upset. Shani never cried. 'He's a worthless nothing. How were you to know?' Bea leant across the table and handed Shani a tissue before taking her friend's hands in hers, giving them a reassuring squeeze. 'You're worth ten of him, and don't you ever forget it.'

Shani pulled her hands away and straightened her top. Bea could tell she was embarrassed and that it was time to change the subject.

'Paul, how's Guy?'

'Still wonderful.' Paul kissed his fingers. 'In fact, I believe I've met the only other truly perfect man in the entire universe.'

'Who's the other one?' Shani teased, a little colour seeping back into her face.

'Me, of course. Guy's perfect, though. He's kind and generous, and happy to take our relationship as slowly or as quickly as I like. He says he's happy to be with me and get to know me properly.' He winked at them. 'We're having so much fun going out together.'

'I think I'm going to cry again,' Shani sniffed, pulling the used tissue out of her sleeve and blowing her nose.

'For heaven's sake, what is wrong with you?' Paul teased. 'Are you sure you're not pregnant? My mum always goes on about how emotional she was when she was expecting me.'

'What?' Shani frowned. 'I told you I'm not, so please stop going on about it, will you?'

'I only meant... Never mind.' Paul shrugged.

Bea had had enough of the bickering. 'I've got tons of washing to catch up on,' she said, thinking about Luke upstairs in her bathroom. 'And knowing you,' she pointed to Paul, 'you'll need an in-depth chat with Shani about her revelations about Harry.'

'Yes, and I think you should speak to Luke. We've been asking him about Leilani and he insists she's nothing more than a friend. Maybe you were wrong about her,' Shani said, grabbing her bag. 'You're obviously attracted to the bloke.'

'Maybe, but I need to sort out this business with the house before I can concentrate on anything – or anyone – else,' she said.

'I haven't told you about Luke interrogating me the other day, have I?' Shani asked, raising her eyebrows. 'It was when I phoned him in a panic about the water leak.' Bea listened silently, wondering what she was about to say. 'He asked how you were, and when I said you were on holiday in New York he seemed rather surprised. Although, to be honest, I did have a sneaking suspicion he already knew you were away.'

'Did he ask who I was with?' Bea felt a familiar knot forming in her stomach.

''Fraid so. And by the disappointment in his tone, he wasn't impressed.'

Maybe he did feel something for her, Bea thought, aware she should be keeping her distance – at least emotionally – from him.

'The next day, I passed that new coffee shop on the corner of New Street and King Street, and he was having a coffee with that Leilani.'

'Leilani,' Bea murmured, her mood flattened, reminding herself that it was probably just as well, then at least she wouldn't be tempted by him again. 'Never mind. Anyway, it's Christmas soon and I think we should chat about what we're all doing.'

'I have to spend the day with my parents, as usual,' Shani groaned. 'I've no idea why, they never seem to enjoy themselves and always end up rowing.'

Paul pursed his lips together. 'I know we were planning on sharing a turkey *à deux* here, Bea, but Guy has asked if I'll meet him at his flat after he's finished at the restaurant. He insisted you must come too, so no arguments.'

Bea shook her head. 'I'm not going to interrupt your first Christmas together. I'll be fine here.'

Paul scowled. 'No chance. It'll be your first Christmas alone and without Annabel, I'm not having you feeling sorry for yourself here.'

'I'll be fine,' she insisted. 'Anyway, Dad's asked me to join them this year.'

Shani swung round from the doorway. 'And you said yes?'

'I did,' Bea lied, laughing at the disbelief on her friends' faces. 'The wedding's coming up and I thought I should try my best to build some bridges before the big day.'

'Rather you than me having to put up with Joyce for an entire day.' Shani laughed. 'She hates you.'

Bea laughed. 'I know, which makes it more fun that Dad invited me, don't you think?' Seeing she'd convinced them, Bea watched them leave, heads together as they chatted about their Christmas plans. By the time they discovered the truth, she'd have spent a quiet but peaceful day alone with a bottle of champagne and having watched several films on TV.

After they'd left, Bea went to speak to Luke. He didn't seem to notice her arrival and Bea made the most of watching him work. Bent over the pipes, she could see the muscles in his back through his T-shirt.

Luke turned and caught her appreciative stare. 'What's so amusing?' he asked, pulling his jeans up a bit. 'Were you laughing at my backside?'

'Hardly laughing,' she said, aching to cross the room and kiss him. 'And anyway it wasn't your back I was looking at.' She cleared her throat. 'I was wondering if you wanted a drink?'

'I'm fine, thanks. Nearly done for today.' He sat back on the heels of his plaster-splattered boots. 'I was wondering if you'd like to come for dinner on my boat some time?'

Taken aback by the unexpected question, Bea raised her eyebrows in surprise. 'Yes,' she said, without thinking. 'I'd like that.' Then, remembering what Shani had said about Leilani, shook her head. 'But I'd better not.'

'Why?' He stood up and studied her face, his intense gaze and closeness making her wish she could change her mind.

'Because you have a girlfriend and I'm not going to be anyone's second choice.'

'You really can't find it in yourself to trust me, can you?' he said his smile vanishing. He turned his back on her to continue with his work. 'When you finally realise I'm not the guy you seem so desperate to presume I am, I hope it's not too late.'

15

JANUARY – ICY BREEZES

Bea was walking along Grève de Lecq beach with Paul and Shani. They wanted to stay occupied and keep Shani from dwelling on her situation with Harry. Bea's phone rang.

She struggled to retrieve it from her jeans pocket. 'Hi, Mel, how are you?'

'Fine, but I can hardly hear you; it's a terrible line.' She sounded put out that Bea wasn't available for her usual lengthy chat whenever Mel called.

'It must be the wind. I'm on the beach.'

'Huh, rather you than me. Anyway, I phoned to ask if you had bought the tickets for us to have a table at the charity ball this weekend?'

'Charity ball?' Bea turned her back to the wind in a vain attempt to muffle the noise.

'Yes, for Burns Night, the one with the black-and-white only dress code.'

'Oh, yes,' Bea remembered, thinking she needed something to wear. 'The tickets arrived in the post while I was away.'

'Great. I don't suppose you've managed to find the time to shop for your outfit yet?'

'You presumed right.' She pulled the collar on her jacket up higher to shield the phone from some of the wind.

'Then we must arrange to go shopping to get ourselves sorted,' continued Mel. 'And Shani, she needs to find something a little less, um, obvious.'

'Mel, don't be rude.' Bea wondered why her sister felt the need to put people down like she did.

'What was that all about?' Paul asked, pacing along beside her, pedometer attached to his jeans.

'Only Mel,' she puffed, doing her best to keep up with him. 'About Burns Night. We bought tickets, remember?'

Shani and Paul looked at each other vacantly for a moment. 'Never mind the ball, we still can't forgive you for lying to us about spending Christmas with your parents,' Shani said. 'Mel told us you hadn't gone, so you must have spent the day on your own. I was horrified to think of you alone in that big house.'

Bea wasn't surprised Mel had told them; she never could keep out of other people's business. She wrinkled her nose. 'I know, I'm sorry about keeping it from you, but I quite enjoyed not having to bother sitting around a dining table.'

Shani put her arm around Bea's shoulder and gave her a brief hug. 'You're impossible, but we love you anyway.'

'I forgive you… sort of. Right, about the ball.' Paul waved Bea on, encouraging her to keep up the pace. She stuck her tongue out at him. 'You could look a little more excited.'

Shani groaned. 'I don't have anything to wear.'

'Which is why I gave in to Mel when she insisted we go shopping tomorrow afternoon. We'll find you something incredible.' Bea stopped, bending over to catch her breath her hands on her knees.

'Sounds okay, but I'll decide what I wear, not Mel.' Shani drew level with Bea and crossed her arms over her stomach.

'Come along you two, we're supposed to be jogging and getting you fit.'

'Stop nagging, Paul.' Bea pulled a face at him. 'You know I hate jogging.' She turned to Shani. 'I can't really afford to buy something for this ball either, but I haven't much choice. I wish I hadn't agreed to go now. I hate the thought of spending money I don't have buying something I'll probably only wear once.'

'Me too.' Shani stretched her calf muscles.

Paul rolled his eyes. 'For pity's sake. Anyone would think the pair of you are ancient, the way you act sometimes. I know you have a lot of responsibility resting on your bony shoulders, little Bea, but you have to lighten up and think "sod the rest of the world" and have some fun.'

'I think I've had my quota of fun for the foreseeable future,' Shani grimaced.

'Well, I haven't,' he shouted.

'I agree with Paul,' Bea said, liking his attitude. 'I think we should treat ourselves. We haven't done so for ages and it is for a worthy cause.'

* * *

'Weren't we lucky finding this closing down sale,' Bea whispered, nodding at Shani's reflection in the mirror when she emerged from the changing room wearing a white, empire-styled dress with a tiny black satin ribbon running under her bust. 'Your boobs seem bigger than they did before.'

'Rubbish,' laughed Shani. 'I think it's just the style of the dress.'

'I adore my dress.' Mel twisted and turned, looking at her reflection from every angle in the one-shouldered creation she'd tried on.

'I'll have to make sure Grant hires a tuxedo soon, otherwise he'll forget.'

Bea picked out a sleeveless chiffon–covered beaded dress and carried it into the changing room. The weight of the dress gave the feel of luxury. Pulling back the velvet curtain from her changing room, she crossed to the mirror. 'I feel really glamorous in this,' Bea said, wishing Luke was to be her partner for the night rather than Tom. She held her hair up at the back of her head. 'I think I'll have something a little Hollywood done to my hair, too.'

'I know we've all got to watch our cash flow, but I think it'll be fun to treat ourselves. We may as well make the most of this.'

'It's perfect practice for my wedding day.'

Shani groaned. 'Why does everything always have to come back to your wedding, Mel?'

* * *

'This is going to be fun,' Bea said, determined to ignore the pain she was experiencing thanks to her exquisite, black four-inch stilettos. She hoped they'd loosen up as the evening wore on.

'Tom, you look *très* James Bond,' Paul said, eyeing his dinner jacket. 'Grant, you've scrubbed up well, too. I'm impressed. I can see Mel's influence here, so don't even try to deny it.'

Bea laughed as Paul, immaculately groomed, bowed theatrically. 'As you see, I've splashed out on a new black silk cummerbund and bow tie.'

They stared in silence when Guy strode into the room. 'Wow,' said Mel, eyes wide.

'Thank you,' Paul said, smiling with self-satisfaction.

'Not you. *Him*,' she said, pointing at Guy. 'You're wasted as a chef, Guy.' Mel shook her head as she stared at the six-foot, dark-haired vision in front of her. 'You should be gracing billboards, not holed up in a stuffy kitchen.'

'I said something similar, didn't I?' Paul linked arms with Guy and smiled up at him.

'Taxi's here!' Tom shouted, taking Bea's hand in his. 'You look very beautiful tonight.'

Bea sat in the taxi and smiled at him, trying not to think about Luke, wondering if he'd be at the ball too as the car took them to the manor in St Ouen. Arriving outside the huge white marquee, especially erected in the walled garden, Tom helped each of the women out.

'This is amazing,' Bea gasped, trying to take in every detail as light dripped from the grand crystal chandeliers overhead. Circular tables covered in crisp white linen tablecloths showed off rose and lily of the valley displays.

'Stunning,' Shani agreed, taking a glass of apple juice from the waitress. Bea caught her eye and when Shani smiled, she pushed away the nagging doubt and picked up a glass of chilled champagne.

'Not drinking tonight?' Mel asked, as a pipe band welcomed the guests to the event. Shani ignored her. 'It is pretty incredible,' Mel said, barely able to contain her excitement. She pulled her chiffon wrap over her shoulders and took a glass of Buck's Fizz.

Paul threaded one arm through Shani's and the other through Guy's and led them further into the room.

Tom took Bea's hand and squeezed it gently, leaning down towards her. 'Did I tell you how beautiful you look this evening?' he whispered.

She kissed him on the cheek. 'Only about twenty times. But hey, carry on if you feel you must.'

He studied the table plan and pointed to the middle of the

room, near the dance floor. 'This is perfect,' he said. 'We won't miss anything sitting here.'

The Master of Ceremonies welcomed the guests, announced the arrival of the seigneur. Bea wondered what it must be like to own this beautiful place. Once he and his wife were seated, everyone took their places.

'Did you know that Charles II gave this seigneur's ancestor the land where New Jersey now stands as a thank you for letting him come and stay here?'

Bea did recall her father telling her the story. 'Yes, it's why they named it New Jersey. I told some Japanese clients that a couple of years ago and I'm sure they didn't believe me.'

'It does sound a little far-fetched,' Paul said. 'I can see why they'd find it a bit unlikely.'

Bea couldn't help noticing Shani's quiet mood, but didn't want to draw attention to it, especially with Mel there.

'These savoury tartlets are to die for,' Mel declared, rather louder than Bea suspected Grant would have liked. She lifted her napkin to hide her giggling. 'How can anyone make stinky goat's cheese and red onions taste so heavenly?'

A grey-haired couple on a nearby table turned to glare at Mel reproachfully. Grant pulled a face, but Mel simply winked at them. 'Try it,' she said to the woman. 'You won't regret it.'

'Mel, that's enough.' Bea gave her sister her fiercest glare, which was difficult when she couldn't stop smiling.

'I hope Paul's happy,' Shani whispered to Bea as they watched Guy and Paul walk across the dance floor. 'He deserves to be.'

'I agree. He's been a good friend,' Bea said, her words tailing off as she spotted Luke talking to two older men at the far end of the room.

'Blimey,' Shani sighed. 'Luke scrubs up well.'

'He does, doesn't he,' Bea agreed, barely able to think straight at the transformation. She was about to force her eyes away from him when he seemed to sense her and gazed directly back at her. She smiled before looking away, but couldn't help glancing back at him to find him still watching her. He raised his glass to her and before turning back to continue his conversation.

'He could make a fortune on the telly,' Shani said, having another look at Luke. 'And I'd love to know why you insist you're not interested in him, Bea, because I can't think of one reason, especially since he insisted there's nothing between him and Leilani.'

Bea wished she could share why with her friend. She took a gulp of her drink to steady her pounding heart.

'Everything all right?' Tom asked, returning from the gents and looking around to see what had diverted her attention. 'Everyone seems very quiet at this table. It's time to get the party started, you lot.'

She struggled to retain her composure and cleared her throat. 'Yes, it is,' Bea replied, her voice high and shrill. 'I can't get over what an incredible place this is,' she added, to cover her loss of composure.

'I'm taking this as a practice for my wedding,' Mel announced, glancing around the room. 'It's given me a few ideas about décor and seating arrangements.'

Bea desperately wanted to sneak another look at Luke but forced herself not to. What was wrong with her, she wondered, annoyed at being so flustered.

The small band upped the tempo and volume of their background music as the Master of Ceremonies announced the first dance. Tom took Bea by the hand. 'Come on, let's show them how it's done.'

She shrieked when he pulled her to her feet. 'As long as you're not expecting me to be any good at this waltzy sort of dancing.'.

He placed one hand lightly on her waist. 'It's nothing to worry about. Just follow me and try to relax and enjoy yourself.'

She did as he suggested. 'Hello,' said a baritone voice that haunted Bea's dreams. Tom tensed and looked over Bea's shoulder at Luke.

'Good evening, Luke, Leilani.' Tom smiled stiffly, continuing to dance without faltering, unlike Bea who accidentally stood on one of Tom's feet. As they passed, Leilani narrowed her heavily made-up eyes at Bea, but Bea forced a smile at each of them still trying to count steps in her head.

'I didn't know they were here,' Tom murmured.

'Me neither,' she fibbed, wondering if she'd misread Tom's accusatory tone. And why she was lying to him? They danced to several more songs but didn't pass Luke and Leilani again. Bea supposed they must have returned to their table.

As soon as she and Tom were seated again, and seeing Tom busily texting on his phone, she subtly motioned to Shani that she was going to the ladies'. Shani followed. 'That man is so hot,' Shani grinned, spotting Luke. 'You could burn your fingers on him.'

'I know,' Bea agreed quietly, trying to get used to Luke's new, scrubbed-up appearance.

'Leilani seems very possessive for someone who's supposed to only be his friend, don't you think? Like a lioness protecting her... well, not her young exactly, but you know what I mean.'

Bea laughed. 'I do. I wish he hadn't asked me to dinner on his boat the other day. I don't want to think of him as being two-faced, like Simon.'

'Now that is depressing.' Shani reapplied her matt-red lipstick. 'Then again, after what happened between you both that night, maybe you could be right. Don't worry about it now. You're here to enjoy yourself. Make the most of this brilliant party.'

Bea nodded, wiping away an eyeliner smudge. 'I'd better actually go to the loo, I suppose.' She washed her hands and decided she needed to get a grip.

Bea returned to her seat and watched Paul, who was looking happier than she had seen him in years. Someone coughed quietly next to her ear and she turned and came face to face with Luke, crouching down next to her in between her and Tom's chair.

'Hi. I was wondering if you'd dance with me,' he asked, his arm resting on the back of her chair. He looked at Tom. 'You wouldn't mind your beautiful partner having just one dance with an old friend, would you?'

'Not at all,' Bea said without waiting for Tom's reply. Luke took hold of Bea's hand and led her onto the dance floor.

She could sense Tom's eyes boring into the back of her.

'Thank you,' Luke said. 'You're looking incredibly beautiful tonight, although I have to admit I miss seeing those bunny slippers.'

'Stop it,' she said, trying not to laugh. 'What are you playing at?' His aftershave sparked an array of delicious feelings coursing through her.

'Can't a friend ask his pal to dance?' he whispered in her ear, holding her closer.

Bea swallowed. She could feel the hardness of his chest against her breasts. Her mouth was almost completely dry. 'Of course you can,' she replied breathlessly.

'I didn't think you were seeing each other any more,' he said, the heat of his hand firm against her back.

'We work together and neither of us had a partner for the evening.' She wasn't sure why she felt the need to explain herself to him.

'I could have been your partner, if I'd known you were free.'

Bea dismissed the idea. 'But you're here with Leilani, aren't you?' she said, feeling him tense slightly.

'We're friends, Bea – that's all.'

'Just like Tom and me.'

He watched her silently for a few moments, his expression dark, and Bea had to concentrate on not looking away from the intensity of his gaze.

'If I can believe you when you tell me nothing happened in New York, why don't you listen when I tell you that whatever happened between Leilani and me is all in the past?'

Bea breathed in his citrusy aftershave and glanced up at his perfect lips. Damn Tom for telling her about the investigation. An icy breeze seemed to grip her insides at the reminder.

'Bea?'

She couldn't allow herself to be with him. She couldn't lose her house. But at least she had her appointment with Mr Peters in the next few days. She took a deep breath. 'There's too much going on in my life right now for me to get involved with someone, Luke.'

'I could help you sort out whatever it is you're dealing with. You only have to ask.'

She wished it were that easy. She relished being in his arms. This was the most she could allow herself for now. It would have to be enough. 'Thank you.'

'I wish you'd tell me what's holding you back,' he said, lowering his head to whisper in her ear. I wish I could, too, she thought, her entire body tingling when he kissed her lightly on the neck. The music ended. Bea went to move away, but he held on to her. 'One more dance?'

She let him take her back in his arms. 'Luke, we talked about this.'

'No, we didn't. You decided that I wasn't right for you but I've got no idea why, and I don't believe it's because of Leilani.' His breath was hot against her neck. She wanted to kiss him, feeling almost light-headed. 'I can't begin to imagine why you think Tom's better suited to you than me.'

'I told you, we're just friends.' Bea took a deep breath to control her emotions. She daren't give him false hope. She gazed up at the desolate expression in his deep blue eyes and wanted him more than she had ever wanted anyone in her entire life. She swallowed, aware that she had to come up with some excuse for her behaviour. 'Anyway, you're not ready for the kind of relationship that I want.'

'You don't know that.'

'I do. And about that night...'

'What happened that night was amazing.' He stopped dancing for a moment and stared at her.

She made a step to force him to dance again, not wishing to draw any more attention to them than was necessary. 'Please keep dancing,' she pleaded. Luke moved once again.

'Is it because Tom makes you feel safe, is that it? Is that what you want?'

16

FENCED OFF

'Right now, yes it is but only because I see him as a friend and work colleague.' She turned her head away from him but not quick enough to avoid his lips grazing hers so lightly she wasn't certain whether she'd imagined it. She had never wanted to kiss anyone so desperately, but she owed it to herself to be sensible.

He sighed and let her go. 'I'm sorry you don't trust me, Bea. I wish you did.'

'It's time you went back to your friends.'

He fell silent. 'If that's your final word on the matter, then I'd better escort you back to your table.'

Bea forced a smile onto her face, not wanting anyone to see how upset she was. 'Really, there's no need,' she said, turning her back on Luke and returning to her table as he followed. Tom watched in silence as Luke held out her chair for her. He gazed down at her briefly before returning to Leilani and his friends. Leilani put a lean, tanned hand on his shoulder and nodded over to Bea. Bea smiled and looked away.

'She resembles a rather elongated great Dane, don't you think?' Paul whispered in her ear.

Bea giggled. 'That's a little mean, Paul. I wouldn't mind having legs as long as hers.'

'Nah, you're little and cute, like me,' he said, winking. 'Who wants to be a beanpole like her?'

'Thank you.' Shani glared at him. 'There's nothing wrong with being tall and skinny.'

'Yeah, whatever.' Paul pulled a face and Bea laughed.

Tom's phone bleeped. 'I'd better deal with this,' he said, making towards the direction of the gents.

She heard the band strike up a tune, and as Tom returned she went with him onto the dance floor when he took her hand. 'I wonder what we would have been like if we'd married?'

Startled by his observation, Bea hesitated. 'I'd hate to think,' she said, making a joke of it.

'We never argued much and got along pretty well.'

Bea agreed, hoping he wasn't going to try and ask her out on a date again. 'I suppose we did.'

She glanced at her watch, pleased to note it was nearly the end of the evening.

* * *

'You and Tom were getting a little cosy tonight.' Shani said, pulling up the duvet in Bea's spare room. 'Is there something you want to tell me?'

Bea looked out of the window through the darkness towards the coast of France. 'Er, no. Don't expect any gossip from me. He's off to Manchester to meet with a client tomorrow, so won't be at the office for a few days. Sorry to disappoint you.'

'A relief?'

'Yup.' Bea sat on the end of Shani's bed and rubbed her sore feet. 'I don't know why I let you persuade me to wear those shoes. They nearly killed me.'

Shani puffed up her pillow and leant back. 'They didn't seem to bother you when you were dancing with Luke.' She held up her hand to stop Bea from interrupting. 'I know you insist there isn't anything going on between you, but I caught the two of you exchanging looks tonight. Several times.'

Bea sighed. 'Let's not talk about him, Shan,' she said, wriggling her toes and groaning. 'I'm glad you're staying here tonight, it's lovely knowing there's someone else in the house for a change.'

'Why not?' she said, obviously ignoring Bea's request. 'I don't care what you say, I know you well enough to see you fancy him like mad, which means there's some other reason you're keeping your distance, and I've no idea what it can be.'

Bea stared at her tired reflection in the dressing-table mirror. God, she looked awful. 'It doesn't matter what I think or feel about him though, does it?'

'Why would you say that?'

'Because he's with someone else,' she said, hating her voice for cracking like it did and giving away the depths of her feelings. 'I know he keeps insisting he isn't, but they go everywhere together. And she stays with him most of the time.'

'Maybe she's the one who's after him and he doesn't realise it?' Shani tilted her head, her face sad. 'Or have you thought that maybe he believes you and Tom have more going on than you actually do?'

'Why would he even think about me when he's with someone as beautiful as her?' Bea walked out to the hall. 'Who knows? Anyway, I'm shattered. I'll see you in the morning.'

She went to her bedroom, closed the door behind her and sat down heavily on the end of the bed. Shani opened the door and stood in her doorway having followed her. 'You're gorgeous too,' she said. When Bea laughed, Shani added, 'And you're far more fun than she could ever be. I'm sure Luke isn't really interested in anyone as shallow as her, model or not.' She turned to leave the room, then looking back tapped the side of her nose. 'There's something going on between the two of you that I don't understand, but one of these days I'm going to work it out, or force you to tell me what it is.'

The next morning, Bea woke early and got up quietly hoping not to disturb Shani. After a while, she dialled Luke's number. 'Yes?' croaked a deep female voice.

Bea panicked and slammed down the phone. Leilani. She was furious with herself for daring to believe Luke when he said they weren't together. Bea pushed her jealously to the back of her mind. She paced her bedroom trying to work out the best way to contact him without having to hear Leilani's self-satisfied voice, finally coming to the annoying conclusion that she would simply have to wait.

Bea was frustrated that she hadn't arranged to see him. She knew she should keep her distance, especially when his girlfriend was right there in his bed. She pictured his toned body wrapped around Leilani's perfect limbs and felt a sick feeling deep in her stomach. However hard she tried to remember what Tom had told her about Luke, she still couldn't help her feelings. It didn't help when he acted the way he had done at the ball. She needed him to know he couldn't play with her emotions. He had a girlfriend, and it wasn't fair on either of them to play games.

She didn't want to wake Shani, so decided that maybe today was the perfect day to resume her attempt at jogging. Despite her best intentions, she hadn't been since that day at the beach with Paul and Shani. A run on the beach would do her good, she decided, so she dragged on her tracksuit and tatty trainers. She pushed a few pounds into her pocket so that she could buy the newspapers on the way home, grabbed her phone and drove to Grouville bay.

Bea remembered to stretch her legs gently to warm up and took a few deep breaths of fresh air. 'Ahh.' This was more like it. She walked down the cobbled slipway and gazed appreciatively at the sea and the surfers as they rode the rolling waves on their colourful boards.

She decided to start slowly. 'Phew,' she grumbled, finding even a gentle jog tiring, 'this is far harder than it looks when Paul and Shani do it.' After about a hundred and fifty yards she was panting, and if it hadn't been for the other runners pacing along the beach, she would have allowed herself to collapse in a heap face down onto the damp sand.

Bea forced herself on for as long as she could bear. She could hardly breathe. Her chest was tight and her calf muscles burning. There was nothing for it but to casually slow to a walk and then stop. Bea stood feet slightly apart, hands firmly on thighs, bent over, red in the face and gasping for air.

Having managed to slow her heart rate to near-normal, she turned to walk back up the slipway to the catering van, hoping to compensate her efforts with a Galaxy and a large coffee, when her phone rang. With shaking fingers, she pressed the green button as she paced along, eager to reach the liquid refreshment she had promised herself. 'Hello?' she panted.

'Is everything all right?' Luke whispered. 'I saw I had a missed call?'

'Argh,' she screeched, tripping on a stone and landing in an ungainly heap, cracking her knee on the concrete path, grazing her hand and sending her phone flying with a loud clatter. 'Shit, shit, bollocks,' she grimaced, rubbing her knee and brushing away the tears of pain that seemed to come from nowhere. She grabbed her phone. 'Luke, I—'

'Stay where you are, I'm coming to get you,' she heard Luke shout as she put the phone to her ear. 'Where did you say you were?'

'Just off the first slipway, Grouville beach,' she breathed. 'But I'm —' the phone went dead. 'Fine,' she added. Bea held the phone in front of her and stared blankly at the screen. 'Sod it.'

She pulled up her trouser leg and winced at the blackening bruise and beads of blood on her knee, then remembered Luke was coming. 'Oh, hell.' She covered her leg again and tucked loose blonde strands of hair behind her ears to try and look reasonably human. He was going to see her unwashed and sweaty, and after only having run a short distance. It then occurred to Bea that he didn't have to know how little she'd run before nearly suffering a coronary. And anyway, what did that have to do with anything?

Yes, let him come, she decided. Let him think she did this thing every Sunday, like Bea was damn sure Leilani did. An annoying image of Leilani, her endless, toned legs in the tiniest micro shorts, pacing comfortably along the beach sprang uninvited into Bea's mind.

Bea hobbled towards the van. 'Morning, Des,' she said, trying to sound cheerier than she felt now that she'd managed to regain some composure.

'Bleedin' 'ell, Bea, you bin runnin'?' he teased, taking in her dishevelled appearance. 'That's not like you, my love.'

'Yes, but keep it to yourself, won't you?'

'Want your usual?'

Bea nodded. 'Yes, please.' She tidied up her hair and smiled when he handed her a coffee, Galaxy bar and her newspaper. 'It won't do any harm people thinking I take regular exercise, will it?'

'What people's that then?' he asked, scratching his head as Bea paid him.

She spotted Luke running towards her. 'Bea, what happened?' he demanded urgently.

She turned to Des, her eyes wide with embarrassment. 'People like him.' She motioned discreetly, doing her best to ignore her stinging knee.

He stifled a guffaw with little success. 'See ya next week then, love.' He winked.

Bea turned to Luke. 'Morning.'

'Morning? What happened?' he panted, looking her up and down. He pushed a hand through his messy fringe. Bea was painfully aware his hair was still tousled from racing straight over from his bed.

She stared at him silently, intent on remaining as composed as possible. 'Nothing, why?'

Luke's concerned expression morphed into one of fury. He grabbed her by the elbow.

'Hey,' she glared at him, 'my coffee.'

'Sod your coffee, you said something had happened,' he accused angrily.

Bea shook him off. 'No, I didn't. You presumed something was wrong. You cut me off before I could finish what I was saying.' She turned and walked off.

He soon caught up with her. 'Do you realise how infuriating you can be sometimes?'

'Now you listen to me.' Bea glared at him.

'No, you listen. When I phoned you back, it sounded like something dreadful had happened. I thought you were hurt.' He noticed her torn tracksuit. 'There's blood seeping from your knee.'

She glanced down at her leg. 'I slipped when I answered your call. I was slightly out of breath, that's all,' she sniffed. 'I'd been for a run.'

He thought for a moment, confusion spreading across his angry face. 'You sounded like you could hardly breathe,' he continued, frowning. 'That must have been some run. Why didn't you phone me back if there was nothing wrong? You knew I was coming to find you.'

She stopped, leaving him to stride ahead for a couple of paces. He retraced his steps. 'Bea, you phoned me at some ungodly hour this morning, remember?'

'Surely Leilani can't be very impressed that you've come here to meet me?'

Luke shook his head. 'I didn't feel the need to tell her, if you must know. So now that I'm here, you may as well tell me what was so damn important it couldn't wait?'

Bea shrugged. 'I called but only because I wanted to arrange to see you, then when you cut me off so abruptly the best thing seemed to just let you come here.'

His hands fell by his sides 'You wanted to see me? Why?'

'To discuss this thing.' Bea was beginning to feel a little awkward. This wasn't going to plan. He was supposed to have — what? She wasn't quite sure.

'Thing?' he mocked. 'Are you still drunk from last night?' Bea stared at him in silence, trying to figure out what to say next. 'Well, go on then. I'm waiting.'

'Luke, your behaviour last night was ridiculous.'

'How?'

'Coming over to our table, insinuating things by staring at me, and then again when we were dancing.'

He looked down at her. 'You're lecturing *me*?'

'I'm just saying!'

He ignored her protests. 'Do you realise how badly you're behaving?' He stared at her, his eyes searching hers for answers. 'I thought there could be something between us, but it seems I was wrong. Fair enough. But I've caught you looking at me as if you're searching my face for an answer to something, and I've no idea what it is.'

Bea couldn't look him in the eye. He was right, only she couldn't tell him the truth.

'Fine. I'll leave you to carry on with your jogging, then.' He marched off towards his car. 'Bloody woman,' she heard him curse.

Bea watched him leave, wishing she could afford not to care about his past. If only Simon didn't want half of her house, if only she didn't need to keep her job to be in with a chance to get that sodding mortgage. She walked towards her car, pulling her keys from her pocket as she balanced the coffee and paper in one hand. If only bloody Tom hadn't told her about the investigation.

She dropped her bar of chocolate, hearing it break in its wrapper.

17

FEBRUARY – PRUNING DEADWOOD

Bea didn't have to look at the calendar to know it would have been Annabel's birthday today. She stood outside her kitchen door, holding the neck of her coat closed as she drank her coffee and stared across the garden. 'I miss you,' she whispered, glad to be alone with her memories. Bea wished she could go back one year to the birthday treat she'd surprised Annabel with. 'It isn't every day you're seventy,' Bea recalled saying when Annabel had expressed horror at how much her gift must have cost. 'It's from me and Simon. He arranged everything – the mystery walk with the Kew guide and tickets for Les Misérables. We have him to thank for this, really.'

Was it only me who was shocked at Simon's double life? she wondered. She shook her head and held tightly on to her mug. No, Aunt Annabel had always been fond of him, too. Bea tried not to think how devastated her aunt had been when she'd discovered him with Claire. She hated to think that Annabel's heart attack could've been brought on by that devastating night. She breathed in the crisp, frosty air and swallowed the lump restricting her throat. She'd shed enough tears for Simon, and her aunt would hate for her to spend today crying. No, she'd begin her day by visiting Aunt Annabel's grave and take her some of her favourite orange roses.

'I know they're shop-bought,' Bea murmured, aware that there were one or two others near the immaculate grave, 'so I've brought you hyacinths, too. There's one in blue and one in pink.' Bea smiled. 'You never could decide which colour you preferred.' She breathed in the familiar scent, remembering many winters watching her aunt planting the bulbs and then watching them flower on the kitchen windowsill. It was a tradition she was determined to continue.

She picked up the vase and, noticing there wasn't any water, sat back on her heels to get up and fetch some.

'Here, let me.'

Startled by Luke's voice, she stood up quickly, nearly dropping the vase in her hand. 'What are you doing here?'

'Sorry if I'm intruding, but I saw your car as I was driving past and realised it must be an anniversary of some sort. Your mum, or your aunt maybe?'

Bea cleared her throat. 'It would have been Aunt Annabel's seventy-first birthday today.'

'I presume you planted the hyacinths especially for today, then?'

Bea nodded. She could feel herself welling up and turned away from him. 'I was just...'

'Let me.' He took the empty vase from her hand and walked away.

Bea watched him and struggled to retain her composure. She didn't want anyone to be too kind to her today. It would be too much to bear. She crouched back down and placed the hyacinths either side of the wooden cross, pushing their enamel containers slightly into the ground so the wind couldn't disturb them.

'Here you go,' Luke said, handing her the vase, their hands grazing lightly.

'Thank you,' she said, placing the roses into the water. She rested a hand on the cross. 'I can't wait for this ground to settle so I can order a proper gravestone. I gather you have to wait about a year, though.'

'Yes, something like that.' He placed a hand lightly on Bea's shoulder. 'I hope you didn't mind me stopping. I'll leave you in peace now.'

Bea put her hand up until she could hold his fingers. The warmth of his touch on her shoulder was strangely comforting. 'I don't mind. Thank you for looking out for me, it was kind.'

As his footsteps receded along the narrow path, she could almost hear her aunt's approval. Aunt Annabel liked strong men. Her Antonio had been a well-built man, always needing a formidable team of polo ponies to take his bulk. She'd like the idea of Luke working with his hands. She never did understand people's preference for working in offices. Bea's breath caught in her throat as emotion got the better of her, and she cried for a few minutes. 'I'm so lost right now,' she whispered, placing her hand on the cold wood of the cross. 'Surely things will improve soon.'

Bea arrived at her father and stepmother's home a short while later. As usual, it hadn't occurred to either of them that today might be a day when Bea wouldn't want to discuss wedding plans. But it was easier for her to get it over with than to row about it endlessly, so she fixed a smile on her face and went in.

'I've invited Tom,' Bea heard Mel say as she let herself into the house. 'He doesn't have a partner either, so I thought Bea— Oh, there you are.' She seemed confused by Bea's unhappy expression. 'I was saying, you're pairing up with Tom.'

'I'd really rather not, Mel.' She had no intention of staying any longer than necessary.

'Now, now, girls,' her dad said, standing up to give her a bear hug. 'No fighting. Mel's right, though.'

'It's not a problem, but why should it matter if I take someone or not?'

'Because then I can deduct your "plus ones" from the invitees.' Mel took her crystal-covered biro and scrawled out the writing next to Bea's name and then Tom's on her printed out spreadsheet.

Bea scowled at her sister. What was she on about? She looked at her dad for a clue.

'Mel and Joyce have got a little enthusiastic with their invitations, and Grant has finally put his foot down.'

'Not Grant,' Mel groaned. 'Dad's the one being selfish.' She pulled a sulky face at him. Bea could remember when that princess-look of hers used to work, around the age of five. She tried not to be irritated with her sister.

'Thank you, Melanie,' Joyce snapped, entering the living room carrying a plate of biscuits. 'I think your father is being perfectly reasonable about this.' She looked Bea up and down. 'I thought we said ten-thirty, not eleven o'clock,' she said, looking pointedly at her watch. 'I have a list of items to work through today, Beatrice. We can't all be spending time wallowing.'

Bea ignored her and sat down, soothed by her father's glare in Joyce's direction as he left the room. She knew he'd have a go at Joyce when she'd left, but a part of her wished he'd do it in front of her for once.

'Melanie tells us she's inviting Luke and his glamorous girlfriend. You and Tom will have to team up, and no argument.' She hesitated for a moment. 'I do believe though that refusing to allow any more than one hundred people in the marquee is probably a little too conservative, Eric,' she shouted in the general direction of his study. 'Your precious lawn will always grow back if we do decide to hire a larger marquee.'

'I think a hundred guests are more than enough,' Bea said,

happy to support her father. 'You can't have that many friends, and neither side have large families, do they?'

'Beatrice, I'll thank you to keep your opinions to yourself,' Joyce snapped, raising her chin in her usual aggressive manner when anyone dared to disagree with her. Bea remembered being terrified of Joyce when she was little, until she saw Annabel stand up to her and give her hell. Bea smiled to herself. That was the night when Annabel told Joyce and her father that Bea would be moving in with her for good. It had been the happiest day of her life, until her wedding day.

'Are you listening to me?'

Bea blinked and tried to recall what Joyce had been saying. 'Of course.'

'You've had your big day and I won't allow you to ruin your sister's, whatever misguided loyalties you might have about that date.'

Bea concentrated on not giving in to her temper. She glared at Mel. 'I'm sorry if I think choosing Aunt Annabel's first anniversary is a bit insensitive.'

'You're so selfish.' Joyce pursed her thin lips together. 'You've always thought more about that old woman than you did anyone else.'

'You wonder why?' Bea murmured under her breath.

Her father returned to the room. 'What's all this commotion?' He looked over at Joyce, who for once kept quiet. 'I told you that I wanted this to be a calm chat, so let's keep it that way. Mel's day should be as perfect at yours was, Bea,' he said, ignoring Joyce's badly concealed moan. 'I agree the date is unfortunate, but it's booked now. Maybe it's not such a bad thing to have something happy for us all to focus on.'

'Maybe,' Bea said, unconvinced. She was the only one who'd had any affection for Aunt Annabel. She suspected her father had a soft spot for her too, being his first wife's sister, but never dared show it, probably because Joyce always seemed so sensitive about any reminder that she wasn't the first woman he had loved. Not wishing to give her father more grief than he suffered most days, Bea nodded.

'Mel tells me she's come up with a way for you to keep Simon away from the house?' her father added.

'An injunction, but he's retaliated by getting his lawyers to send me a letter threatening a court date on the tenth of May.'

'Probate ends on the tenth of May,' her father said quietly. 'He doesn't waste any time, does he?'

'No, but I suppose whatever happens it'll be a relief to get it all finalised at last.'

'Have you been to the bank yet?' he asked. Bea nodded. 'No luck?' Bea chewed her lower lip and shook her head. 'Never mind, you'll have to keep trying. You know I would help if I could.'

Joyce stood up. 'Don't you dare say if it wasn't for this wedding, Eric.'

'I wasn't going to, Joyce. This wedding might be expensive, but even this couldn't pay for half that house.'

'Yes, well, some people don't know when they're well off, do they?' Joyce snapped, giving Bea a pointed glare. 'Your sister doesn't have a house of her own yet.'

'Mum, stop it,' Mel said, slamming down her biro. 'Annabel was nothing to me. She was Bea's mum's sister, so why would she include me in her will? Honestly, you do irritate me sometimes.'

Bea didn't know who must looked more stunned at her sister's uncharacteristic outburst at her mother – her, her father or Joyce. When no one spoke, Mel took hold of Bea's wrists. 'Look at your hands,' she said, inspecting Bea's ruined nails. 'A farmer would have better fingernails than you.'

'I doubt that,' Bea replied, noticing that they did need attention.

'But I promise I'll get a manicure before your wedding.' She thought it was the least she could do. 'Do you want to come with Shani, Paul and me to a winter fayre this afternoon after we've finished here?'

'She's not going anywhere until we finalise these arrangements,' Joyce snapped.

Mel thought for a moment then smiled. 'Oh, go on then. Where is it?'

'Gorey Village, near Shani's parent's house. Her mum is chair of the Women's Voluntary Guild, or something like that. Shani phoned me last night and asked if I could muster up some helpers.'

Mel glanced up at her. 'Why's that? I thought her mum was the most organised person in the entire cosmos.' She smiled at her mum. 'Apart from you, of course.'

'They've lost some of their regulars to a stomach bug. They just need helpers for two of the stalls. I couldn't really say no to helping Shani out.'

'It sounds like a good idea to me,' Bea's dad said, giving her a kiss on the cheek. 'It'll give you a break from all this wedding talk, Mel, and you from house worries, Bea. You two should get going. We've agreed that we won't be hiring a larger marquee now, and we know your plus one and Tom's are being removed from the list, so that's progress. By the time we've pruned the deadwood,' he raised his voice a little, 'and Joyce realises our neighbours from twenty years ago do not need an invitation, then I think the numbers should tally pretty well. We can discuss this again later in the week.'

'How can I refuse, then?' Mel said. 'Grant's busy and these preparations are stressing me out. I'm happy to get away from them for a bit.'

'And I need a break from the smell of paint and white spirit.' Bea smiled, relieved to be leaving.

* * *

'It's so busy here,' Bea said, seeing so many vehicles in the car park. The only spot she could find was between two shining Range Rovers, and with her lousy parking skills she thought it preferable to park on the road.

'What is it about bangers and not washing them?' Mel looked back at Bea's ancient Mazda.

'I daren't,' Bea joked. 'The rust is holding it together.'

Having been given their orders for the day, Bea led the way to their pitches. It never ceased to amaze her how Shani, being so tall and slim, had such a matronly mother whose steel-grey hair, pulled back into a tight chignon, framed her powdered face with dark eyes that never missed a trick. Bea was sure her thin lips had never uttered a kind word to anyone.

'Step to it,' she bellowed. 'I want these stalls ready for visitors as soon as possible.'

'Blimey,' Mel groaned, indicating the elderly women scuttling around the room at Mrs Calder's orders. 'This lot are terrified.'

'Aren't you?' Paul laughed. 'Even I wouldn't cross the old bag.'

'Hey, that old bag is my mother.' Shani punched him on his shoulder. 'Only I'm allowed to criticise her.'

'I can see who'll be heading up the next generation of old bags,' he laughed, before running off with a tray of cakes meant for someone's stall.

'Steady on, young man,' Mrs Calder's voice bellowed across the room. Voices hushed, and Bea giggled as Paul mouthed an apology. 'Right. Melanie and Paul, you are to man the second-hand bookstall, and Beatrice and Shani you can take the preserves.' Mrs Calder pointed to the rickety trellis tables.

'Come along,' she continued. 'Jump to it. Lady Dulbury will be arriving in half an hour to open the fayre and your stalls need to be immaculate before then. And don't lose your money bags. Oh, and a photographer from the Gazette will be coming so don't let side down.'

'Whose bright idea was it to help out?' whispered Paul to Bea. 'I'd rather be moping by myself than being bossed around here.'

'Stop messing about.' Shani took hold of Bea's sleeve. 'Come with me.'

'I think you're already starting to morph into your mother,' Paul grinned. Mel grabbed his wrist and dragged him to their stall.

'No. No. No, Mrs Baxter, not like that.' Mrs Calder pounded over to where a poor white-haired lady fumbled with a disintegrating Victoria sponge.

'Quick, let's look busy,' Shani said, frantically tidying up their stall.

Bea didn't argue. 'You must take after your dad.' She raised a playful eyebrow.

'Thankfully, I do. When I was small I was sure I was adopted, and even had the guts to ask her once.'

'That's brave,' laughed Bea. 'What did she say?'

'Nothing, she told me not to be so rude and sent me to my room without any supper.'

At the laughter, Shani's mother walked over to them. 'I presume by the chit-chat that you two are satisfied with your presentation?'

'Yes.' They nodded, almost standing to attention and trying not to laugh.

She surveyed the trestle table and its contents before sighing loudly, her whole body quivering as if to emphasize her concerns. 'It'll have to do, I suppose. You are amateurs, after all.' She clapped her hands together and marched off once more to check on the others.

* * *

The jostling and elbowing in front of their stall slowly began to subside. 'We've done extremely well, don't you think?' Shani said.

'Most of our jars have been sold,' Bea agreed proudly. 'Even the boxes hidden under the table are almost gone.' Bea looked down at her own bag containing two jars of damson and raspberry jam she'd bought for herself and her parents. She took the last few jars from under the table. 'I'll pop these on the stall to see if we can sell them too.' She stood, her arms full of jars and sensed someone standing at the table.

'Can I help you?' she asked, looking up.

Luke held a carrier bag full of books. 'Yes, please.'

18

MOLEHILLS

Startled, Bea dropped two of the jars. 'Damn,' she said, as one hit her foot and Luke instinctively reached to catch the other before it hit the ground.

Luke held it up triumphantly. 'Well done,' she said, impressed by his quick reaction and ignoring her aching foot.

'Well?' he asked, waiting for a reply.

Bea frowned. 'Sorry?' Why did she find it so hard to stay focused around him?

Luke indicated the jar in his hand. 'Can I buy a couple of pots?'

'You can buy as many as you like,' she said retrieving the jar from the floor and placing the rest neatly onto the table. 'I wouldn't have thought this was your sort of thing.'

He looked around at the other stalls. 'I could say the same about you. My mother is on the committee with that old battle-axe over there.' He inclined his head in Mrs Calder's direction.

Bea leant towards him, 'Lower your voice,' she whispered. 'That's Shani's mother.'

Bea pressed her lips together to stop laughing when Luke's eyebrows shot up. 'Poor girl. Doesn't take after her, does she?'

'No, thankfully,' Bea smiled. 'So, do you always help out at these things then?'

He shook his head and shuddered. 'No, only when they're held around here, which luckily is only once a year. My mother always asks me to help with any heavy lifting, and I don't really mind. It's a bit of fun, and I'm usually paid with a couple of ciders and Jersey Wonders from the stalls.'

'What a surprise,' Leilani said, suspicion souring her voice as she sidled up to Luke. 'When Luke suggested we come, he didn't mention *you'd* be working here, Beatrice Potter. Isn't it delightful how we keep on bumping into each other? I suppose we should expect it on this tiny island.'

Bea ignored her insistence on saying her name incorrectly and forced a friendly smile, determined to be pleasant. 'Leilani, have you been enjoying the fayre?'

'It seems a little more interesting now I see you're here. I thought there would only be old ladies fighting over tea cosies.' She snaked her arms through Luke's. 'Lukey,' she said, in a sickly-sweet voice. 'I've seen enough. Let's go and do something fun.' She took one of his hands and began pulling him away. 'Ta-ta, Beatrice,' she said over her shoulder in a mock English accent.

Bea ignored her and caught Luke's eye. He mouthed an apology and smiled.

'God, I hate that rotten cow,' Shani said from behind her. 'I'm thirsty, do you mind holding the fort for a bit?' She crossed her legs as only someone expert in yoga could manage. 'I can get us some lemonade after I've visited the ladies' room.'

'Go ahead.' Bea watched Shani walk off, wondering what was different about her.

'Young lady,' said a tiny old woman in front of her. 'Will you help us?' Bea nodded, hoping Shani wouldn't be long with that drink. Her throat was parched, and she wished she'd thought to bring a bottle of water along. 'We've just enjoyed the most delicious afternoon tea and were advised that the jam served with the scones was being sold at this stall. But we can't decide between the raspberry and the damson.'

'How about buying one of each?' Bea asked, giving them her brightest salesman smile.

'We only want one jar each though,' the shorter of the two women replied.

'Well, why not both buy a different one and if you have a spare container at home you can take half from each of the jars and swap.'

After a short debate, they agreed. 'Splendid idea, that's what we'll do.'

At the end of the day, Shani's mother thanked them for all their 'admirable effort'. 'Quick, let's make our getaway before she finds anything else for us to do,' Paul whispered as they hurried over to Bea's car. Bea rested two jars of jam on the roof as she unlocked her car door.

'Here, give those to me.' Paul reached for the jam.

Shani quickly snatched them off the roof. 'No chance. These are mine and Bea's; you said you didn't want any, so it's too late now.'

Bea watched as Shani held the jars high above Paul's head. Distracted by the way Shani's sweatshirt pulled against her stomach, something occurred to her. Bea's mind was in turmoil. How had she not noticed? Why hadn't Shani said anything to her? For once she was relieved that the others chatted continuously all the way to their homes to give her a chance to process the realisation. Bea dropped Mel off first and then Paul, eventually arriving back at The Brae.

'Come on, let's get inside,' she said to Shani, barely able to contain herself.

As soon as they were in the kitchen, Bea turned to her. 'I can't believe you're pregnant and you never said anything.'

Shani's mouth dropped open, then her face slowly reddened. 'How do you know?'

'Seriously?' Bea stared at Shani's rounded stomach. 'Harry?' Shani nodded. 'How far along are you?' Shani didn't answer, but sat down lowering her head into her hands. 'Shani, when's the baby due?'

The doorbell rang as they stared at each other in silence. 'What's going on in here?' Paul frowned suspiciously as he walked into the kitchen.

'I thought you were going straight to meet Guy?' Bea said, wishing she'd been left alone with Shani at least until she'd learned everything there was to know.

'I was, but I forgot to give you this bag of treats before you dropped me off.' He held out a brown paper bag. Neither of them spoke. 'Have I missed something?'

Bea looked at Shani and then back at him. 'She's pregnant.'

Paul dropped the bag onto the table before sitting down heavily. 'And she didn't tell us?'

Bea squeezed Paul's shoulder. If she was upset with Shani for not confiding in her, how bad must he feel? 'I had no idea.' He shook his head slowly. 'Shan?'

'So, was that business about Harry needing a scan all nonsense?'

Shani nodded and took something from her bag. 'Here, I can see you're both practically holding your breath,' she said, holding out a piece of paper towards them. 'It's a scan of the baby.' She pointed to the black and white image.

'I can't believe it.' Paul murmured, snatching the picture from her fingers and studying it.

'Do you hate me, Bea?' Shani looked at Bea for the first time.

The pleading in her eyes made Bea well up. She walked round the table and gave her a hug from behind. 'Don't be stupid. Of course I don't hate you.' She hesitated, then couldn't stop herself from adding, 'I am disappointed, though.'

'I was dreading that,' Shani said, wiping her eyes with a tissue. 'I'm pregnant with a baby I didn't plan or originally want while you lost the one you wanted so badly.'

Bea shook her head angrily. 'That's not why I'm disappointed. I can't believe you kept this from me.' She looked at Paul. 'Us,' she said, correcting herself. 'Why did you keep something this important to yourself? Why try to cover it up?'

Shani sighed. 'You have so much going on already, and you—' she jutted her chin out at Paul '—are in love for the first time since being heartbroken. I thought you both had enough happening in your lives.'

'And?' Paul didn't sound convinced. Neither was she, decided Bea.

'Then I discovered Harry was married and had no idea how to tell you.'

'Idiot.' Paul took her hand for a moment before squinting at the scan. 'I'm sorry, but I can't make this out. What exactly am I looking at?'

Bea pulled out a chair and sat at the table taking Shani's hand in hers. She hated seeing her friend in such turmoil. Shani was always so open with them both, or so she'd always thought. She must have been really concerned about upsetting them to keep something this monumental to herself.

'It was devastating when I lost my baby,' Bea said quietly. 'And I admit I do find it difficult to come to terms with that, but it doesn't stop me being thrilled for you.' She touched Shani's arm. 'You're going to be a lovely mum. You know that, don't you?' Bea hoped she was managing to reassure her. 'You having a baby will be something we can all look forward to. Something good we can enjoy. I can't believe you've been going through this by yourself though.' She took a deep breath, hating to think of the turmoil Shani must have been experiencing.

'What about Harry?' Paul asked. 'What did he have to say about the baby?'

'After the scan and we knew I was pregnant, he admitted he was back with his wife.'

Paul groaned. 'You poor thing.'

'I don't think I believed his business partner when he told me Harry was married, so to hear Harry calmly tell me about her was a bit hard to take in.'

'I'm not surprised,' Bea said, wishing she could confront Harry and give him hell for what he'd done to her friend. 'We're here for you though, Shani, whatever happens.'

Paul glanced at the kitchen clock. 'Damn, I'm late to meet Guy. You don't mind if I race off, do you? He starts work soon and I need to see him about something before then.' He bent down and kissed Shani on the cheek. 'Don't fret about this. Sod Harry, you've got us two and we'll be all the support you need.'

'We'll catch up with you later,' Bea said. 'Don't worry, Shani and I can carry on chatting things through.' She waited for him to give Shani a quick hug and reassure her once again. Something occurred to her, but Bea waited for Paul to close the door behind him before speaking. 'Can you stay at the flat with a baby, do you think?'

'I don't think so. That's another thing I need to discuss with Paul.'

'I hope you know the baby doesn't make any difference to my offer for you to move in here.'

'Really?' Shani narrowed her eyes. 'Are you sure it wouldn't be too much? I did love it here. Too much, probably.'

'I can't have you in some tiny bed-sit when I'm rattling around by myself here. Let's face it, Shan, I have six bedrooms and only use one for me and another as an office. It's the perfect solution for both of us.'

'But I wouldn't be able to pay you much as I won't be working for a few months.'

'I've thought about that, but to be honest every little will help. It'll also be company. I didn't realise how lonely I would be living in this place all by myself. The only problem I can see us having is with Paul. He's going to be upset to lose you as a flatmate. It's going to be bad enough for him not having you every day at work, without you moving out, too.'

'I know,' Shani said, thoughtfully stroking her baby bump. 'How am I going to tell him?'

'Maybe I could ask him to move in here, too?' Bea suggested. They all got along well together, and another person helping towards the mortgage would be beneficial.

'What if the baby is one of those that cries all night?' Shani asked, looking worried.

'Then you'll just have to have one of the rooms at the back of the house,' Bea teased. 'I'm joking.' She patted Shani's arm when she looked concerned.

'I'd love to live here. I can't think of anywhere else I would rather be. I'm not sure if Paul will move here too, but he won't mind as much if he thinks he's welcome too.' Bea saw Shani looking thoughtful and waited for her to speak 'How should we sort out paying for things?' She raised a hand when Bea went to interrupt.

'I'm not moving in here without paying my way. You can't afford it, and it's against my principles.'

Bea wasn't surprised Shani was wanting to get things straight before agreeing to live at The Brae. 'I don't mind what you want to do, I'm just relieved we've agreed you should move in here. That's a start.'

It mattered to her that Paul didn't feel excluded, so to ask him too would be perfect. She knew it would suit Shani to move in, having heard her rave about living in the countryside with the orchard and areas of the garden many times in the past. Bea suspected she would enjoy parking her baby's pram in the garden's fresh air, knowing it would be safe there.

'Do you know,' Shani said eventually, 'even Harry's lack of interest in our baby can't dampen my mood now I know I don't have to start traipsing the streets finding somewhere suitable to live.'

'I think we both need a celebratory cuppa,' laughed Bea.

Shani opened the bag Paul had left to reveal spongy cakes. 'Jersey Wonders, perfect.'

'I thought you'd say that,' Bea said, happily. 'Full of fat and sugar, and perfect for celebrating baby news. Mmm, these are still warm.'

19

MARCH – DARKEST DAYS

Bea struggled to decipher her aunt's handwriting. Why had she ever thought she stood a chance of keeping up with her aunt's good work? She was already finding it impossible.

She picked up a bag of snapdragon seeds and opened the twisted top, trying not to lose the precious seeds her aunt had collected from her garden the previous year. Bea dipped a small container into a tub of compost and went to pour it into some little pots, accidentally knocking over the seeds and scattering them over the floor. She threw down the pot and burst into tears of frustration.

Why was she bothering with all this? Simon was right. Aunt Annabel wouldn't be here to see any of it, and no one else was interested in the damn garden. She sat down on an old wooden stool and sobbed.

'This bloody house,' she groaned. Maybe she should sell it and move on. As soon as the thought entered her mind, Bea knew it was an irrelevant one. Even overwhelmed as she was by everything she'd lost – her aunt, her marriage and her baby – she knew she couldn't lose this house, too. Anyway, where would Shani and her baby go if she did sell it?

How had it come to this? When had her happy marriage become a sham? Had she even been in love with the real Simon, or had she only seen in him what he wanted her to? Mel had once accused her of marrying Simon too quickly because she was desperate to create the happy family she'd lost when her mum had died.

She blew her nose on a crumpled tissue and went back into the house. Though it was early, she opened a bottle of rosé and lit a fire, then sank into the huge sofa in the darkness of the drawing room with only a box of tissues for comfort. The soothing golden glow of the fire did nothing to improve her mood. She started on her way to get hideously drunk, unsure how else to block everything from her mind. She was in love with a completely unsuitable man who could end up causing her to lose her job and, if she wasn't extremely careful, her freedom, too. What the hell was she playing at, and why was everything so complicated?

The bottle empty, Bea decided to get another from the fridge. The lights in the house flickered once and then went out. Bea carefully made her way to the window. She looked out but couldn't see any other lights nearby. 'A power cut.' That was all she needed on top of everything else.

Turning too quickly, Bea caught her temple on the corner of an open cupboard door. She winced in pain. Putting fingers up to her head intending to rub it better, she felt the warm stickiness of blood. 'Damn, that hurts,' she moaned. Stunned and a little wobbly, she padded over to the sink to soak a wedge of kitchen roll in cool water to help stem the blood trickling down the side of her face.

Bea held the wet mass up to her head as she returned to the drawing room and sat. Her head was pounding. Maybe it was time to go to bed. No more melancholy for her. Enough now. She got up slowly, surprised at how dizzy she felt.

The phone rang on the table next to her. 'Hello?'

'Bea? Is that you?'

'Who's this?' she asked, cupping the phone in between her ear and chin.

'It's Luke. I wanted to apologise if I've seemed a bit snappy with you.' He was silent for a moment. 'Are you all right?'

Why had she answered the phone? She knew she was in no state to talk to anyone about anything, especially him, and certainly after finishing a bottle of wine. The last thing she wanted to do was say the wrong thing.

'I'm fine, thanks.' Bea wiped away a random tear from her puffy eyes with a handful of damp, disintegrating tissues. 'Night.' She put the phone down. She would sleep down here tonight. It was cosy, and the fire should keep going for the next few hours.

Sometime later she became vaguely aware of a banging noise. Bea dragged a fresh tissue from the near empty box and blew her nose. The banging was repeated. She pushed the blanket off and ambled blearily over to the door peering tentatively around it to see who was making so much noise. Her eyes focused on Luke staring back at her; he didn't seem happy. She pulled back the heavy door. 'What's the matter?' she asked blearily, her voice sounding odd even in her drunken state.

* * *

Luke couldn't believe his eyes. With one hand holding a clump of bloodied tissues to their head and the other clinging to the door frame, the person vaguely resembled Bea. Except this person had a pale face, eyes so puffy they were almost closed, and mussed hair that stuck up at angles around a blotchy face.

'Luke, can this wait until tomorrow?' Bea asked, pushing her hands through her untidy hair and beginning to push the door closed.

Luke couldn't imagine what could have happened to her. Dread filtered through the pit of his stomach. He put his hand out and caught the door before it slammed shut and followed her silently inside. The only light was coming from the fire in the grate and the moonlight through the windows. Without saying a word, he sat down opposite her as she settled onto the sofa and made herself comfortable again. She seemed unaware that he was still in the room.

'Bea,' he said, keeping his voice as gentle as he could. 'How did you hurt your head?'

He watched as she slowly raised her hand and lightly touched the cut. 'Ouch,' she said, flinching, her gaze troubled. 'I think it was on a cupboard door. Stupid, really.'

Luke forced what he hoped was a reassuring smile. 'Is there anything I can do?'

Bea stared at him silently. He felt a pang of sadness at the obvious sadness in her eyes. Something must have happened between the fayre and now. 'Is it Simon?' he asked.

She thought for a moment and then nodded slowly. 'I'm such an idiot,' she murmured sleepily, touching her head once more.

'No, you're not,' he soothed. 'We can talk about this in the morning.' He leant forward and checked her cut. It was difficult to see clearly, but he thought the bleeding had stopped.

'I don't think it's deep. We can get it looked at properly in the morning. Why don't you get some sleep?' He watched her lie back and close her eyes, amazed she complied so readily. He pulled a chenille blanket from the back of the settee to cover her and sat back down, watching her silently, the flickering shadows from the fire taking him back to that memorable evening they'd slept together.

He added several logs to boost the fire and tried to make sense of his jumbled emotions. He felt protective of her and wished he and Bea were closer and that she would let him take care of her somehow. He pictured her with Tom at the charity ball. He hated having to watch Tom with Bea. Why did she seem to trust Tom when all she seemed to do was push him away? He wished he knew what was holding her back. Was he wrong to think Bea had feelings for him? Or was it just wishful thinking on his part?

* * *

While preparing coffees in Bea's kitchen the next morning, the phone rang and Luke answered it. 'Hello?' he said absent-mindedly, stirring sugar into the steaming black liquid.

'Who's that?'

'Who's this?'

'I asked first— Oh sod it, it's Shani.'

'Luke,' he volunteered, trying not to sound too amused at her obvious surprise.

Silence. 'Er, morning, Luke. Um, is the lady of the house there, please?' Shani asked, excitement clear in her voice. He suspected she assumed he and Bea had slept together because he was in the house so early.

He placed the coffees and two plates of buttered toast on a tray. 'She is, but she's a little caught up now. Can I ask her to give you a call when she comes round?'

'Comes round? Is she okay?'

Damn, thought Luke. Why had he used those specific words? He thought for a moment and, remembering what close friends the two women were, knew he had to fill her in on the previous evening. 'Shani, she's not all right.'

'What do you mean?' Luke could hear the breathless concern in her voice.

'I phoned her last night but she didn't seem to be her usual self.

She wasn't particularly happy to see me when I popped round here to check on her, but I couldn't in all conscience leave her.'

'You've been there all night?'

'Yes, I'm about to wake her now.'

'I'm glad you stayed with her. Do you know what's wrong?'

He wished he did, he thought, but didn't say so. ''Fraid not. She has a nasty cut to her temple, and will no doubt have one hell of a headache this morning. I don't envy her.' He hoped he hadn't said too much and felt sure Shani needed to know exactly what happened in case Bea tried to make light of everything. She needed help sorting whatever it was out, and her best friend was the perfect person to help her.

'She's got rather a lot on her plate, and to be honest I've probably added to her troubles.' Shani groaned. 'Unfortunately, her problems aren't things anyone else can help with. Simon is very controlling, and she's going to have to find a way to sort him out finally. I've got a niggling feeling there's something else wrong, but she hasn't confided in me about it. Look, I'm going to come right over.'

'Thanks,' he said, relieved Shani was on her way. He knew Bea wouldn't be happy to see him there when she woke. Hell, he thought, he'd be horrified to find her sitting watching him after a heavy night too.

Up until now, she'd always seemed strong and independent, so in charge of everything. Seeing her in such a state last night had concerned him. She seemed fragile and he couldn't help wondering if her biggest concerns were losing the house she loved so much. He had to agree with Shani though that there must be more to it than that. But what?

Shani arrived and thanked Luke for sitting with Bea for the night. 'Let me know how she is, will you?' he asked, writing his mobile number on the notepad by the door.

'Will do,' said Shani, concern for her friend written all over her face.

As he opened the front door, she called to him. 'Luke?'

'Yes?'

'How will you explain to your girlfriend where you've been all night?'

'She's not my girlfriend.' She might not be, he thought as he walked down the front steps, but Leilani was still going to be impossible, and probably throw a tantrum over him staying out all night, especially when she discovered he had been at Bea's.

* * *

Bea heard the front door close and stretched, wincing in pain. She recognised Shani's voice and watched through blurry eyes as her friend entered the room. 'Oh, my head,' Bea groaned, pushing herself up slowly. 'Hey, how did you get in?'

Shani stared at her thoughtfully. 'Luke.'

Bea frowned and tried to process Shani's words. 'Luke's here? I don't understand. Ow.'

'He told me you were in a really bad way last night and didn't feel he should leave you alone.'

Realisation dawned on Bea. 'Oh no, I think I remember.' She looked up at Shani, another movement that hurt like hell. 'Even my eyes hurt.'

'I know, and you look a mess.' Shani held out a mug for her to take. 'Drink your coffee, then you can freshen up. You'll feel much better after that.'

Bea, having no strength to argue, was happy to let Shani take charge. Seeing her puffy face, swollen eyes and bruised and cut temple in the ornate mirror on the wall, her heart sank to think that anyone, let alone Luke, had seen her in such a state.

After luxuriating in a hot bath, she took a couple of painkillers and was soon feeling a little better. Shani wanted her to see a doctor to check she didn't need stitches, but Bea insisted it wasn't necessary. Instead, she suggested they go out for some fresh air.

They walked along the paths in between the World War II gun placements and bunkers at Noirmont Point.

'Is it because of the baby?' Shani asked eventually. Bea shook her head. 'What's bothering you, then? I'm sure you're keeping something from me and it's making me anxious.'

Bea wished she had the freedom to share what Tom had told her about Luke's problems.

'You can tell me anything, you know that, don't you?' Shani said.

Bea caught Shani's eye but didn't mention that she had never imagined she might keep her pregnancy a secret from her. She needed to find a way to explain things to Shani without breaking the confidentiality code she had to abide as a trust officer. She spent her working life looking after others' trusts and companies and it went against her principles to discuss business when she shouldn't.

'Bea?'

Bea paused. 'Look, it's not that I don't want to tell you, but I'm not allowed.'

'Can you tell me who it's to do with then?'

'I can't tell you that either, sorry. It's nothing for you to worry about, though. It's more to do with work.'

'Tom.' Shani pulled a face. 'I might have guessed.'

'Sorry?' Why was Shani always so intuitive? 'Why do you mention Tom?'

Shani stopped walking and stared at her, hands on her hips. 'I knew he'd be involved somehow.'

Bea shrugged. 'It's difficult, and Tom hasn't actually done anything wrong.'

'So tell me. You work for the same company and he is your manager, after all.'

'He knows something that he felt I should be told, that's all,' Bea eventually confided.

Shani stared at her, a confused expression on her face. 'This has something to do with Luke, I presume?'

Not comfortable looking Shani in the eyes, Bea bent to smell a narcissus. 'You don't know anything of the sort. Anyway, I've told you I can't discuss it.'

'How come Tom can tell you, then? I don't get it.'

'He told me to make sure I didn't inadvertently get myself into a difficult situation.'

'With Luke.'

Bea rolled her eyes. 'Will you forget about Luke? Please drop it.'

Shani shrugged and began walking again. 'All I know is that something is playing on your mind and I don't like it.'

Bea put her arm around Shani's waist. 'Neither do I, but there's nothing I can do about it.'

Shani stroked her rounded stomach. She stopped and gave Bea a reassuring smile. 'It'll all work out, just hang in there.'

'I hope you're right.' If it doesn't, she was just going to have to simply deal with it.

Shani snuggled into her red woollen scarf and pointed out to sea. 'I wonder if Luke's boat is out there? It does look a little rough today.'

'I doubt it. He's moored at St Catherine's over the other side of the island. I suppose living on his boat while he does up his cottage is an obvious thing to do for someone who loves the sea.' She inwardly cringed at the thought of him spending all night watching her sleep. What had she said to him? God, her head was still pounding. 'Anyway, I have more pressing matters to worry about. I need to sort out this money for Simon.'

Shani groaned. 'If only you could discover what this Jersey Kiss thing is and maybe you could sell it. If your aunt left it to you in her will then it must be worth something.'

'I know,' Bea said, shivering and doing up her ancient Burberry mac. 'But I've looked everywhere for it. There's no paperwork that I can find, no paintings that look valuable, and certainly no jewellery. If I don't find a way out of this financial mess, I'm going to have to seriously consider selling The Brae, and I can't bear the thought of losing everything Aunt Annabel worked so hard to achieve. I'd feel as if I'd let her down badly, not to mention you and the baby.'

'I know you would, but you shouldn't.' Shani paused. 'We need to discuss my rent.'

Bea shivered.

'Bea,' Shani said. 'I know it's awkward talking about these things, so I've contacted a rental agency and explained my situation. They suggested I pay you about two hundred pounds per week. Do you think that's enough?'

That sounded fine to Bea. She needed approximately one thousand four hundred pounds each month. 'Are you sure it isn't too much for you?' Shani was a supervisor at the gym, not an owner.

'I'm happy as long as you are.'

Bea smiled. 'That's great. I can let Mr Peters know when I meet with him tomorrow.' It had been much quicker working this out with Shani than she'd expected. Then again, Shani never liked to waste time messing about.

'I wish I could afford to help you out more,' Shani said, tightening her scarf slightly. 'Why's it so bloody cold? It's March, for heaven's sake!'

'I'm sick of this weather too.'

'What time is your appointment?'

Bea groaned. 'Nine o'clock. It's the third time he's seen me, and the poor man keeps trying to help because of my aunt, but we're not getting far. He can only do so much, I suppose. I'll be able to find out exactly what that will be tomorrow.'

* * *

'Mr Peters will see you now,' the secretary said, showing Bea through to his wood-panelled office.

'Ahh, Ms Philips,' he said indicating a chair and opening a file on his desk. 'I've studied your income and expenditure and the amount you're hoping to borrow.'

Before he could continue, Bea told him about Shani and how much she'd be contributing by way of rent.

He listened in silence and made a few calculations. 'Have to admit, I can't quite see how you'll be able to make the monthly payments.' Bea sat up straight, determined not to let him see how much his negativity was upsetting her. 'Ms Philips, much as I would like to help you, especially as an old friend of your aunt, I'm afraid that at this moment I will not be able to sanction a loan for the full amount.' Bea opened her mouth to speak, but he continued. 'Even with your friend moving in, I'm afraid you'll still be short on funds.'

Bea chewed anxiously on her lower lip. 'I have to find a way to keep the house.'

'I'm sure you do, but I'm governed by procedures and must decide based on those. I suggest you go home and maybe discuss this with family members, see if there is something they can maybe do to help.'

'I'll do my best,' Bea assured him, knowing full well that she wouldn't get anywhere. 'My ex-husband wants his money now and I'm not sure how my family can afford to help me.' She stood up and shook the bank manager's hand. 'I'll do what I can and get back to you, if that's all right?'

'Yes, of course it is. I can arrange for part of the amount, but it would be less than a third of the value of the house and not the fifty per cent you were hoping for.'

Bea forced a smile. 'It isn't enough, but I'd be grateful if you could put the offer in writing for me, so at least I know what I can borrow.'

'My secretary will forward it to you in the next few days, and should you find an alternative source of funds, then we can arrange to finalise the paperwork at that time. Best of luck, Ms Philips.'

Bea made to leave, and then turned to him. 'Mr Peters, I've been wondering if perhaps you might recall my aunt mentioning something called A Jersey Kiss?'

His eyes widened, and he thought for a moment. 'Can't say that I do. What exactly is it?'

Bea shrugged. 'My aunt left it to me, but no one seems to know what it could be and we can't find any records about it.'

He tapped his ink blotter with his pen and stared out of the window, looking as intrigued as she'd been when the lawyer first told her about the mysterious legacy. 'I do remember her mentioning some sort of gift to you. I know she was very proud of it, but I can't say for certain that she was referring to this Jersey Kiss. Could it possibly be a piece of jewellery? Her late husband enjoyed commissioning intricate pieces for her.' He shook his head slowly. 'I'm sorry, I wish I knew. Maybe it's a painting, or a sculpture that you've not noticed before?'

Bea hadn't thought to check the house or garden for sculptures. She smiled gratefully. 'Thank you, you've been very helpful.'

* * *

'Right,' said Shani, when a flustered Bea visited her at the yoga studio. 'We'll have to speak to Paul and let him know I'll be moving in with you sooner than expected. He'll understand our motives, I think. You could always consider renting out a couple of the other rooms, too.'

Bea hoped Shani was right about Paul, and feeling only slightly less panicky, hurried off to work to make up the time she'd taken for her appointment.

She sighed heavily as she arrived home at the end of the long, arduous day. Taking off her navy coat she flung it over the back of a chair.

Later that evening, as Bea was microwaving a lasagne dinner for one, Paul phoned. 'The soon-to-be mother has informed me that my loss is to be your gain.'

Bea tried to make out if he was happy or not about Shani's news. 'Yes,' she acknowledged cautiously. 'We thought if you didn't mind, Shani would have much more space living here with the baby, and of course there's the garden for all the fresh air she needs.'

'Hold it right there,' he interrupted. 'You don't need to give me the prepared speech. I understand. After all, our lease doesn't allow children, so we'd only have to move anyway. Stop worrying.'

'Tell her everything, you little cheat,' Shani shouted in the background.

'Thank you Shani,' he snapped. 'I was just about to do that.' Bea could imagine Paul's large blue eyes glaring at Shani in mock rage. 'Guy has asked me to move in with him and we've been trying to figure out a way to break the news to her ladyship. We were even contemplating finding a two-bedroom cottage so Shani could move in with us. Now she is to abandon this unexceptional abode, Guy and I can get on with searching for our new home sooner than we anticipated.'

Bea gave a sigh of relief. 'Well, that's one less problem to worry about. I'm glad to have been so helpful to you both,' she laughed. 'Tell Shani to let me know when I can help move her things here, though I'm not sure about the rent.'

'No, you don't,' Shani said, taking the phone. 'This isn't just a room I'm renting; it'll be two soon, and you're letting me have use of all the house and gardens. I'm not arguing, Bea. If this isn't arranged in a fair way, then I can't accept your offer to move in.'

'Shani,' argued Bea. 'You can't afford it.'

'And you can't afford not to accept it. It's the going rate. I'm not a charity case, and my parents have offered to help me with the rent while I'm not working. Well, my father has. For once he's over-ruled my mother, and I have the feeling she'd been given a stern telling-off because she was far nicer to me than usual when I popped in to see them yesterday.'

Bea could tell Shani was calmer about the situation now her parents were coming around to the idea a little.

'I'll also make sure Harry agrees to assist in some way,' Shani added.

'All right, I give in.' Bea thought for a moment. 'We can put in a certain amount per week for food, and I'll cover the household bills myself. Yes, that's what I'll do. I'll feel much happier then.'

Bea could hear Shani murmuring to Paul and knew by her muffled voice that her hand was clamped over the receiver as she discussed the finer points of their arrangements. 'Paul's nodding at me, so he thinks we're on the right track. Okay, we'll do it like that. This is going to be exciting, don't you think?'

It would be fun, and the thought of having someone to chat to late into the night cheered her up no end. 'It'll take us back to our boarding school days.'

'You only boarded for two terms before your aunt insisted you came back to Jersey,' Shani teased. 'I was left there for an entire year after you'd gone.'

Bea went back to her notes and added in Shani's agreed rental payments. It made her income appear much healthier. It was more than she had intended asking Shani for, but however generous it seemed, she still couldn't make the figures work to cover the payments needed to keep the house.

Bea heard a noise outside and realised she hadn't checked the post. She went to the hall to see what delights the postman had delivered. 'Great,' she groaned, opening the court order Simon had threatened her with. 'This is a nightmare.' She chewed the end of her biro. 'Damn Simon for wanting so much.'

20

APRIL – HOME TO ROOST

The phone rang, interrupting her thoughts. 'Bea, it's Tom. I've been thinking.'

'You have?' she said half-heartedly, staring down at the letter from the lawyer's office.

'I think I should host a dinner party. Maybe invite several friends, what do you think?'

A dinner party? Bea was stumped and not exactly sure why he was asking her opinion. 'I don't see why not. You haven't really entertained in your flat yet, have you?'

'No, and I want to show my new friends that I've moved on from Vanessa.'

Bea rubbed her stiff neck. She must have been looking down for too long, she thought. Bea leant her chin in her hand. 'Fine.'

'Will you help me with the food?'

Ah, so that was it. Bea thought for a moment. He sounded so unsure of himself she didn't like to refuse. 'Okay.'

'Brilliant. Thanks, Bea.' He hesitated for a moment before adding. 'Is everything all right?'

'I'm having a lousy day, that's all,' she explained, trying to sound friendlier. It wasn't like he was the one demanding money with menace. 'Being broke isn't improving my mood. Who are you thinking of inviting?'

'Us, of course' he replied, his voice softer. 'Your two friends, Paul and Shani, plus Mel and Grant, and Luke and Leilani.'

Bea's mood took another nosedive. He'd meant *her* friends. And what about Guy? 'Don't forget Guy.'

'Oh yes, sorry.'

She ignored his reaction. 'Why would you want to invite Luke and Leilani?' she dared to ask, her stomach doing somersaults. She hadn't seen Luke since the night of the power cut. She shuddered to think how humiliating it would be to be to see him again.

'They appear at the same parties we go to, and anyway I have to deal with him in business, so why not? I don't think we'll ever hit it off, but she seems very pleasant. In fact, she was the one who phoned me the other day and suggested we should all meet up.'

'She did?' Bea tried to work out what Leilani's motive could be. She wondered if Luke knew anything about it, but doubted it. Maybe he'd turn down the invitation anyway.

'Yes, so it'll seem a little odd if I don't. I thought if I hosted then at least it would be over and done with.'

'I suppose so,' she replied. 'As long as you don't talk business, I'd hate to let anything slip about this damn investigation. Any idea how much longer it should go on for?'

'I don't know exactly, but it won't be too long now.'

Bea sighed. 'Do they still think he's guilty?' She didn't dare hope he'd give her the answer she wanted.

Tom didn't speak for a few seconds. 'I'm not sure. His ex-partner's the main culprit, that I'm sure about. Luke is probably guilty by association more than anything, but we still have to make sure we don't let anything slip about it, okay?'

'Yes, of course.' She couldn't help smiling. Guilty by association wasn't the same as consciously committing a criminal act. That had to be better, surely?

'Fine, then it's settled. I'll give everyone a call and plan it for a week on Saturday. I'll let you know how you can help closer to the time. Speak soon.'

She put down the phone and took a deep breath.

* * *

'Blimey, how on earth did you cram all this stuff in your room?' Bea said over her shoulder, as she carried yet another box of books from her car into the house. 'Couldn't you have weeded out the ones you've read and donate them or something?'

'I love my books.' Shani pulled a bag over her shoulder and took a bin bag of clothes in each hand, then followed Bea up the stairs to her bedroom at the back of the house. She dropped the bags on to the bed and leant against the windowsill, staring out over the orchard beyond. 'This is a perfect view,' she panted. 'I can't think why you don't have this room.'

Bea emptied the bags. 'I prefer the view of the veggie garden, although I admit nothing beats this when the apple blossoms are in full bloom.'

Shani leant out of the window and breathed in deeply. Bea couldn't help smiling. It was going to be so lovely having someone share all the wonderful things about this place. 'I don't know how to thank you, Bea. You've been a life saver offering me this room.'

'Rubbish.' Bea shook her head. 'I need your money and you and the baby need a roof over your heads. I think we're even. Don't you?' Bea shrugged. 'Anyway, I've been looking forward to having you here. We're going to have so much fun.'

Shani faced her and leant against the wall, resting both hands on her rounded stomach. 'Thank you for not making me feel like a parasite.'

'Stop it,' Bea said, upset to hear her friend talking about herself in such a dreadful way. 'You're only feeling like that because Harry has treated you so badly.'

'Maybe. I suppose I should be happy he has promised to help me out financially, even though he still insists he doesn't want anything to do with the baby.'

Deciding to change the subject, Bea indicated the clothes. 'Why don't you start putting some of these away before they crease too badly? I'll go and fetch another couple of bags. If we keep at it, we should be finished in an hour or so.'

'Hey there,' shouted Paul up the stairs. 'We've brought another car load.'

'Grab what you can and bring it up here,' Bea bellowed back. Bea laughed at the mountains of coloured fabrics Shani was folding into neat piles on the crumpled bed. 'We're going to have to start putting boxes in the attic soon, I'm not sure there'll be enough room down here.'

Paul walked into the room and held up a pair of Shani's size eight jeans. 'I doubt you'll be wearing these for a while.'

Bea snatched them out of his hand. 'For that remark you're going to have to take these boxes up to the attic.'

'What, now?' He grimaced. 'I hate attics. Filthy places, full of smelly old things.'

Amused, she forced a stern look on her face. 'And while you're there you can have a rummage to see if there are any paintings that could be the Jersey Kiss. I don't remember Aunt Annabel wearing any unusual jewellery, so it's probably a painting.'

'Fine.' He picked up one of the boxes and left the room. He waved Guy to follow him. 'You can come with me; I'll need you to hold the torch.'

'You do know he's going to have a ball up there,' Shani laughed. 'He's so nosy it'll be his idea of heaven, especially if he does find this painting.'

Bea doubted he'd find anything worthwhile. All she remembered being stored in the attic was old furniture and a few trunks of clothes, some of them dating back to when her aunt was at boarding school decades ago. 'I've been meaning to go through everything, but the thought of all the spiders hiding up there in the eaves is enough to put me right off.' She shuddered.

'This is so embarrassing. I didn't realise I had so much. And these things.' She held up the jeans. 'Paul's right, they may as well go to charity. I can't imagine ever fitting into them again.'

'Yes, you will.' Bea took them from her and folded them. 'You'll lose all your baby weight in no time. When you go back to work all that yoga will pull everything back together before you know it.' She placed the jeans back on the bed.

They separated Shani's boxes into items she wanted to keep in either her room or the baby's, and boxes to go into the attic. 'I'm exhausted. All this lifting and moving things around is harder than you think.' Bea fanned her hot face with a gym brochure. 'It'll be good to store that lot out of the way, at least until we know what's happening with this place.' Bea tried not to think of having to move out. 'If I do stay here there's more than enough room to give you your own living room, if you like.'

'Are you two actually going to help us, or are you expecting me to cart this lot up those rickety steps?' Paul complained, shouldering the door open and struggling into the room laden with a box stuffed full of ornaments. 'I found this on the landing. You don't half have a mountain of tat here, Shan.'

'Nothing interesting up there, then?' Bea asked.

Paul shook his head, brushing a cobweb from his hair. 'I've had a quick peek, but nothing that could be your painting. It's very dusty and full of trunks, a scary coat stand covered with strange-looking furs, and old bits of furniture. I think you'll need to sort it out at some point.' He shrugged. 'Even if you don't find what you're looking for, maybe your aunt kept some of your mum's stuff up there.'

His suggestion gave her a jolt. She'd approached her aunt so many times when she was small about her mother's belongings, but Aunt Annabel had always rebuffed her, saying that it was too upsetting for her to go through them. She'd promised to show Bea at some point, but they'd never done it. 'I suppose I can look at her bits now without worrying about upsetting Aunt Annabel. I don't think there's anything mysterious up there, though. I just think she missed mum so much she hated thinking about losing her.'

'Strange, when you think what a tough old bird your aunt was,' Shani said, thoughtfully.

She nodded. 'I'll leave you to it and put the kettle on,' Bea said, leaving the room mainly to have a moment to herself. She'd got so used to not being allowed into the attic, apart from the time she'd snuck up there when her aunt was out, but it hadn't occurred to her to look through much then.

Bea called them to sit at the kitchen table. 'At least we've found homes for most of your bits,' she said enthusiastically.

'Yeah,' Paul agreed, finishing off a custard cream with relish. 'Thank heavens you had the baby's room for us to fill, too.'

'No need to be sarcastic. Anyway, I don't understand where I hid all this stuff at our tiny place.' Shani pushed her hands through her short, unwashed hair looking confused.

'I do, your room was always a tip.' Paul rolled his eyes. 'I'm not going to know what to do with all the space now you've gone.' He laughed when Shani pulled a face. 'I'm only joking. I'll miss you really.'

'Anyway,' Bea said passing them their drinks, 'we can take the next few weeks to go through the rest of your stuff and whittle down what you don't need and maybe do a car boot sale. We're going to need to decorate the baby's room soon anyhow and can do it all then.'

'At least we have Tom's dinner party to look forward to,' Guy added.

'That's another problem,' moaned Shani miserably. 'I have to find something I can still fit into.'

Bea gave her a reassuring smile. 'That's one thing you don't have to worry about. I have more than enough baggy clothes to lend you.'

'Great. What will you wear?'

'No idea. I'd like to buy something new. We know my financial status though, so that's out of the question.'

'Why don't you ask Mel if she has anything you could borrow? You look as if you've lost weight recently,' said Paul. 'I have a sneaky suspicion you haven't been eating properly. You don't want Simon to think you're losing weight because you're missing him.'

'I can always make some meals for your freezer if you wish,' Guy offered. 'From what I hear of your ex-husband, he would like the idea of you pining for him.'

Bea shuddered at the thought. 'Ooh, don't say that.'

Paul leant back in his chair and sighed contentedly. 'I think that's a great plan, Guy. Thanks.'

Bea welcomed the offer. 'Normally I'd say not to worry, but the thought of eating your food is too good an offer to turn down.'

'Yeah, thanks,' Shani agreed.

Bea noticed how pale and exhausted she suddenly seemed. 'Right, I think it's time we let Shani go and have an early night. Don't you agree, boys?'

'I'm fine.' She stroked her stomach gently.

Paul shook his head. 'No, Bea's right. You look worn out.' He motioned to Guy for them to leave. 'I think it's time we left you in peace and made our way home, too.' Paul stood up and took the empty mugs to the sink. 'I wonder what Tom will expect you to make for Saturday, Bea?'

'I don't know yet.' She followed them to the front door. She was dreading Saturday but didn't want to admit that to her friends. She would just have to put a determined smile on her face. After all, she mused as she waved goodbye to them, how awful could it possibly be?

21

HEAT AND SHADE

'Chateaubriand?' shrieked Shani as they pottered in the garden a few days later. 'How the hell do you cook that?'

'No idea.' Bea waved her secateurs in the air. 'And before you explode, I've already told him that if he wanted Chateaubriand then he'd have to make it, and that he should serve something else instead.'

Shani stood with one hand on her stomach and the other on her back. 'What, like tuna melt or spag bol, you mean?'

'I'm holding a weapon, Shani.' Bea pursed her lips and narrowed her eyes.

'Scary. Ow! Damn roses. And what did he say to that?'

'Guess.' Bea cut several roses and put them to one side. 'He said he was only joking, and you know how useless I am at knowing when people are joking.'

Shani stopped sucking the blood from her pricked finger and shook her head slowly.

Bea laughed. 'Why are you staring?'

Shani smiled and sighed. 'Did we miss something in those teen movies we always used to watch? How don't we know about ways to avoid men who are full of their own self-importance?'

Bea shrugged. 'I've no idea. Now stop moaning and get on with what you're doing. At least we've both decided what to wear. That's some sort of achievement.'

'True,' Shani said. 'You look lovely in that red shift dress and nude shoes of Mel's.'

Bea pushed down the cuttings in the bucket with a polka-dotted gloved hand. 'I still can't believe she agreed to let me borrow them.'

'She wants us to get together for the final wedding arrangements next week, so she's probably trying to keep in your good books. I can't think of any other reason she's lending you clothes right now.' Shani winced and rubbed her bump rapidly. 'Ooh, I'd place bets this baby is going to be a professional rugby player. He kicks like a horse.'

'Sit down for a bit and take a break.' Bea indicated the low wall by the driveway.

'You never did say what he's going to cook for Saturday.' Shani sat down carefully.

'No idea. It's a shame Guy hasn't been asked to do the cooking, don't you think?'

'I'd be looking forward to it far more if he was. I'm surprised he was able to get a night off on a Saturday, too. I've got a feeling the poor chap was forced into it.'

* * *

'Perfect timing,' said Tom, opening the heavy bleached oak door and pecking Bea lightly on the cheek. He turned to lead her towards the kitchen. 'Come and check if this is okay, will you?'

Bea lifted the foil and breathed in the smell of the perfectly cooked joint. 'Looks and smells great.'

'Mel will kill you if you get fat on her dress,' Shani whispered from behind her.

Tom covered the meat, careful not to splash his immaculate chinos and pink shirt and then walked with her into the neutrally decorated lounge. He poured Bea a glass of wine from a crystal decanter.

'Thanks, just what I need.' She took a sip and carefully placed the glass down on the dining room table, noting that it looked as if a ruler had been used to place each piece of cutlery at precise distances from the other. 'Juice?' he asked Shani.

Paul and Guy arrived. 'Shan, you're looking voluptuous, for once,' Paul said, pointing at her boobs. 'You look so different with those, or are you wearing a clever bra?'

'Stop teasing her,' Guy said, hugging Shani. 'You're looking very beautiful tonight.'

Shani smiled. 'It's me and a clever bra. I thought I'd make the most of having something to show off for a change.'

Tom marched over to them, holding a glass of wine in each hand. 'Great to see you both here,' he said, fawning over Guy. 'I've done my best, but the food won't be to your standard.'

'I'm certain it will be delicious,' Guy assured him. 'It is a treat not to be the one catering for once.'

Tom smiled looking unsure whether or not he was being teased. 'Well, we'll soon find out.'

The doorbell rang. Tom hurried to welcome Mel and Grant in to the apartment. Luke and Leilani followed closely behind. She was wearing a short, olive-green shift dress that Bea thought looked very expensive. Tom and Grant stared at her, both forgetting to close their mouths for a few seconds.

'Shani, you look blooming,' Luke said, seemingly oblivious to the intense focus on his partner. 'Hello, Bea, it's good to see you again.' He pushed back his hair. 'Red suits you.'

The soft tone of his baritone voice sent Bea's stomach into rapturous somersaults. 'It's good to see you too,' she replied, her voice a little higher than she liked.

After a few drinks, Tom showed everyone to their seats and served the main course. Bea noticed Luke's designated chair was diagonally across from her own and couldn't help sensing his gaze as they dined.

It took until the delicious New York cheesecake that Tom admitted buying from the French patisserie in town for Bea to find a break in Leilani's constant chatter.

'How's it been living on the boat?' she asked Luke, thinking of the recent storms.

'Exciting is probably the best way to describe it,' he said, his blue eyes twinkling. 'Summer's definitely the best time to live on-board though, when there's little rough weather.'

'Have you always had boats?' Shani asked. 'I hate them and once got sick before the ferry had even left the harbour.'

Luke smiled sympathetically. 'Sailing doesn't suit everyone. I've always had boats, from very small ones when I was a teenager up to this one which I saved for. I wanted a boat like Trojan for years and when the opportunity arose to buy her, I was determined not to miss it.'

'Sounds very *Swallows and Amazons*,' Paul laughed, sounding slightly drunk. 'Can we come and have a look on board?'

Tom frowned at him and turned to Luke. 'What type of boat is it?'

Luke sighed dreamily, 'She's a magnificent Rampart, forty-two-footer.'

Tom didn't seem any the wiser and Bea decided he had no more idea about boats than she did. 'When was she built? If you've lusted after one since your childhood, she must be something special.'

'She's much older than me. She was built in 1955 and is made of wood. She takes more looking after than a fibreglass boat, but I love the character of these older boats.'

Bea couldn't help noticing how his eyes sparkled as he spoke lovingly about his home.

'Where's she moored?' Shani asked, dabbing her mouth with her napkin.

'In the marina most of the time, and I've been sleeping on her while I'm carrying out the renovations at my cottage in St Catherine's.'

'Is that allowed?' Shani asked. 'Aren't there regulations about living on boats?'

'Not really.' He gave Bea a meaningful glance and half smiled. She flushed at the memory of their trip to the Écréhous together.

'Luke doesn't stay there by himself all that much,' Leilani interrupted, nudging Luke, her innuendo blatant. 'Personally, I can't see what all the fuss is about. It's an old boat and not very high spec as far as I can tell, and let's face it, this is hardly the climate to be living on-board, is it?'

Luke didn't seem to mind her criticisms. 'It probably depends on what you're used to.'

By the time Tom served coffee in the comfort of the cream living room, Leilani was holding court, telling stories about her experiences on the catwalk.

Shani and Guy whispered, their heads bent close as they amused each other in one corner of the room. Bea watched silently as Luke walked over to her and sat down. Leaning back into the cream leather settee, he turned his body towards her. 'Shani tells me she's moved into The Brae?'

Bea nodded.

'I could have helped her move if I'd known. I gather she had more than she expected hidden away at her flat.' He smiled, his eyes twinkling in amusement.

'I've no idea where she was hiding it all.' Bea said, still astonished by the enormous number of items Shani had brought with her. 'It's all stored away now though. It's made me realise I should also tidy up my attic; the Jersey Kiss could be stored up there somewhere.' She took a sip of her drink and relaxed further into the seat. 'It's lovely having her in the house,' Bea admitted, staring into her half-empty glass.

'I've missed you,' he murmured, so quietly she wasn't sure if she had imagined it.

Bea blinked in surprise and saw his serious expression. 'Sorry?' She glanced around the room, relieved no one appeared interested in their conversation.

'You heard me,' he said gently, not taking his eyes away from her. 'I've enjoyed being with you tonight. Can't we put everything behind us and start again?'

Bea didn't have to consider his invitation. 'Yes, of course,' she said, wishing it was that simple.

He smiled and Bea felt her heart pounding. She studied his rugged face.

'Is everything all right?' he asked. 'You're looking a little tense this evening.'

Bea shrugged. 'It's nothing.'

'Bea,' Luke said, placing his hand on hers. 'If you tell me, maybe I can help.'

Why not, she thought. If he was crafty enough to find a way to launder money, then maybe he could come up with some idea for her to sting Simon. She told him about the court order and her desperation to sort things out.

Luke thought for a moment.

'I have a suggestion you could try,' Mel said, sitting down next to Bea. 'You could apply for a Martin order.'

'What's that?' Bea had heard of a Mesher order, where the wife is given enjoyment of the home until an agreed time – usually when the youngest child had finished their secondary or tertiary education. They didn't have children, though. 'I've never heard of it.'

'I have,' Luke said thoughtfully. 'They're pretty rare though, aren't they?'

Mel nodded. 'I don't know why I didn't think of it before. Too much time listening to my mum fretting about this wedding, I suppose.'

Bea wished she'd hurry up. 'What is it though? Tell me.'

Mel leant closer to Bea. 'It's where the sale of the property is postponed until the person living in the house dies or remarries.'

Bea narrowed her eyes in disbelief. 'You seriously believe Simon would agree to sign over The Brae to me? Just like that,' she clicked her fingers.

Mel added, 'If he wants you to hurry with the decree absolute, he might.'

'You never know,' Luke said. 'It's worth a try.'

'He wants me to pay him out and the only way I can do that is to get a loan if I want to keep it. I'll ask him, but I'm pretty sure he'll tell me to bugger off.' She sighed, wishing Mel's suggestion had been remotely achievable.

'Think about it,' he said, 'maybe there's a way to persuade him.'

'I'm sure we'll find some way round this,' Mel said. 'We just need to keep thinking.'

'Listen up everyone,' Leilani said, standing in the middle of the room. Bea tried not to show her annoyance at her interrupting their conversation. Leilani held up an almost empty wine glass and beamed pointedly at every one in the room. 'Lukey didn't want me to say anything tonight,' she said, her immaculate lipstick somehow unmarred by the three-course meal. 'But I'm too excited to keep it to myself any longer.'

Bea looked quizzically from Leilani to Luke. 'I've no idea what she's talking about. She never could cope with much alcohol,' he joked, raising his eyebrows. Bea grinned, wondering what Leilani was about to say.

'Lukey and I are to be married,' she squealed, theatrically throwing her arms wide.

'What?' Luke's eyes widened. Bea's heart pounded, but she couldn't move.

'Aren't we, darling?' Leilani blew a kiss at Luke who sat motionless, staring at her in silence. 'We haven't had a chance to choose a ring yet.'

Bea, a stabbing jolt in her solar plexus, tried her best to make sense of what she'd just heard. She looked away from Leilani and focused on the cream carpet, desperately trying to gather herself. She heard Luke swear under his breath and felt him push himself up from next to her, watching as he crossed the room in one stride to his bride-to-be.

'I think it's time we were leaving,' he announced, his voice a monotone and his expression like granite as he took Leilani firmly by the elbow. 'Thank you for a wonderful evening, Tom.' He shook Tom's proffered hand before turning to Bea. 'It was good catching up with you.'

Bea, unable to form any words, looked straight into his eyes, making a valiant attempt at hiding her confusion and hurt. I'm a fool, she thought, forcing her mouth into a smile which she suspected more resembled a grimace.

'Good for Luke,' Tom cheered closing the front door behind them. 'I never saw that coming, did you?' he asked Paul sounding happier than he had all evening.

'Nope.' Paul stole a glance at Bea. She tried her best to reassure him by trying to look pleased for the newly engaged couple. Paul stood thoughtfully for a moment. 'I suppose when you feel the time is right to do these things, you just get on and do it.'

'Well,' Mel interrupted defensively, 'at least they won't be able to book anything before my wedding day. I don't want Leilani over-shadowing me.'

'She couldn't do that,' Grant said, for once saying the right thing. 'You're far prettier than she could ever be.'

'Aww, thank you. Now, don't forget we're meeting on Monday lunchtime to visit the florists with Mum,' Mel said, oblivious to any undercurrents. 'I think I've decided about the flowers.'

Bea was relieved to find that the party seemed to have reached a natural end. She accompanied Shani to the kitchen to make a start filling the dishwasher. 'What the hell was that all about?' Shani hissed over her shoulder.

'I'm meeting Mel at the florists.' Bea emptied the dregs of the wine glasses in the sink and began washing the fine crystal glasses.

'You know what I mean. What the hell was that business with Leilani and her engagement?' She flicked Bea lightly with a tea towel. 'I saw you all cosied up on the settee with Luke, and also the stunned expression on your face when she made her announcement.'

Bea stared at the bubbles on the glass she was washing. 'I'd rather not talk about it.'

'I'm sorry. I don't know what he was saying to you, but I'd bet a pound to a penny he didn't see that coming either.'

Bea turned to face Shani. 'He knew it was coming, he didn't even flinch. He certainly didn't argue with her,' she snapped. 'I'm so confused. I think he means one thing and then something happens to make me realise I've totally misread the situation. I've made a bit of a twit of myself. It doesn't matter, I'll get over it,' she insisted, wishing she could find a way to cut off her feelings for him.

'Hey, girls.' Tom strode into the room. 'Don't worry about clearing up. My cleaning lady has agreed to come in for an extra couple of hours tomorrow morning to do it all.'

Shani shrugged. 'You don't have to tell me twice. We may as well head for home and leave you in peace.'

'Thanks for a lovely evening.' Bea gave Tom a kiss on the cheek desperate to appear as if nothing was wrong with her. 'Everyone had a wonderful time.'

'Yes, I thought it went well. I'll see you at the office on Monday. Thanks for coming.' Tom returned to Mel and Grant in the lounge.

'Come on, let's go,' Bea said. It was time for her to stop wasting emotion on someone who was already spoken for. Enough was enough. Bea knew it was time to move on from Luke and focus on her future. She had a lot to sort out, and now was the perfect time to get on and do it.

22

MAY 1 – THE SCENT OF LILIES

Bea sniffed the intoxicating perfume from the lilies of the valley she'd picked in the garden, then scrolled through her phone to find her lawyer's number. It was nine days to Simon's D-Day, and she was relieved she had taken the day off work. She was also glad she'd thought to use the same lawyer her aunt always used.

'I'm sorry, Annabel's house is considered part of your marriage settlement,' he said, shuffling papers. Bea didn't know how he ever found anything on his untidy desk. 'I know it seems very unfair to you, and that she would be unhappy to think of Mr Porter bene-fiting in any way from her death. I think the best option is to include in my court papers the confirmation that your aunt had booked an appointment to see me before she died.'

'Do you think it'll help?'

'I can't be certain, but it will show her intention to speak to me about matters. The judge will base his judgment on the legalities of each case, not the emotions behind them.'

Bea chewed her lower lip; this was so frustrating. 'What about the Martin order?' Bea needed some good news. She wasn't sure how much longer she could muster the strength or finances to keep up this fight against Simon.

'Realistically, unless you have something with which to bargain, or a way of persuading your ex-husband, then you'll be hard pressed to get him to accept. By agreeing to the order, he will, in effect, be giving up any rights to the property, or any monetary gain from its sale.'

'I can't see him doing that. But you think it's worth a try?'

'You won't lose anything by speaking to him. I could write to him formally with the suggestion, but sometimes these things are better dealt with on a more, shall we say, personal level.'

Bea also knew how much a letter from him would cost. She checked her watch, concerned that she was being charged for every six minutes he spoke to her. 'I thought I'd try to talk to his girl-friend,' Bea said, picturing going to Claire's apartment and knocking on her door.

'Worth a go. And Beatrice? Your aunt was a close friend of mine for many years, I want you to know how proud of you she would have been.'

Bea swallowed the lump in her throat. 'That's kind of you to say, I appreciate it.' The last thing she wanted to do was sell The Brae, but if all else failed she would have little choice. She didn't relish the thought of having to move Shani out, either. Not when she'd been so relieved at the thought of moving in. But whether she liked it or not, Bea knew she was running out of options, as well as time. She glanced up at her wall calendar. *1st of May, only nine days until court.*

She thought through her plan and decided that the best chance she had with Claire would be when Simon was away on one of his business trips. Unfortunately she had no idea if he had any booked in the next few days. She would just have to hope that she timed her visit to their apartment when he was out.

* * *

Later that evening, Bea was pleased to find Shani in the living room watching television. 'What's the matter?' she asked, noticing the grim look on Shani's face. Then it dawned on her. 'Mel's phoned, hasn't she?'

Shani groaned dramatically and threw her head back against the sofa. 'She ranted on for over an hour tonight.'

'Oh no, poor you,' Bea winced at the thought of her friend having to listen to her sister moaning.

'Poor me, indeed, I had to keep moving the phone from one ear to the other, they were getting so hot. I thought she'd never ring off. She can't take a hint, even a big one like "sod off Mel, I'm knackered". Thankfully, Grant started complaining in the background about their dinner getting cold.' She pushed herself up and followed Bea through to the kitchen.

'What's the latest, dare I ask?' Bea busied herself making them both a mug of tea.

'Apparently Mel saw Tom with Vanessa,' Shani said. 'What do you think they're up to?'

Bea couldn't care less. 'Who cares? I think they're trying to make each other jealous, or something childish like that. I'm not going to get caught up in his problems.' She pulled her hair back into a ponytail and twisted a band around it. 'I suppose Mel wants us to meet with her wedding planner again, then?'

''Fraid so, and she needs us to help her put the seating plan together next weekend. I couldn't think of an excuse quick enough to get out of it.'

'Balls.'

'Balls indeed.' Shani pushed her swollen fingers through her short black hair. 'The further along I get in this pregnancy the less my brain seems to connect. And, as if it couldn't get any worse, guess who's coming to help?'

'Please don't tell me Joyce will be there, too?'

Shani nodded slowly, an agonised expression on her tanned face. 'Correct.'

'Thank heavens we've only got another few days of this wedding stuff,' Bea said.

* * *

'You'll never guess what?' Mel asked, surrounded by fake flower arrangements, white, pink and grey chiffon and several heavy black folders at the wedding planner's studio. 'I bumped into Leilani the other day and she insists they're having an enormous wedding in early September.'

A tingling sensation shot through Bea's chest. She concentrated on not changing her expression.

'So soon?' Shani asked. 'How are they managing to book everything at such short notice?'

'No idea.'

Shani frowned. 'They'll either have to put the date back to next year or just have a smaller wedding, I imagine.'

'Can't see that happening,' Mel scowled. 'Bea, what's the matter?'

'Nothing.' She wasn't in the mood to confide in her sister. 'I'd just rather get on with these wedding plans than waste time wondering what Leilani and Luke are doing.'

'Quite right.' Joyce raised her eyebrows pointedly at Mel. 'About the table decorations, I have a folder here with several cuttings from recent bridal magazines.'

Shani took one of the folders and flicked through it.

'There are some strange ideas in here. Look at this one.' Shani pointed at an ostrich feather standing in a small iron base in the shape of a bride's shoe with tiny brides and grooms hanging from it at odd angles.

'There'll be none of that tat on Melanie's tables, thank you very much,' Joyce insisted.

Bea winked at Shani. 'I think Shani's hormones are giving her strange ideas.'

'Well at least my wedding photos are going to be incredible.' Mel gave them a confident nod.

'What do you mean?' Shani looked at Bea and raised an eyebrow.

'Now that Luke is to be Grant's best man, of course.' Bea couldn't think of anything to say. What was her sister up to now?

'It did take a bit of persuasion from Grant.' Bea had assumed an old school friend was going to be his best man, but didn't say so. 'Since our engagement party, they've spent quite a lot of time together,' Mel continued. 'Don't forget they go way back. Grant says he still feels guilty for breaking Luke's nose during a rugby match years ago.'

So, that's how it happened, Bea mused, picturing it.

'I just wish Leilani didn't have to come. No doubt she'll look amazing,' Mel added.

'I bet she will,' Bea and Shani said in unison.

'And you,' Mel nodded at Bea, 'as my maid of honour will be partnered with Luke now. Won't that be fun?'

'Yes.' Bea suppressed a sigh. The sooner this wedding was over and done with, the better as far as she was concerned.

23

MAY 2 – BLOOMING FABULOUS

Bea couldn't believe how large Shani's stomach had grown in the last couple of weeks and had to concentrate on not staring at it. She was relieved that the wedding would soon be over, and could concentrate solely on her legal problems and her friend's baby. It was only seven days until the first anniversary of Annabel's death and Bea was dreading it. She couldn't believe her aunt had been gone for almost a year.

She had kept a low profile socially and, as much as she missed seeing Luke, she felt it was the only way to deal with being in love with someone she couldn't have. She wasn't sure why he was keeping away, though. It was going to be difficult enough seeing him at the wedding, and hoped she remembered to watch every word she said to him.

'Have you thought more about Mel's hen night?' she asked Shani. 'We've already left it a bit late.' The sun had just forced its way out through a layer of thick clouds after a particularly forceful shower. Everything in her garden shone as Bea pulled on her Wellington boots in anticipation of a couple of hours of therapeutic weeding.

'Really? I thought she didn't want to do anything. How about arranging a night at Effervescence, that's probably the easiest option?'

'Effervescence, that's a brilliant idea.' Bea thought for a moment. 'What about Joyce? It's not the sort of place I'd imagine her liking.'

'Tough. We need to book somewhere I can sit for most of the evening.' She patted her baby bump. 'We can eat and then enjoy the show.'

'It's the show that worries me.' Bea grimaced. She'd been to see the brilliant sketch show with the hilarious drag queens before and it was perfect for a hen party, but not one that included Joyce.

'Why?' Shani pulled a cushion behind the arch of her back and leant against it.

'Some of the jokes can be a bit rude.'

Shani straightened the loose-knitted jumper over her stomach. 'Yeah, I forgot about that. Well, it's either that or a quiet meal somewhere.'

'Why don't we ask Mel? We don't want to upset her and have to deal with Joyce's moaning, too.'

'True,' Shani laughed. 'She's tense enough about the whole thing already, especially now there's the threat of Leilani competing with her in the bridal stakes.' Shani winced. 'Sorry, I didn't think before speaking.'

Bea took a weary breath. 'You've nothing to be sorry for. I've got no interest in Luke or Leilani,' she lied. 'I'll give Mel a ring now.'

Bea came back from the phone. 'Surprisingly it's Effervescence, and Mel told me Joyce will be fine, especially if we open a bottle or two of Laurent-Perrier Rosé beforehand. She also said Guy and Paul are welcome.'

'Girls,' Paul said, stepping in through the French doors. 'Mel just texted about her hen night. Excellent choice.'

Bea stood. 'I may as well take these damn things off, I can see I'm not going to get any peace this morning.' She kicked off her beloved wellies and pushed her feet into her bunny slippers. 'I can't wait until it's over.'

'What, the wedding, the court date, or my giving birth?' Shani rested her hands on her rounded stomach. 'It's like some sort of countdown.'

'Have you heard from Harry at all?' Paul asked.

Shani's shoulders drooped. 'I don't expect to now. I'll just contact him when the baby's born, and we can take it from there.'

Paul stroked her shoulder. 'Sorry, that was a bit insensitive of me.' He turned his attention to Bea. 'I heard Tom's put his new apartment back on the market. Why would he do that? He's only just bought the place and probably hasn't even finished paying for that expensive furniture. It doesn't make sense.'

'How do you know all this?' Bea wasn't naive enough to think there was no truth in what Paul was saying.

Shani sighed. 'You can't do a thing in Jersey without everyone knowing your business.'

24

MAY 8 – MOONBEAM

Bea knocked at the door. She'd checked her watch and knew from experience Simon would probably be at the seventh hole on the golf course by now.

'I'm coming, hang on...' The door opened. Claire stared open-mouthed at Bea.

'I'm sorry to bother you without phoning first, but I thought you might not agree to see me,' she said, staring at Claire's unkempt appearance.

'And you would have been right,' Claire snapped, tightening her dressing gown belt. 'What do you want?'

'I'm sure you're sick of Simon ranting about our finances and about me?' she asked, knowing how Simon went on about matters he couldn't control.

'You're not kidding.' She looked Bea up and down. 'Simon seems to think – and I have to say, I believe him – that you're only dragging this out because you can't bear to let him go completely.'

Bea hid her irritation. Did this woman seriously believe such nonsense? 'Claire, the only person who's causing unnecessary anguish for us all is Simon. I inherited that house. I love it and don't want to part with it.'

'Yes, but he's entitled to half. He told me.'

'I was left the house by my godmother, I shouldn't have to pay him any part of it,' she said, not quite sure she believed what she was saying. 'It's not as if he needs the money, is it?'

Claire frowned and shook her head. 'No, I suppose not.' She stepped back and motioned for Bea to enter their apartment. 'Why don't we sit down?'

Bea walked in and sat down on one of the sumptuous cappuccino-coloured suede sofas. 'It's beautiful,' she said, aware how this place and hers were at opposite ends of the spectrum when it came to interior design.

'Thank you.' Claire sat opposite her. 'You were saying.'

'Yes, Simon doesn't need the money, and if you want our finances to be settled so that he can be granted his decree absolute and be free to marry you, then all he has to do is sign a Martin order.'

'A what?' Bea explained that it would mean that Simon would transfer the property outright to her. 'And you think he'll agree to that?'

Bea shrugged. 'It's down to you to persuade him.'

'Me?'

'Think about it. I want to move on, whether Simon believes it or not. If we sort out the problem with the house, then the divorce can be finalised. You can marry Simon and your baby will be born into the sort of family unit I know he'd rather be part of.'

'I suppose so,' Claire said thoughtfully, chewing a broken fingernail.

'If you can't get him to agree to this, then you'll need to ask yourself how much influence you have over him, despite carrying his baby. Also, I'm sure it must be a worry that he left me and moved on to you without any conscience at all. What's stopping him from doing the same to you?' she said, aware what she was saying must upset Claire, but not caring for once. 'Don't you want to prove to yourself how important you are to him?'

'I have to admit, you are voicing some of my concerns.' She looked at Bea, her puffy eyes showing some uncharacteristic softness. 'I feel bad about having an affair with Simon behind your back.'

Bea shrugged. 'Yes, well, that's all in the past,' Bea insisted. 'We need to think ahead now. I'm sure you want me out of your life as much as I want to be away from it.'

Claire nodded. 'Absolutely.'

'You'll talk to him then?' Bea could barely contain her excitement.

'I will.' Claire stood up. 'He's not going to like it though, you do know that?'

'I do, but I think it's time Simon put someone else's emotions before his own. If you're going to have his baby then you need to know that your feelings matter. Maybe you could mention that to him, too.'

Bea left the apartment. She couldn't help smiling at the thought of Simon's reaction. 'Let him try and talk himself out of this,' she said as she unlocked her car door.

* * *

The night before the wedding Bea tried on her cerise bridesmaid dress and matching bolero jacket with its three-quarter-length sleeves. She hadn't been sure about the style, but they'd shortened the skirt a little and now it felt a bit more like something she'd choose to wear. She picked up the matching satin shoes and handbag. The only thing Bea hadn't agreed to was having her shoulder-length hair cut into a neat bob. It would never be sleek like Mel's; she had far too many curls. 'Anyway, I like it wild and lose,' she murmured stubbornly, accepting a fascinator being clipped into her hair was going to be as far as she'd go. Bea let Mel book her in for a manicure after her sister had shrieked in horror at the state of her nails and was surprised to realise she was looking forward to dressing up the following day.

She stepped into her bubble bath to enjoy an hour's reading before trying to get a decent night's sleep, but had only managed a few pages when her mobile rang. She ignored it, grateful when it stopped, but then it rang again. Clearly the caller was determined.

'Bugger,' she grumbled, stepping tentatively out of the bath and dragging a towel around her. 'Shan, why are you calling me on my mobile? I thought you were staying in tonight.'

'I am.' Her voice was strained. 'I'm in my bedroom.' There was a brief pause and some panting. 'I'm in labour.'

Bea gasped. 'Don't panic.' She threw her phone down on her bed. Then, dragging on her dressing gown, she ran down the landing to Shani's room. 'Are you all right?'

Shani was bent over, one hand on the bed and the other on her back. 'I need to get to the hospital.'

'But the doctor said you'd have hours!'

'I've been having contractions for hours. You don't think I'd have called you at the first twinge, do you?'

'Why the hell not?' Bea snapped, immediately feeling mean for panicking. 'Sorry.' Bea's heart hammered in her chest as she tried to remember what they should do next. 'Quick, let's get you down to the car.'

'If you're driving me to the hospital, I think you had better get dressed, don't you?' Shani groaned and held onto her back. 'Ouch, this hurts.' She panted a few times until the contraction passed. 'I think I've still got a bit of time.'

'What do you need me to do?' Her brain had gone into meltdown.

'Take a deep breath. That's it. Now another one.' Shani rubbed her back and smiled at Bea. 'This is scary, but I can't help feeling excited now that it's time.'

'Me too,' Bea said, concentrating on trying to look calmer than she felt.

'I'll get myself down the stairs and give Paul a quick ring while you dress; he should be here in no time.'

Bea left Shani panting and phoned Paul. 'Oh my God,' he shrieked. 'Give me ten minutes max.'

She ran to her room and grabbed the grass-stained jeans and tatty off-white sweatshirt she'd been wearing earlier. 'Right, I'll take this.' Bea picked up Shani's overnight case and ran down the stairs to the car.

With trembling hands she carefully fastened the seatbelt around Shani's huge stomach. 'Where's Paul?' She paced back and forth on the gravel. 'We should have arranged to meet him at the hospital.'

'Calm down, I can hear him,' Shani shouted, wincing in pain.

'Why don't we just take his taxi?' Shani suggested, waving Paul over as he paid the taxi driver.

'No need, I'll drive,' Paul insisted.

'No you won't.' Bea snatched the keys back from him. 'I'm fine, I'll get us there.'

'Bea, will you please do me a favour and give Paul the car keys?'

'What for?' asked Bea, hysteria rising in her voice with each word.

Shani patted her lightly on the hand. 'Because I want to get there in one piece and you're making me nervous. Why don't you have a stiff drink and go back to bed and try and get some sleep before the wedding tomorrow?'

Paul took the keys from Bea's hand and gave her a kiss on the cheek. 'Stop stressing. We'll be fine, and I promise I'll call you as soon as baby puts in an appearance.'

'But I want to be with you.' Bea pushed her head into the window.

'I know you do, and I love you for it,' Shani soothed. 'But to be honest, Bea, for once in his life, Paul appears to be strangely calm and I need that right now.' She winced and sucked in her breath. 'I think we ought to be going. Paul will call you as soon as anything happens.'

Paul turned on the ignition and the car flew backwards, only stopping when it collided with Bea's low granite wall. Bea didn't bother checking her car, and suspected Paul wasn't as calm as he was making out.

Shani puffed. 'Take it easy. I only asked for you because I thought you'd be a safer bet than her.' She waved Bea away.

'What?' Paul screeched, becoming more panic-stricken.

'Why am I the calmest one here? Everything's fine; this is all perfectly normal. Now get a grip and let's go. I should have taken your taxi and left the two of you here to be hysterical together.'

'That's enough,' Bea shouted, opening the driver's door. 'Get in the back, Paul, I'm driving.' Not waiting for him to argue, she grabbed hold of his jacket and pulled him out of the car.

Shortly after setting off, Shani frightened them both by bending forward, one hand on the dashboard and the other on the mound of her stomach and starting to puff and pant again. 'Phew, that was a bad one.' She winced, her face flushed with the exertion. 'At least it's the middle of the night and we don't have to worry about traffic.'

With almost pathetic relief Paul pointed to the lights ahead. 'Hospital. There's the hospital.'

'Thank heavens for that,' Bea whispered, as they pulled up outside.

'You've both done very well. Now let me out of the car.' Shani pushed herself up out of the seat. 'I'll make my way in and start the registration process. You two park the car and bring my case.'

Bea nodded and watched her amble off, marvelling at her bravery before wheel-spinning towards the car park. Reaching the entrance Shani had indicated, Bea rang the bell. 'This is terrifying.'

Eventually a tired-looking midwife unlocked the door. They followed her up to the labour ward and waited in the hallway. 'What checks do they have to do anyway?' Bea wondered.

Paul paced along the tiled corridor. 'Why is it so quiet in there?'

Bea shrugged. 'I suppose they're getting her changed and checking the baby is actually on its way.' She hoped it wouldn't be too long until they could join Shani; Bea couldn't bear to think of her being alone and frightened.

'I'd be panic-stricken if I were her,' Paul said, reading Bea's thoughts.

Bea sat down on one of the chairs and tapped her foot on the floor. 'Why won't they call us in?'

The door finally opened, and the midwife waved them over. 'Shani's ready for you both now.' She smiled at Paul. 'You don't need to look so terrified. Everything's fine.'

Bea walked in first, her eyes widening at the sight of Shani lying with her long, slim legs up in stirrups.

'And there's another contraction,' the midwife said cheerily. 'Come in quickly, you two, and please try to stay out of the way.'

'Glad you could— argh! —both make it,' Shani grimaced.

Bea felt lightheaded and doubted it was due to the intense heat in the room; the look of pain etched on her best friend's face was alarming. Paul shielded his eyes from the bottom end of the bed. 'They could face the top of your head towards the door,' he grumbled. 'Or have a warning note outside.'

Bea glared at him. 'Don't be such a baby,' she said through

clenched teeth. She took Shani's hand in hers, grimacing when Shani almost crushed her bones with a vice-like grip. 'Ouch, Shan, can you let go a little?'

The young nurse smiled. 'If either of you think you're going to faint, then go outside. You'll find a water cooler in the hallway.'

Paul shook his head. 'We'll be fine.'

'Phew, that was a bad one,' Shani said, turning to smile at Paul. 'You look worse than I do.' The midwife examined Shani once again. 'Surely I'll be ready to push soon.' The woman nodded.

This was going to be a long night, Bea thought. Maybe the thrill of watching new life entering this world was a little over-rated. She decided should she ever feel broody again, she would just visit this place; it would soon put her off wanting babies.

'She's had a baby,' Paul shouted down the phone to Guy two hours later, his voice trembling.

'Well, that's a relief,' he teased over the loudspeaker. 'What sort of baby?'

'What do you mean, what sort? A baby.'

'Is it a boy, or a girl?'

'Oh, a girl. She looks like a little moonbeam, so cute and tiny. I think they said she was three kilos or something, though I've no idea what that means.'

Bea pulled a tissue from her sweatshirt sleeve and blew her nose.

'Congratulations,' Guy said. 'I can't wait to give her a cuddle.' Paul said he'd see him later and ended the call. 'You need to take it easy,' he told Shani, and then frowning over at Bea. 'You're looking a bit washed out.'

'You don't look so hot yourself.' Bea peered down into the clear bassinette and felt a tug at her heart as the baby took her little finger in her hand.

'Gorgeous, isn't she?' Shani yawned and although her face was puffy from the exertions, Bea thought she'd never looked more beautiful. It felt strange to see someone as tomboyish as Shani looking so maternal and serene. She could tell by the adoring way Shani was gazing at her baby that she'd be an incredible mother, with or without Harry's involvement.

'You were so brave.' She hugged Shani, careful not to disrupt the drip in her arm. 'She's perfect. I'm sorry I was so panicky before.'

'Don't be silly, you were both brilliant. Bea, you'd better get a move on; didn't you have to be at Joyce's like an hour ago?'

Bea took a moment to understand what Shani meant. 'What?' She rubbed her eyes and yawned. 'The wedding, it's today.' Bea said, wishing she didn't have to rush off.

'You go and have a fantastic day. Give Mel my love.'

Bea retied her ponytail and checked her watch. She blanched. 'I'm so late.' Bea pulled an agonised expression, making Shani smile. 'I don't want to go.'

Shani giggled. 'Behave yourself, you'll look gorgeous, and you're going to have fun. Take photos and send them to me.'

'I will.'

'Oh, and Bea – thanks for everything. You've been a star.' Bea sniffed, aware her chin was starting to wobble. She blew her nose. 'No, don't you dare start crying,' Shani said, welling up. '*I'm* allowed to – no one's going to see me for hours yet. Mel and Joyce will never forgive you if you ruin the photos with bloodshot eyes and a big red nose.' She pushed her friends away gently. 'Go on, I'll see you both when it's all over.'

Bea shook her head and took one last look at the baby. 'Right, here goes,' she said, trying to raise a little enthusiasm for the next few hours. 'The wedding's finally here.'

'I need a coffee so strong you could stand a ruler in it,' Paul said, rubbing his face with his hands.

'Bugger coffee,' Bea laughed, hurrying down the corridor towards the car park. 'I think I'll need a couple of vodkas before I'm in the mood to face this lot.'

25

MAY 9 – ARCHWAY OF ROSES

Bea drove home in a haze of emotional exhaustion. She didn't care what the time was; she had no intention of leaving her house until she'd had a quick nap and freshened up with a hot shower. She phoned her dad to let him know she'd be about an hour late and to ask him to break the news to Joyce and Mel as best he could.

After her nap she showered and washed her hair, unable to stop thinking about the emotional night she'd shared with Paul and Shani. She couldn't imagine anything more worthwhile than giving birth. She allowed tears to flow as she scrubbed her face. 'No time for regrets,' she murmured, grabbing her electric toothbrush and cleaning her teeth before splashing her face with cold water.

After dressing, she drove to her dad's house. 'Hello, darling,' her father said, smiling at her, relief obvious. 'Give me a kiss and hang up your clothes, then come and let me show you inside that monstrosity.'

She looked past him to the enormous white marquee covering most of the back lawn of his beloved garden. 'Red carpet?' she said, wondering how long the whole construction had taken, down to the carpet that meandered from the driveway into an entrance decorated with an elaborate archway made up of hundreds of deep red roses, lilies and a mass of greenery. 'Wow. You don't do things by half, do you, Dad?'

'This display wasn't my idea.' He puffed on his pipe. 'When your stepmother refused to lower the number of invitees, I had no choice but to hire this damn thing. The temporary lavatories cost as much as a smaller marquee.'

Bea hoped he'd manage to relax at some point and enjoy the day. 'Don't let Joyce catch you smoking again,' she whispered, following him into the massive space.

'Let her.' He straightened one of the chairs. 'Look at the top table. We're going to die of heat sitting in front of the windows.'

Bea agreed. 'That is incredible though,' she said, indicating the elaborately iced wedding cake displayed on a small round table.

'Don't even try to estimate the cost,' he said, puffing on his pipe.

Bea looked at the tiny clouds of smoke coming out of the side of his mouth and gave him a hug. 'Mel's very lucky to have you,' she said, kissing his cheek. 'We both are.' Chiffon bows were tied round the middle of each chair, matching the bridesmaid's outfits. Bea squinted up at the silky lining of the marquee, lit by cascades of tiny prisms from the crystal chandeliers that would later be muted to a soft glow, which she was certain must have been Joyce's idea.

'She has a thing about lighting,' her dad said. 'I'm sure she needn't have spent quite so much on this wedding. So much of it seems extravagant nonsense.' Bea believed him. 'The damn table arrangements cost more than your stepmother's and my entire wedding. Look at them, ridiculously over the top.'

Bea murmured her agreement as she took in the elaborate creations, a large, cream cathedral candle bound in thin rope and ivy, with even more arum lilies woven into the rope and finished off with large pink feathers. 'Flipping heck, she must have commanded an entire nursery's stock of the things. I'd have been more than happy to help, you know. I have more than enough flowers in my garden.'

'It's almost obscene really, when you think you're paying for all this for only one afternoon. Things have certainly gone up since you and Simon were married.' He turned to face Bea and took her hands in his own. 'Talking of which, I know I can't help you pay him off, but I can help towards your legal fees. And before you argue, I insist. Annabel and I fell out over you many times over the years, but she loved you very much, and she wouldn't have wanted him to have half her house, especially not after what he did to you.'

Bea gave him a hug. 'Thanks, Dad. All I need to do is find a way to prove that Aunt Annabel intended to put a clause in her will to make sure he didn't benefit from her death in any way.'

'I don't see how that house can even be considered a matrimonial asset when he was messing around with someone else. It's not right.'

'Don't worry about me. We've got a brilliant day ahead of us.' She laughed. 'Even if it's all a little over the top.'

'Good girl. You remind me so much of your mother when she was your age.' He put his arm around her shoulders as they walked slowly back to the house. 'I still miss her, you know,' he said, lowering his voice. Bea swallowed the lump in her throat. 'Right, you'd better get in there, they'll be panicking if they don't see you soon.' He stopped, looking thoughtful. 'How come you were delayed, anyway?'

She took a deep breath hoping her emotions wouldn't get the better of her again. 'Shani went into labour during the night. She had a baby girl a few hours ago.' Bea cocked her head in the direction of the upstairs windows. 'I'd better go and make my presence felt.' She hugged him and raced up to the spare room.

'Your hair looks gorgeous, Mel,' she said seeing her sister having her hair primped and curled. Before Mel could answer she raised a hand. 'I've got exciting news. Shani had a little girl last night.'

Mel squealed, batting the hairdresser's hand away. She twisted in her seat towards Bea. 'Is she okay? Is the baby gorgeous?'

Bea tried not to laugh at the hairdresser's irritated expression. 'Yes, they're both doing great, although Shani's a bit tired after everything.'

'Melanie, sit still. You don't have all day to get ready,' Joyce said, taking Mel by the shoulders and facing her towards the dressing-table mirror once again. 'That's wonderful news, Bea. But you're already late and we still have to do something with your hair before you can get changed.'

She held Bea's fascinator up for the hairdresser to see. 'We need this in Bea's hair as soon as she's changed into her bridesmaid outfit.' She gave Bea a condescending smile. 'What a relief Shani didn't spend the night here after all. It would have upset Melanie's entire routine.' She gasped. 'Imagine how ghastly it would have been if her waters had broken over my new spare linen.'

'Mum,' Mel snapped. 'What a thing to say.' Before they could descend into a row, Bea left them and went downstairs to the kitchen to make some tea and toast. She was starving and hoped that breakfast would keep her going for the next few hours.

'Coping?' asked her father, listening out for Joyce's high-pitched voice. 'I'm keeping my distance from those two.' He pointed upstairs. 'They're getting more anxious as the hours pass.'

'I know, they're driving each other nuts already.' Bea buttered her toast and ate it hungrily.

'Thankfully the caterers are here. The florist has left, and it appears that we're keeping to schedule – touch wood.'

'Beatrice, get up these stairs immediately.' Bea grimaced at the sound of her stepmother's command.

'I suppose I'd better do as she asks.' She rolled her eyes.

After being made up and her hair fussed with, Bea was relieved to change in to her outfit, then help Mel with her elaborate dress and veil.

'You look sensational, Mel,' she said, happy to see her sister so excited. For some reason they looked even less alike today. Mel, with her shiny, almost black hair all glossy and up in a French pleat, and Bea with her blue eyes and wild blonde hair that never managed to look very sleek. No wonder people found it surprising to discover they were half-sisters.

'I do, don't I?' Mel said, smoothing down the corset of her dress. 'I can hear the cars. Bea, hurry up and put your shoes on.'

Bea slipped her feet in to the towering heels and went to rescue the small bridesmaids from Joyce. The youngest one's jaw was set. Bea could tell she was on the brink of rebelling. She took them by the hand and followed Mel and her mother out to the cars. The phone rang, but her dad grabbed it. 'Get them in the car, I'll see who this is,' he said, waving them outside.

A few minutes later he joined them. 'That was Tom,' he said. 'He sends his apologies but has been unavoidably detained some-where.' He motioned to the back of Joyce's head as she rearranged her wide-brimmed hat in the back of the second car. 'She won't be impressed to have her table plan out of kilter,' he said, unimpressed with the late cancellation. 'At least Shani has a decent excuse for not being here.'

Bea couldn't imagine what Tom could be doing. It was a Saturday and surely even he didn't have to work over the weekend.

'He said he would give you a call later to explain,' her father added, looking stressed.

Bea sighed. It didn't bother her whether he turned up or not, but she wasn't looking forward to Joyce finding out. She settled into the back of the limousine, soothed by the smell of the vintage leather seats. Her phone bleeped and she saw it was a text from Tom.

> I have something urgent to talk to you about and need your help. Please come whenever you can, it doesn't matter what time. We can have a quick chat. Tx

He'd never asked her for help before. Bea considered his request and replied, saying she'd see him as soon as she could.

She put her phone into the small bag matching her outfit and closed her eyes, making the most of sitting still. Not sure how long she'd dozed off for, she was jarred awake by Joyce hissing directions in her ear.

'Get out of the car, this instant.'

Bea checked her mascara was still reasonably in place and tripped out of the car. 'Oof,' she said, her breath being forced out of her lungs as someone caught her at the last minute before she managed to face plant onto the tarmac.

'You okay?' Luke asked, looking as shocked as she probably did. 'That was close.'

'Stupid girl,' Joyce said through gritted teeth, grabbing the other bridesmaids and positioning them behind Mel as she stepped out of her car. 'Always daydreaming.'

Bea pushed the fascinator from in front of her eyes and back where it was supposed to be. 'Thanks for catching me,' she giggled, more out of shock than amusement. 'That could have been pretty embarrassing.'

'You think it wasn't?' Mel laughed.

'Right time, right place,' Luke said, still holding on to her waist. Their eyes locked and Bea straightened her dress. Luke glanced down at his hands. 'Sorry.' He let go and raised an eyebrow. 'Well, I'd better get back in the church and find the groom. He only sent me out to check if you lot were on your way.'

'See you inside' Bea said.

'I told you he'd look great in my photos.' Mel gave Bea a wink.

Their father linked arms with Mel. 'When you get inside, we'll follow on,' he said to Joyce pointedly. 'Okay, girls, I think this is your moment.'

Bea watched him whisper something in Mel's ear before giving her a kiss on the cheek. She could remember him doing the same thing to her. She gave the little bridesmaids a big smile. 'Ready?' They nodded. 'Come on then, let's help Mel get married.'

She motioned for them to start walking down the aisle and stepped into the church behind them to where Grant and Luke were standing facing the altar. Unable to wait any longer, Grant turned to look past them to the back of the church, where Mel and her father were standing. His eyes lit up in such a way Bea felt sure they'd always be happy together.

Her eyes caught Luke's and her breath caught in her throat. He looked so gorgeous. Her stomach did a lustful flip as they stared at each other. He gave her a little nod and smiled. 'Okay?' he mouthed. Bea nodded, not caring that she'd almost made a complete prat of herself outside moments before.

Joyce waved at her, breaking the spell. Bea passed Paul noticing that he was already dabbing at his eyes with a hankie. She smiled when Guy rolled his eyes heavenward. Poor Paul; the emotion of the last twenty-four hours was beginning to take its toll on him, too.

'Bea,' whispered her stepmother as she reached the end of the aisle. 'We're sitting over here. Girls, come along.' She noticed Luke talking to Grant and showing him the wedding rings. Grant patted his best man on the back and Bea decided she was glad that Luke had been asked to take part after all.

The music changed. Everyone turned to see Melanie begin

walking down the aisle, one arm linked through their father's. Her sister looked so beautiful and her father so proud. He winked at Bea and she felt her throat constrict. Grant took a deep breath as he waited for his bride to reach him. Even by Joyce's lofty standards, Bea could see he had scrubbed up well. She couldn't help thinking how lucky her younger sister was to be marrying the man of her dreams, and in such beautiful surroundings.

Bea looked at her father walking slowly with Mel and thought how handsome he was in his suit and cravat. She wished he'd kept some pictures of his wedding to her mum. They must have made a beautiful couple, she thought, feeling tears welling again. She pushed the thought away. Mel held out her heavy bouquet and Bea stepped forward to take it. She caught Luke's eye just as a stray tear escaped down her carefully made-up cheek. His smile vanished. He stared at her briefly, before focusing his attention directly ahead.

The wedding ceremony seemed to be over quickly, and after endless photos, Bea was relieved to be ushered into the waiting car to be driven back to the house for the reception. She was beginning to feel as if her body was working automatically. She wondered how Shani was getting on and, stifling a yawn, she took her place on the red carpet with the other queuing guests. She listened vaguely to the conversations going on around her, knowing she had never met most of these people before, and would probably never see them again.

She was grateful to finally reach Mel. Bea felt sure her sister had never looked more beautiful or serene. She congratulated Grant with a kiss and automatically took the next hand offered when it dawned on her that it was Luke's.

'Why have you stopped?' he teased, his eyes glinting mischievously. 'Don't think I didn't notice you'd kissed practically everyone else before me.' Bea laughed, feeling strangely lost for words. 'Anyway, why aren't you standing here, too?'

She lowered her voice so Joyce wouldn't hear her. 'Because I was determined not to be.' She went to give him a kiss on the cheek, amused at his annoyance, only for him to turn his face at the last minute and ended up catching him on the mouth.

'That's more like it,' he whispered, looking amused.

Bea, embarrassed to have been caught out by such a simple prank, was about to say something when she was unceremoniously pushed forward by a large woman with a harsh blue rinse. 'Move along, young lady. You're not the only person in this line-up.'

Finding her seat next to Guy, Bea was grateful not to be seated at the top table but couldn't help glancing at Luke every so often who, she admitted, looked more attractive than any man deserved to.

'He really is a perfect specimen, and don't think I didn't notice that kiss he gave you. Not what you would expect from a soon-to-be married man.' Paul sat down beside her. 'Where's what's-her-face, I would have thought she'd be here taking notes and making sure her efforts overshone Mel's?'

Bea had completely forgotten about Leilani. 'I've no idea. I'm sure she must be here somewhere. I've been so busy refereeing the bridesmaids I haven't noticed who's here and who isn't.'

'Your stepmother is ranting over there about Shani and 'he-who-shall-not-be-mentioned' nearly ruining her table plan.' Paul poured them each a glass of wine from bottles sitting on the table. 'She wasn't impressed with Shani's timing, and as for Tom, well, put it this way – I hope he's got leprosy or something nearly as horrible because I can't imagine an excuse good enough to allow him to cry off at the last minute.'

Bea took a sip, relieved to be able to quench her thirst, the coolness of the liquid helping her to feel more awake. 'Poor Shani, as if she could go into labour on purpose.' Bea raised an eyebrow. 'This hasn't been as tiresome as I'd expected, though.'

'Yes, well, you would say that, wouldn't you? Kissing the best man like you did. Minx.' Paul pursed his lips.

'Shut up, Paul,' she laughed. 'You're sitting far too close to me to be that brave.'

Bea just about managed to stay awake through the meal and then the speeches began. Her father's was as wonderful as the one she recalled him giving at her wedding. Then Luke stood up, looking more nervous than she'd ever seen him. He looked over at her and then back down to his notes. She watched him speak and heard the guests laugh at his jokes, and all she could think about was how she wished she didn't have to keep her distance from him.

Paul nudged her. 'They're calling you, sweets.' Bea couldn't figure out what he meant, then Mel waved her over. 'Bea, come here for your maid of honour present.'

Bea blushed. Had they all noticed her gazing at Luke? She went to her sister and accepted a pink Lalique cross. She thanked Mel and Grant before returning to her table, touched by their thoughtfulness.

The music started up and Paul groaned as the band began to play the intro to 'I Will Always Love You'.

'Please not this.' He pretended to push his fingers down his throat. Bea pressed her lips together not wishing her sister to see how funny she found him as Grant led Mel onto the dance floor for their first dance.

Seeing Luke coming in her direction, Bea looked around for Leilani. 'Dance with me,' he said, when he reached her. Unable to think of a reason not to – and not really trying that hard – she took his hand. 'Where's Tom?' he asked.

'He couldn't make it.' She didn't elaborate further.

Luke stared at her for a moment, his expression softening. 'I see. Well, I can't say I'm sorry.'

Bea thought it would be rude to agree with him. 'So, where's

Leilani?' She was enjoying his closeness and didn't really want to know, but felt she should ask.

'California.'

'California?' She stopped moving and frowned at him.

'Keep dancing or everyone else is going to bump into us.' He lowered his head to hers. 'She's modelling, or something. She had an offer she couldn't refuse.'

'Just like that?' Bea concentrated on not slipping on the temporary parquet flooring. Why would someone as clingy as Leilani leave him to fly across the Atlantic when they should be preparing for their own wedding? It didn't make sense.

'It seems both of us have been left in the lurch. We'll have to look after each other for today, won't we?' He pulled her closer to him, as another slow song began.

As much as Bea felt she should be sensible, she was too tired from the excitement of the night before to be bothered fighting her conscience. Anyway, she thought, it felt good being in his arms again.

'I'm enjoying this far too much,' he murmured in her ear, his breath sending shivers up her spine. 'I wish I knew why you're so determined to keep away from me, Bea.'

Bea couldn't think what to say so kept quiet, enjoying his closeness while it lasted. The record finished and was replaced by a faster-paced song. 'Let's escape outside for a bit,' he suggested. 'You can show me round your dad's impressive garden, and maybe we can chat in peace. I'd like to speak to you about something.'

Intrigued, Bea let him lead her out to her father's treasured koi carp pond. It felt a little clandestine having her hand in his, but at the same time the pressure of his hand around hers was sublime. How can something so wrong feel so perfectly natural? she wondered, staring at his broad back as she walked slightly behind him.

'Shall we sit over here?' He pointed to a wooden bench set away from the marquee. It was the very spot her father came to relax every morning with his coffee before anyone else in the house woke up and disturbed him. She sat, relieved to kick off her tight shoes.

'You look very sexy, by the way,' he said softly, sitting down next to her and taking both her hands in his. 'Bea, I have to tell you...' he began, just as his mobile rang. 'Damn.'

'Ignore it,' Bea insisted, her voice barely above a whisper and not bothering to hide her frustration with the caller.

'I can't, unfortunately.' He kissed her lightly on the lips and frowned as he answered the call. 'This won't take a moment, I promise.' He stood up and walked a short distance away with the phone to his ear. 'Yes? Hi. No, it's fine, don't worry.'

Bea felt a little foolish sitting there, then, noticing the serious expression on Luke's face as he paced across the lawn, she decided to leave him to his call and went to return to the reception. He motioned for her to wait. When she shook her head, he raised his free hand apologetically and continued with his call, his face grim. Maybe, she mused as she went back to join the others, it was business. Then again, it was probably his fiancée. The reminder that he had one gave her a pang of disappointment.

She returned to the marquee, feeling a little foolish for getting caught up in the romance of the day and giving in to her feelings for Luke. She was relieved to spot Paul, his back to her. She tapped him on the shoulder. 'Hi.'

He leapt up and hugged her. 'Where have you been?' Bea hurriedly explained. 'Oh, charming, so he takes you away from the throng and then abandons you to some phone call. So, where's his fiancée? I would have thought she'd be here somewhere.'

Bea explained about Leilani's modelling assignment in California. 'Anyway, enough of that. Have you spoken to Shani?' Bea asked, knowing Paul would have phoned her at some point.

'Happy, as you can imagine,' he said. 'She's decided to call the baby Poppy.' He nudged her sharply in the ribs. 'Look out, here comes the man himself.'

Bea saw Luke striding towards her. 'I'm going to have to go,' he said, looking troubled. 'Something's cropped up that I must deal with.' He kissed her lightly on the lips.

'You're leaving already?' She didn't bother to hide her disappointment. There was something going on, but she had no idea what it could be.

'I'm afraid so,' he said, looking unhappy about whatever was troubling him.

She watched him thank her parents and say his farewells to the newlyweds. Then he was gone.

Bea felt strangely bereft and gave herself a mental telling off for being so ridiculous.

'Damn shame, if you ask me,' Paul said, when Luke had left. 'Now you won't know when Leilani will be back, if ever.'

'She'll be back,' Bea said, miserably. 'They're supposed to be engaged.'

'More's the pity.' Paul frowned at her thoughtfully. 'If he's still engaged, then what was he doing dancing with you like that, let alone kissing you.'

'Paul, you know perfectly well it wasn't like that.'

'Yeah, whatever you say.'

Bea was saved from having to argue with him when Mel called her over to let her know it was time she went to change out of her wedding dress. They went up to the spare room so that Mel could change into her going-away outfit.

'Hasn't it been perfect?' she enthused as Bea unzipped her dress.

Bea nodded, delighted her sister had enjoyed the wedding she'd always dreamed of. 'It has; now hurry up and change, or you won't have enough time to get to the airport.'

'Can you believe I'm going to Mauritius?'

Bea smiled. 'No, you're very lucky.'

Mel changed into her new silk navy trouser suit with a little red silk top. Bea brushed out her sister's hair, removing numerous grips, and then helped her downstairs with her suitcase. 'What the hell have you got in here, gold bullion?'

'Only a few things I might need. I like to have a choice.'

'But you're going somewhere hot; all you need are a few sarongs and bikinis. Two hundred of them wouldn't weigh this much.'

'I couldn't decide what to take, so I've taken a few extras, shoes especially. I don't want to look out of place, do I?'

'I don't think that's a possibility. Now let's go and find Grant.'

Bea offered to stay behind to help with the remaining guests, but happily agreed when her dad told her not to worry about it.

'Don't forget to phone Tom back and find out what was so important he couldn't attend your sister's big day,' Joyce shouted over her shoulder, before rushing back into the marquee.

'Take no notice of your stepmother, and don't worry. We've got everything under control. By tomorrow afternoon, it'll look as if nothing has taken place here,' her father assured her, hugging Bea firmly.

* * *

She decided Tom could wait and after racing home to change, Bea ran upstairs, checked Shani's bed and Poppy's cot were perfectly made up for them, and drove Paul and Guy to the hospital.

'This stuff is revolting,' Paul said, forcing down a curly edged ham sandwich in the hospital cafeteria an hour later. He took a sip of his coffee and grimaced. 'I can't believe they're letting her come home so soon.' Me neither, thought Bea, dreamily picturing her own comfortable bed. He pushed his plate away from him. 'I wish we could leave straight away, I'm exhausted.'

'Me, too.' Bea stifled a yawn. 'But she's insisting she's discharged earlier than they'd really like, so has to wait for the doctor to check her and Poppy over before they can go.' She hadn't really thought about it much when Shani had asked if she could come straight to The Brae. Bea had assumed Shani and the baby would be in hospital for a couple of days, giving her time to make sure everything was in place for them before they were discharged. She supposed that they would figure out how best to cope with everything baby Poppy was going to need.

'I wonder what Harry is saying to her?' Guy said, shuddering as he took his first mouthful of sandwich. 'I don't suppose you mind him visiting Shani at your home?'

Bea shook her head. 'No, of course not. I'd rather he saw the baby than not bother. He's probably not that bad a person once you get to know him,' she said, hoping she was right. 'I suppose he'll need time to get used to having a baby around.' She was about to carry on talking, then spotted Luke paying for a coffee at the nearby till. What on earth was he doing at the hospital? 'Luke?' He turned to see who'd called him, a frown on his tanned face. 'Is everything all right?' she asked, seeing how exhausted he seemed and that he was still wearing his best man's suit.

'Not really.' He walked over to her and sat down. 'Why are you here?'

'Shani had her baby last night. Paul, Guy and I are giving her and the father a bit of personal space before we take her home to stay with me. You?'

He seemed to consider what he was going to say next. Bea didn't think she'd ever seen him so sad and couldn't help feeling anxious about what he was going to say. 'I don't think you ever knew my business partner, Chris.' Bea shook her head, wondering where this was leading. 'The phone call I received at your sister's wedding... he was rushed in here with a suspected fractured skull.'

'What happened?' she asked, horrified. No wonder he'd left in such a hurry. 'Is he going to be all right?'

He nodded. 'Yes, thankfully. It turns out he has severe concussion.' He looked as if he was going to say something further, but changed his mind.

Bea wished she could hold him and try to take away some of the pain he was obviously struggling with. There was more to the story, she was certain. 'What is it? Tell me.'

'It's nothing to do with you,' he insisted quietly, taking a sip from his coffee. Lost in thought for a moment he looked at her. 'He was caught at the harbour, trying to abscond from the island.'

'But I thought he went missing ages ago?'

'Three years. He'd sneaked back onto the island and probably never thought anyone would still be looking for him after so long.'

'Is there anything I can do?' she asked, stunned. Sensing he was keeping something from her, it occurred to her that whatever it was involved her in some way. 'Will you tell me what else is bothering you?'

He rubbed his eyes, then lowered his voice to a whisper. 'Fine, but if I do, I want you to try not to hold what I tell you against me.'

Her stomach tensed. Was she finally going to have to hear him confess to his part in the money laundering? She wasn't sure she wanted to hear it after all. 'Why would I do that?'

'Because it's to do with Tom. At least, I'm fairly sure it is. The authorities will just need proof.'

Bea clasped her hands under the table. 'Tom?' Her voice came out in a hoarse whisper.

Luke nodded. 'I know you and he go way back, but how well do you really know him?'

'I assumed I knew him very well.' She thought back to Luke's insistence that Tom wasn't all he seemed. She rested her hands on the table. 'Why?' She swallowed. 'What he's supposed to have done?'

Luke took a deep breath. 'I think he's probably involved in Chris's activities, but I'm not sure how yet.'

Bea felt as if she'd been slapped. 'Seriously?' She shook her head in disbelief. 'I don't think you understand how serious an allegation that is.'

'I can see you're shocked. I didn't mean to upset you.'

She struggled to take in what she'd just been told, but something niggled at her. 'You can't be serious about Tom. I know you don't like each other, but this is ridiculous. What grounds do you have for accusing him of anything? Anyway, why would Tom have anything to do with anything illegal?' She closed her mouth to stop herself from saying anything further. He still hadn't mentioned money laundering, and to tip him off now would be stupid. She wasn't going to lose her house and risk prison.

'Money problems, that's why.' Luke looked around to check he wasn't being overheard and leant closer to her.

Bea shook her head. 'I can't believe this.' She felt sick at the thought of Tom accusing Luke if he had been the one involved in illegal activities.

'Chris had Tom's contact details on him when they brought him in, so he's obviously contacted him recently. Chris knew he'd be arrested if he showed his face back here again, so he must have thought coming here worth it to risk a prison sentence. I assume Tom got sucked in to his scheme in a moment of weakness, and once you're involved with these things, I imagine it's almost impossible to back out.'

'I feel awful,' she said, wishing she'd not believed Tom so readily.

'Don't be silly, it's not as if you could have done anything.' He studied her face for a moment. Was he looking for assurance? she wondered.

'No, but I can do something about it now.'

Luke grabbed her wrist when she went to stand. 'What do you mean? Listen, Bea, I don't have time to argue, but you need to promise me that you'll let the authorities deal with Tom. I was hoping to get to the bottom of this myself, but I've had to hand all the information I've gathered to them.'

She didn't answer.

'You don't know who else could be behind this and I don't want you getting involved. It could be dangerous.' He turned to walk away, pulling his car keys from his pocket.

'Well, I happen to believe I *am* involved,' she said. 'He's my manager.' Damn, she'd said it.

Luke turned and scowled at her. 'I don't care what he is to you, you need to stay away from him. Let the authorities sort this out. Promise?' He sighed wearily. 'I'm aware that money laundering is about the worst thing you could be involved with in business, and that if you mention this to him, you'd become involved and you don't need that.' He sighed wearily. 'Tom is dangerous. And my guess is that he won't think twice about implicating you, if he hasn't already.' He stared at her questioningly for a moment. 'I really have to go. He'll probably suspect that the authorities have been informed by now, as well as the police. Even the nicest people can turn when cornered, Bea, and despite what you may believe, Tom isn't a nice bloke.'

'You leave Bea to us,' Paul, who had sat quietly listening, said. 'She can be hot-headed sometimes, but she's no fool.'

Luke stared at her. 'I have to go. Bea, please don't do anything rash.'

Bea was too stunned to realise Luke knew the dangers of tipping someone off to reply. Did he realise she had been suspicious of him all this time? She hoped not.

'Don't worry, we'll make sure she doesn't do anything stupid.' Paul glanced at Bea, and Guy stroked her rigid back. 'He's right. If Tom can do this, then you never really knew him at all.'

'I can't sit here and do nothing,' she said, frustrated by the injustice of it all. 'Anyway, I agreed to go and see him at his flat later.'

'What did you say?' Luke stopped walking away and hurried back to her. She repeated what she had said. He took her face gently in his hands. 'Then make an excuse. You mustn't try and deal with this yourself. Please leave it to people trained for this.'

Bea relented. 'Fine, I will.'

'Thank you.' Luke's hands fell away.

After Luke had left, they were allowed to see Shani. 'I thought you were only going to be twenty minutes,' she grumbled, pulling on her jacket and smiling down at her sleeping baby.

'How was Harry?' Paul asked, settling himself at the end of the bed.

'He was okay.' She shrugged and couldn't quite hide a satisfied smile. 'He's promised to set up a standing order for Poppy. It's not what I hoped for in terms of a father for my baby, but it serves me right for getting into this mess in the first place. He said he wants to see her occasionally though, so that's something. He believes she should know her father, but that I can only contact him via the surgery.' Shani straightened her baggy top, and Bea couldn't help suspecting her friend was trying very hard to appear braver than she felt. 'It's better than nothing, and maybe one day he'll tell his wife about his other daughter. For now though, I have to be satisfied with that. At least he's acknowledged her and I could tell he regretted the way he's treated me.'

'It's a start,' Bea said, giving Shani a hug. 'It's going to be lovely having you both at The Brae. The house needs a bit of life put back into it.'

'Thanks, Bea.' Shani stood up and winced. 'I think I'm going to need a rubber ring to sit on for a few days.'

Paul grimaced. 'Too much information, thank you,' he said, picking up Shani's overnight bag. 'You can take those,' he said to Guy, indicating the two flower arrangements she'd received. 'Let's get a move on. I need my bed even if the rest of you don't.' He narrowed his eyes at Bea and gave her a pointed look. 'We all need to get to our beds, don't we?'

Bea pulled a face. She still felt the need to see Tom and find out what he was up to, even if the others thought it a bad idea.

Shani stopped them before they left the room. 'Hold on. What's going on? Tell me now, or I'm going to keep you all waiting, so you can't get home.' She picked up the baby and gave her a cuddle.

Bea listened while Paul explained about their meeting downstairs with Luke. 'You see, Miss I'm-gonna-take-charge has decided to ignore Luke's advice.'

'I never said that.' Why did Paul know her so well?

Paul tilted his head to one side. 'You might not have done, but we all know what you're like when you make your mind up about something.'

Shani put the baby back in her crib and sat down carefully on the edge of the bed. 'What are you up to, Bea?'

Bea groaned, closing her eyes with tiredness. 'Come on, Shan, I'm exhausted.'

'We all are, but no one's leaving this room until I hear you tell Tom you won't be seeing him tonight.'

Knowing when she was beaten and too tired to argue any further, Bea dialled Tom's number and spoke to him briefly.

'He wasn't very happy,' she said after the call ended. 'I've agreed to meet him in the office early tomorrow morning instead. I can chat with him there, before I leave for court. Happy now?'

* * *

Bea settled Shani and Poppy into their bedroom and saw Paul and Guy off in a taxi. She couldn't help thinking that maybe Tom had been using their relationship so that he had an alibi for Vanessa. It would have allowed him the space and time to arrange meetings with his criminal connections. She still couldn't quite believe he was callous enough to do that, or be involved in anything illegal. Then she recalled his furtive calls during their trip to New York.

She wasn't sure what emotion she felt more strongly – fury with Tom and his involvement in something so underhand, or indignation that he had used her in any way. She couldn't believe she had remained friendly with him all this time and not suspected his occasionally erratic behaviour. Surely she should have noticed something? She yawned. She was exhausted and would find out more in the morning, whether he liked it or not.

26

MAY 10 – FINAL HARVEST

Bea woke to a balmy, sunny day. The stillness of the morning did nothing to help calm her nerves. D-Day. If only Simon had agreed to the Martin order she wouldn't have to sit across from him in court today. She stood in the shower, certain Claire would have put the idea to him, but unsurprised he hadn't agreed to it. 'There's still time,' she whispered, as she rubbed her legs dry with a large fluffy white towel. Maybe not though. Simon had never taken the decent way out of anything.

'You'd only have been suspicious if he had agreed to it,' Shani said sagely, a snoring Poppy in her arms as they sat quietly in the garden a little later. She checked her watch. 'You're not due in court until ten-thirty, and who knows, maybe Simon will have agreed to your idea by then? He was probably too busy taking part in one of the posh Liberation Day parties yesterday to be bothered phoning you.'

'You think?' Bea raised her eyebrows but not her hopes at the thought. 'I suppose I was caught up with the wedding and little miss here having just been born.' She held back from mentioning how hard it had been trying to enjoy the wedding when she'd been grieving for Aunt Annabel.

Shani kissed Poppy's forehead. 'No, I don't. You're just going to have to face him in court and hope for the best.'

Bea made a few more notes to the already lengthy list of points she hoped to bring up at the hearing. 'At least by this afternoon I should know whether I'll be keeping my home.'

Shani placed her free hand on Bea's arm. 'Whatever happens today you mustn't worry about what Annabel wanted for you. She loved this place and her garden, but above all she loved you. You would have been what worried her. So, whatever happens, we'll deal with it. I promise I'll be there every step of the way.'

Bea sniffed back the tears. 'Thanks, Shan. I know she only wanted the best for me. My whole life the only constant thing has been her and coming here. I don't know how I'd bear to sell it.'

Bea swatted away a fly. 'I suppose I'd better get moving if I'm to meet Tom. He wants to chat to me before the others get to the office and I daren't be late for my own hearing.'

'Best of luck in court.' Shani gave her a one-armed hug, waking Poppy who immediately began to cry. 'Are you sure you don't want me there? I could always ask Mum to look after Pops for a couple of hours.'

Bea shook her head. This was something she needed to do herself. 'I'll be fine. One way or another I'm going to be okay. I promise I'll phone you as soon as I know anything.'

* * *

Bea parked the car in the closest space she could find to the office and hurried through the car park. She could have done without this, she thought as she waited to cross the road. If Tom was involved in something illegal, she would feel guilty for not picking up on any suspicious behaviour. Tom was her manager and she worked closely with him each day. The lights changed, and Bea stepped out into the road.

'Bea, wait.'

She stopped at the urgency in Luke's tone and stepped back onto the pavement. 'What are you doing here?' she shouted angrily, as Luke ran up to her.

'I know you're unhappy to see me here, but when Shani told me you were going to meet Tom, I had to stop you.' He bent over, hands on his thighs as he recovered from the exertion of running. 'I called your house, but you'd already left,' he panted. 'You can't go in there.'

'Of course, I can.'

'No, listen. Tom is going to be arrested.' He kept his voice low as others passed by. 'I'm sorry, but he's definitely involved in something with Chris and there's enough evidence now to arrest him.'

Bea felt sick. 'Seriously?' Had Tom insisted she meet him at the office to implicate her in some way? It dawned on her that Tom wouldn't have given a thought to her future, to try and save himself. What the hell had he been going to ask of her? 'Do you think Tom was trying to entangle me in all this in some way?' She could hardly believe she was accusing him of something so terrible.

Luke shrugged. 'Who knows? I think he was desperate for someone to help him.' He stared at her silently for a minute. 'And you're probably the obvious one to ask, as his colleague and friend. I'm sorry, I know this must be hard for you.'

They both looked up as two police cars came around the corner and parked outside the office. Bea tensed. If Luke hadn't stopped her when he did, she'd be in there now. She began to tremble at the prospect of what might have happened.

'Come here,' he murmured, taking her into his arms and holding her tightly. 'I'm sorry this has happened, Bea'

She put her arms around him, enjoying the comforting hug. 'I can't believe he'd expect me to go along with something like that. The very first thing we're trained to do is look out for cases where people might be laundering, although I've never experienced anyone doing it, until now.' She looked up at Luke. 'He knew he'd get caught eventually, surely? The authorities here are so on the ball about this sort of thing.'

'He must have done.' He sighed. 'Who knows what happened to make him do this.'

Bea stepped back from him. 'But what about you? Chris was your business partner.' She thought of the documents Tom had shown her about the investigation into Luke's business dealings. Were they false and Tom's way to ensure she didn't suspect him in any way? Bea stared into Luke's eyes trying to ascertain whether she was being naive to believe him like she had believed Tom.

'You surely don't think I'm involved in all this, too?' He narrowed his eyes, then widened them as a thought came to him. 'You actually suspect that I'm the one who's involved with Chris, don't you?'

Even now she couldn't tell him about the paperwork Tom had shown her. 'I'm trying to be logical. Both you and Tom suspect your business partner of being involved in money laundering activities. Tom has...' Damn, she wasn't allowed to say what she desperately needed to.

'Tom has shown you proof, is that it?' He glared at her. 'So now you think I'm here to twist your mind into helping me cover up for what? My involvement?'

Bea hated seeing such hurt on his face, but after falling for Tom's lies had lost any confidence in her powers of judgement. She rubbed her temple with her fingers, trying to ease the headache that felt like it had her brain in a vice. Tom. Luke. Both could be involved in one way or another, purely by their association with

Chris. Both were clever enough. Tom had shown her proof, but as she stared into Luke's eyes his disappointment in her hurt like a physical pain.

'I'm sorry, Luke, but I can't talk to you about this.' He looked aghast and she hated herself for what she must say. 'I really want to, believe me, but legally I can't.'

He looked stunned and raised his hands before dropping them back down to his sides. 'I understand – I think – but please do one thing for me.'

'What's that?' Bea waited for him to speak, wishing more than anything that she worked in some other profession.

'Do not go into that office. If you trust nothing else I've said to you, please do as I ask just this once. You can call Tom later. If I've lied to you about his arrest, he'll still be around for you to chat to; if he's not, you'll know I was telling the truth.'

* * *

'You're quite clear what's going to happen?' her lawyer asked her for at least the third time since they'd arrived at the Royal Court.

'Yes,' she said struggling to focus with so much already on her mind. 'I'm going to leave all the talking to you, unless they allow me to ask one or two questions.'

'That's correct.' He glanced down at the buff folder in his hand and pushed his tortoise-shell glasses onto the bridge of his nose. 'I put in a request for you to speak when we filed the papers a couple of days ago, and if the judge does ask you to speak, you must keep to the point. Be clear and do not bring emotions into it at all. The legal points are all that matter to the court. And it will be on that basis that a decision will be made as to whether your ex-husband be awarded half the value of the house.'

Bea sighed, feeling helpless for the second time that day. 'I understand. No emotions.'

'Easier said than done, don't you think?' Luke walked up behind her. Confused, Bea turned to him. Her stomach did a flip and for a second she forgot her nerves. 'What are you doing here?'.

'It's my hearing today.'

Bea nodded, not sure how to react. 'Ahh.'

Luke leant closer to her and lowered his voice. 'I've been thinking since we spoke earlier. Tom told you they were investigating me, didn't they?' Bea didn't reply. He looked relieved. 'I suspected there was something holding you back whenever we—' he hesitated and looked to see whether or not the lawyer was in earshot '—saw each other, and I know it took a while for me to twig, but when my lawyer showed me some paperwork with Tom's signature on it, I realised he was involved in reporting my case and the reason why I'm here today.'

'Tom reported it? He never said.' Bea clenched her teeth together to stop from saying something improper in the hallowed corridors of the Victorian Royal Court building. 'Why would he do that if he was implicated?'

'Who knows?' Luke shrugged. 'Don't be too angry, he was proved to be right about my partner, wasn't he? Maybe Tom hoped that by implicating me he was putting a smokescreen around himself. What he didn't realise was that I've been waiting for Chris to return to the island, or slip up in some way, so he can be prosecuted and I can try to recoup some of the money he embezzled from me.'

A door closed loudly behind them. She recognised Simon's clipped tone as he approached. She closed her eyes to steady her temper and felt Luke take her hand. 'I have a feeling it's going to be one hell of a morning for both of us.'

Bea forced a smile. 'It seems so,' she said, determined to ignore

Simon until she was inside the court room. Bea couldn't believe Luke appeared so relaxed. She felt sick with fear about probably being forced to sell her home, while Luke was looking at a possible jail sentence. 'How can you look so calm?'

'They're only going to decide whether there's a case to be held today, nothing more, thankfully.' He sighed and bent his head down a little. 'And I'm not as calm as I probably seem.'

Simon walked over and stood next to them. 'Beatrice,' he said, ignoring Luke. Bea noticed Luke's amusement at Simon's arrogant behaviour and was relieved he stayed by her side.

Simon glared at Luke, obviously unhappy that he wasn't leaving them to talk privately.

'So, you decided not to accept my offer, then?' Bea said, hating that her voice trembled slightly.

Simon's eyebrows knitted together. 'I hardly call expecting me to hand over what's legally mine without recompense a reasonable offer. I certainly have no intention of being forced by you, or by Claire, into doing something that stupid.' He gave Luke a pitying look. 'Watch yourself with this one; she's got more of a sting than you'd think. She might look all sweet and angelic, but she can stand up for herself with the best of them.'

'I've worked that out for myself,' Luke answered, giving Bea a cheeky wink to show there were no hard feelings between them and probably to irritate Simon. She relaxed a little. 'I like that Bea doesn't allow anyone to bully her.'

'Oh, it's like that, is it?' Simon sniggered. 'Good luck to you, mate, she'll turn on you one day, too.'

'If she does, I imagine it'll be my own fault.' Luke watched Simon walk away. 'What a jerk.'

Bea sighed. 'He is a bit of an arse, isn't he? I listen to him and sometimes can't believe I ever thought I was in love with him.' It occurred to her that even if she did lose everything at least she wouldn't be married to Simon any longer.

Luke's lawyer approached. 'Mr Thornton, we need to go through now.'

Luke thanked him. 'I'd better be off.' He gave Bea a quick hug. 'Good luck. I hope the judge comes up with the right verdict for you.'

'You, too,' she said, holding him tightly for a moment, trying to take a little resolve from his bravery. 'And I'm sorry I was so awkward with you. I had to watch what I said whenever I saw you in case I inadvertently tipped you off about the investigation.'

Luke gave her a reassuring smile. 'Don't worry. My advocate explained that you could have got years in prison, and in your position, I'd have also kept my mouth shut.'

'Tom obviously showed me the paperwork to keep me off the scent about what was going on with him and Chris.'

'I suppose so. He must have known that if you suspected me, you'd keep away from me, and also be suspicious of anything I said.'

'I still find it hard to believe he could be so sly.'

'All I'm bothered about is that you believe me now.'

'I'm being summoned,' she said spotting her advocate waving her over. 'Bye then, and good luck in there.'

'You too,' he said, before walking calmly towards the main courtroom where the magistrate would hear his case. She took a deep breath and entered the smaller wood-panelled courtroom ready to face Simon and her own future.

* * *

Bea sat impatiently, waiting for the procedures to be read through and the French swearing in to be announced by the greffier, and couldn't help thinking how smart and dignified the officer of the court was as he carried out his duty. Resolving to follow his example, she folded her hands in her lap and listened as each case was heard. Eventually, it was her turn. Her advocate stood and, referring to the papers he'd filed with the court, began his reasoning why Simon should not be awarded half the value of The Brae.

When Simon's advocate had finished, the judge addressed Bea. 'You have expressed a wish to speak, Ms Philips?'

'Thank you, yes.' Bea took a deep breath determined to hide her anger towards Simon. 'I understand that because I was still married to my ex-husband when my aunt died and left me The Brae it was considered a matrimonial asset, but I'm making a request for the court to consider my aunt's wishes for her home when the decision is made.'

He looked down at his notes for a moment. 'I believe your aunt, Mrs Annabel Juarez, had booked an appointment with her lawyer who has confirmed his belief of her intention to change her will.'

She could almost feel Simon's irritation at her daring to speak, but didn't care. She owed it to Aunt Annabel to fight her case as strongly as she could. 'I'm certain of it. The day after my aunt discovered Simon's— I mean, Advocate Porter's association with Claire Browning, she told me she intended adding a clause to her will ensuring he didn't benefit in any way from her death.' Bea's voice cracked at the memory of her aunt's anger and her sorrow that she would die within three days of the conversation.

The judge turned his attention to Simon. Bea wondered if he knew Simon personally. After all, Simon was an advocate and no doubt represented his own clients in front of this same judge. Bea willed herself to remain positive.

'I agree, the whole situation is very unfortunate.' He turned to whisper something to his greffier, who nodded and handed him a sheet of paper. He spoke to Bea once again after reading it. 'I'm advised by your aunt's lawyer that she did indeed arrange the meeting and that they had a conversation on the telephone prior to that meeting where she advised him of her intentions towards Advocate Porter. Also, according to your papers, despite your best attempts to raise the value of half your property known as The Brae, you've been unable to do so.'

Bea didn't dare move. She concentrated on breathing, aware that she was gripping a little too tightly on the wooden partition in front of her.

'You have, however, been able to raise a figure amounting to a little under one third of the value of the property through a mortgage. Considering all that I've heard today, I'm going to award Advocate Porter the value of one third of the property. I realise you will still have to fund a further ten thousand pounds to meet the required amount I am awarding to him, but feel that one third is the fair amount in this case.'

Bea wasn't sure if she'd heard correctly. Had she managed to keep her house? She didn't have to sell? Simon's angry whispers to his legal counsel echoed across to her, and she relaxed slightly, still unable to believe what had happened. It wasn't an outright win, but she still had her house and could find the means to buy Simon out. 'Thank you very much.'

She turned to her advocate and shook his hand. She'd done it. It was all over. Finally.

The greffier announced the following case. Bea sat down on the leather seat and lowered her head in her hands, just about managing to stifle her laughter. She could stay at The Brae. She hadn't let Aunt Annabel down.

Her excitement died down and she sat up straighter, composing herself once again. She wondered how Luke was getting on in the next-door courtroom.

27

MAY 11 – SECRET GARDEN

Since Tom's arrest, Bea had given the police a statement and was allowed to go. She still couldn't get over Tom's involvement. Bea cringed at the memory of not trusting Luke enough to believe him the previous morning. Bloody Tom had a lot to answer for.

Her bank manager, Mr Peters assured her that he hadn't changed his mind and that she could have the money to pay off most of her debt to Simon. Bea didn't mind about needing to locate another ten thousand pounds to cover everything; she'd worry about that tomorrow. So what if she would probably be broke for years? The main thing was that she'd managed to keep her house and Annabel's pride and joy. She swallowed the lump in her throat. 'I did it,' she whispered. 'You knew I could, didn't you?'

She realised the house phone was ringing and ran inside to answer it. 'Hello?'

'Bea, please don't put down the phone, I need to explain everything to you.'

Bea shuddered hearing Tom's self-pitying tone. 'No, Tom, I have no wish to hear anything you have to say.'

'You must let me explain,' he whined.

'I think I've listened to far too much of what you've had to say. You're sly, vindictive and your callous disregard for anyone else makes me sick. As far as I'm concerned, you deserve all that's coming to you.' She ended the call without giving him the chance to reply. Bea went to leave the room, but the phone rang again. She left it for a few seconds, then realising the caller had no intention of giving up, answered. 'I told you I had nothing to say to you, and I meant it.'

'Who's rattled your cage?' Mel asked, amused.

'What are you phoning for, you're on honeymoon.'

'I know, and Mauritius is gorgeous, isn't it honey?' she shouted to Grant.

'This must be costing a fortune, Mel. Is everything okay?'

'Better than okay, in fact.' Bea took a breath to speak, but Mel continued. 'Shut up and listen, Grant said I can only talk for two minutes because the roaming charges are astronomical. Guess who we bumped into at the airport?'

'Who?' Bea asked politely, wishing she'd bought a cordless phone so she could go outside and sunbathe.

'Leilani.'

'Leilani?' Bea stopped dreaming about the sun and paid immediate attention. 'But I thought Luke said she'd taken a modelling assignment in California. Are you sure it was her?'

'Of course I'm sure. How many six-foot models do I know?' she teased. 'She was furious with Luke.'

'What did she say?' Bea asked, intrigued.

'It turns out she didn't choose to leave him, whatever he may have told you. She sat him down one day over lunch with the intention of fixing their wedding date and getting all the plans underway.' She could hear Mel taking a long sip from her drink. 'That was delicious. I'll have another daiquiri please, hon.'

'Go on,' Bea urged impatiently. 'What happened?'

'Apparently Luke told her in no uncertain terms he had no intention of making any commitment to her. Typical bloke.' Bea could barely breathe. 'When she argued that everyone assumed they were engaged, he reminded her she'd been drunk and announced it without any encouragement from him. He told her she shouldn't expect him to marry her simply because she'd tried to back him into a corner by telling everyone he was going to.'

'Really?' Bea felt breathless at the unexpected news. 'What happened next?'

'Melanie, your two minutes are up,' Grant shouted in the background.

'I'm on the bloody phone to my sister. You get me that daiquiri and then I'll get off the phone.'

Bea couldn't help feeling sorry for Grant. 'Poor bloke, you don't have to be so rude to him.'

'Shush and listen. What was I saying? Oh yes, well, apparently Luke pointed out that if she were to settle down now, at the peak of her career, she'd be doing herself a disservice. He suggested she return to the States and not waste her talent as a model.' Mel giggled. 'Or something like that. I think she exaggerated a bit, but I think he told her to go and get on with her career as a kind way of getting rid of her.'

Bea considered Mel's words. 'I can't believe all this.'

'Hang on a sec, you haven't heard the best bit yet,' Mel whispered sounding even more excited than she had done seconds before. 'Grant's on his way back, so I have to hurry. Leilani believed Luke would fight for her. She called his bluff by telling him about this modelling assignment she was offered in America, saying that if he didn't commit to her then she'd accept it and they'd be finished, for good.'

'No.' Bea was impressed with the girl's gall.

'Yes.' Mel laughed. 'He called *her* bluff, and told her she should take the assignment. That was the day before my wedding. The morning of the wedding he dropped her off at the airport on his way to the church. We met her when we checked in later that day. Can you believe it?'

Bea was stunned. 'But I don't understand,' she whispered, trying to take all this news into her head. 'Why would he let me believe she had left him and gone off like that, when really it was him who forced her hand?'

Bea suddenly felt better than she had done in weeks, months even. Leilani had gone and wasn't coming back – not for the foreseeable future, anyway.

'Hey, I only told you because I thought you'd be interested. I feel a bit bad for her though,' Mel admitted. 'Poor Leilani was devastated.'

Bea was amused at her sister's change in tone. She took a deep breath to calm down. 'You're right, I'm not surprised she was upset.'

Fuelled with this news, Bea ended the call and ran upstairs to find Shani and tell her everything.

'You've got to phone him,' Shani insisted, holding out a smelly nappy.

Bea grimaced and took it between her forefinger and thumb and placed it into a nappy bag.

'Don't be so dramatic, it's a nappy – it won't bite.' She rolled her eyes. 'Maybe it's time you let Luke know how you feel?'

Bea wasn't so sure. 'I don't think so. Mel did say he wasn't ready to commit to Leilani. If I'm going to be with someone, then I want it to last.' Bea picked up the newly changed baby and cuddled her.

'But you're already in love with him,' Shani added unhelpfully.

'I'm not going to argue with you about that.' Bea held the warm baby in her arms and sniffed her fresh baby scent. Even if she couldn't be with Luke, it would have been comforting to hear from him, especially after everything that had happened the day before.

She wondered how his court hearing had gone. 'I think I've probably ruined any chances I had with Luke by not believing him,' she said miserably. 'I know he seemed fine in the court building, but I've no idea what that verdict was yet.'

'You mean he could still be guilty and involved with all that laundering business?'

'I doubt it, but it is a possibility.' Her instincts told her he wasn't involved, but they'd also told her Simon was the love of her life and Tom a good friend. What did she know about anything?

Shani carried Poppy downstairs and placed her carefully into her pram. 'I'm going to take her for a walk to the shops,' she said, looking happier than Bea had ever seen her. 'Do you need anything?'

Bea shook her head, unable to speak for a minute as her emotions threatened to overwhelm her. 'No, thanks. Enjoy your walk.'

They couldn't have been gone more than five minutes when Bea, flicking through the envelopes in her hand, spotted the usual bills and another one that stood out. She dropped the bills onto the Bishop's seat and tore open the cream envelope. Unfolding the letter inside, Bea read it twice to take in exactly what she'd been sent. 'No way!' she screamed, dancing crazily around the empty room. She kissed the letter and punched the air. 'Thank you, Aunt Annabel.'

'Shani,' she shouted up the stairs, before remembering her friend had gone out with Poppy. Bea grabbed the phone and dialled Shani's mobile number. 'Shan,' she said, barely able to contain her excitement, 'you'll never guess what's happened!'

'Is everything okay?' Shani asked anxiously.

'It's better than okay – I've discovered what A Jersey Kiss is. Hurry up with your shopping and come back as soon as you can, I've got something to show you.'

28

A NEW LEAF

Bea was so busy skipping around the hallway she didn't hear Luke knock at the front door. 'Oh.' She stopped instantly as he poked his head around the door. Not caring how idiotic she looked she waved him in.

He laughed. 'You obviously beat Simon then?'

'Not completely.' She didn't care about Simon right now, or the outcome of the court case. 'Better than that.'

He looked puzzled. 'You seem very pleased with yourself about something. Hey, I've got a surprise for you.' He held out an envelope, but when she went to take it, he pulled his hand back. 'I know what the Jersey Kiss is that your aunt left to you.'

'Me too,' she gasped, surprised. Luke looked stunned. 'Really, I have, but you go first. Tell me what you've found out.' She could barely contain her excitement. She was touched that Luke had secretly been looking for the mysterious Jersey Kiss and wanted to see what he had to tell her.

'You know the photo I took last autumn of the unusual lilies in your garden?' Bea thought back and gave a knowing smile; it had been under their noses the entire time. 'Well, I showed it to my uncle. He's a horticulturist and he'd never seen one before. He double checked. It seems like your aunt has propagated a new strain of *amaryllis belladonna*.'

'I know, the Jersey lily.' Bea clapped her hands together and squealed.

Luke laughed and nodded. 'Although it's too late this year for any of the big shows, like Chelsea or Hampton Court, my uncle says if you were to show it you would get it noticed all around the world and could make decent money by supplying specialists.'

Bea listened in silence. She hadn't thought that far; he'd obviously done his research.

'Gardeners across the world love discovering new strains of plants, and this one is especially pretty. The money you bring in could help you keep this place. I'm sure he's right.'

Bea stood on tiptoes, took his smiling face in her hands, and kissed him. 'He is.' She held out the envelope she'd received a short while before. 'This came in the post today.' She watched as Luke took the paper out and read it.

'It's the licence for A Jersey Kiss! This is amazing, Bea. I never thought I could be this excited about a plant.'

Bea laughed, 'Me neither. Clever Aunt Annabel. This is the secret that she'd mentioned to me over the years. I never really took much notice – she was always telling me stories about Antonio and I assumed it was something to do with him.' She paused and stared into Luke's eyes, loving that his delight in the discovery mirrored her own.

'Bea, this could be the answer to all your worries. I'm so happy for you.' His mouth broke into a lazy smile. 'I can't believe I've been wracking my brains trying to come up with a solution to your finances. I might have been able to give this information to you months ago if my uncle hadn't been on a cruise when I first sent him the photo.'

'But I have it now,' she said, painfully aware how in love with him she was. He was so genuinely happy for her. She remembered his court date the previous day. 'I suppose the fact you're standing here means you're in the clear?'

He grinned. 'Yes, I am. They decided I didn't have a case to answer, although my partner Chris does.' His smile disappeared, and a haunted look crossed his face. 'I'm afraid it looks like Tom will do time, too.'

Bea couldn't help feeling a tinge of sadness at the person she'd thought Tom to be. It was still hard to take in his part in Luke's investigation. 'I can't believe what Tom tried to do to you,' she said. 'I feel so bad doubting you.'

'Hey, it's not your fault. It's your job to be wary of people. You have to be careful, and it's not like you knew me that well.'

'I do now though, and I'm sorry.'

'Don't say anything more about it.' He kissed her just as she went to reply, then lifted her up in a bear hug, his muscular arms encircling hers. 'You're incredible. Do you know that?' He kissed her until she was dizzy. 'You did the right thing,' he said lowering her back down and becoming serious once again. 'Why should you have believed me? You're a professional and I could have been feeding you a lie, just like Tom did, but you acted as you should have done. We won't mention it again. Now, about your Jersey Kiss.'

Bea kissed him again. 'That one?' she teased, breathing in the soapy scent of his warm skin.

He tickled her waist. Bea screeched. 'No, the other one. The one that's going to make you a great deal of money if you're clever with it, which I'm sure you're going to be.' He took her by the hand and led her through the kitchen and out into the walled garden. 'That one there.' Luke pointed to the area where the lilies had been the previous autumn.

'I'd love it if you'd help me with it going forward.'

'I'll do whatever you like.'

Remembering her conversation with Mel, Bea reluctantly changed the subject. 'Did you know Mel and Grant bumped into Leilani at the airport?'

His eyes glistened with amusement. 'You know what happened then?'

'We seem to have been keeping quite a few secrets from each other up until now.'

'We have.' He kissed her neck. 'That's got to change, don't you think?'

Bea happily agreed. 'She's incredibly beautiful,' Bea said, not enjoying stating the obvious, but wanting everything cleared up between them once and for all. 'I don't understand how you would split up from her.' She wasn't sure she wanted to hear his answer but when he didn't say anything, she continued. 'Why didn't you marry Leilani?'

'Because I love someone else.' Luke's expression turned serious. He didn't take his eyes off her.

Bea eyes widened at his blatant admission. She felt bereft and tried to step back from him but he held on to her. 'What are you doing here, then?'

'I wanted to clear the air between us and find a way to help you sort out your problems with Simon.'

Confused, Bea frowned. 'Why?'

'You know why.'

She struggled to get away from him without any luck. 'No, I don't.'

'I would have thought it was obvious.' He looked down at her, his mouth turning up slightly at the sides.

'No, it's not.'

He kicked a small stone off the path with the toe of his boot.

Damn, thought Bea. He wants me to spell it out to him. She

sighed. 'You told Leilani you aren't ready for commitment,' she said, feeling exposed and awkward, but determined to know everything. 'That's why she's gone, isn't it?'

'Yes, but I meant I didn't want commitment with her,' he said, not elaborating further.

She couldn't think what to say next and knew that the handsome man in front of her was everything she could ever imagine wanting. Unable to say anything else, she turned her back on him and picked up a large twig.

After a short silence, Luke stepped up behind her and took her in his arms. 'Bea,' he said quietly, his breath on the back of her neck sending her central nervous system into overdrive. 'I did tell Leilani that, and I didn't lie. I was trying to let her down gently. To be honest our relationship, which has been more of a friendship than anything else for a few years now, had dragged on for months longer than it should have done.'

Bea stood silently, dropped the twig and let her hands wander up to where his arms held her and gently curled her fingers over the taught muscles.

'I only started seeing her when I thought you were involved with Tom, and even then it was as friends. Childish, I know, but I fell in love with you so quickly that it took me by surprise, and I wasn't sure how to deal with it.' He lowered his voice further. 'Leilani and I haven't slept together in years.' Bea raised her eyebrows, but resisted saying anything. She didn't want to interrupt him or give him a reason not to tell her everything. 'I couldn't understand why you kept pulling away from me whenever we seemed to be getting close. I know now about Tom and the tipping off business, but then it just messed with my mind. After that night we spent together I hoped everything would be okay.'

'And it wasn't,' she sighed, resenting Tom more than ever for keeping them apart for so long.

'What's done is done. I think we should start afresh.'

Bea couldn't think of anything she wanted more. 'I agree.'

He turned her to face him. 'Beatrice Porter or Philips, or whatever your name is now, I love you. Surely you must know that?'

Taken back by his unexpected announcement, Bea couldn't hide her delight. 'How could I?' she asked, unable to take in the enormity of his words.

He held her against him. She could barely breathe, but couldn't be any happier. 'I fell in love with you the moment I saw you at the engagement party,' he admitted, 'when you went the wrong way round the palm to see who was talking to you.' He kissed her neck; Bea was relieved he was holding her tightly so her legs wouldn't give way.

She looked up at the man who she had desperately tried to forget, the same man who now was doing his best to help her to sort out her financial worries and the one who had stopped her from becoming involved with Tom's arrest the previous morning. She knew she loved him more than she could imagine loving any other man. 'You love me,' she said making certain she had heard correctly.

'I do.' He kissed her once again. 'Do you think you'd consider marrying me?'

Bea didn't hesitate. 'Yes, I would. I love you, Luke Thornton,' she whispered, enjoying being able to say the words aloud to him.

'And you know I love you.' He took her hand, leading her slowly back towards the house, past the rosemary, its summery scent wafting in the warm air. 'Maybe now you'll take me up on that offer to have dinner on my boat?'

'I think I could do that,' she laughed.

Luke turned to her, thought for a bit and then, taking a piece of the thin green wire from the nearby trellis supporting her honeysuckle, and fashioned it into a primitive ring. He took her left hand

and slipped it onto the ring finger. 'Not the most beautiful ring, but something to wear until the jewellers open.'

Bea looked down at her grimy hand displaying what was to her the most precious ring in the world.

'What do you say to my proposal then?' he asked, kissing her fingers one by one.

Bea was barely able to speak. 'Does this mean you'll take me back to the Écréhous for our honeymoon?'

Luke smiled down at her. 'If that's what you want, then of course I will,' he whispered, kissing her, just as Bea's honeysuckle fell away from the trellis. Luke put a hand out to catch it before it collapsed on the granite paving. 'I promise you're in safe hands.'

'So it would seem.'

ACKNOWLEDGMENTS

To my wonderful and slightly eccentric extended family, whose actions never fail to provide me with an endless supply of inspiration for my books. One of those is my gorgeous friend, Andrea Harrison, my inspiration for Shani Calder, and Andy Le Lievre, my inspiration for Paul.

Also, to my husband Rob and children, James and Saskia and to my constant writing companions, Jarvis, Claude and Rudi – not forgetting my darling Max who was with me the entire time I wrote this book.

Thanks must also go to the wonderful team at Boldwood Books, especially my copy editor, Gary Jukes and editor, Rachel Faulkner-Willcocks.

Most important of all I'd like to thank you for reading this book and to all the book reviewers for bringing books to readers' attention and for sharing their love of reading.

ABOUT THE AUTHOR

Georgina Troy writes bestselling uplifting romantic escapes and sets her novels on the island of Jersey, where she was born and has lived for most of her life.

Sign up to Georgina Troy's mailing list for news, competitions and updates on future books.

Visit Georgina's website: https://deborahcarr.org/my-books/georgina-troy-books/

Follow Georgina on social media here:

 facebook.com/GeorginaTroyAuthor

 x.com/GeorginaTroy

 instagram.com/ajerseywriter

 bookbub.com/authors/georgina-troy

ALSO BY GEORGINA TROY

The Sunshine Island Series

Finding Love on Sunshine Island

A Secret Escape to Sunshine Island

Chasing Dreams on Sunshine Island

The Golden Sands Bay Series

Summer Sundaes at Golden Sands Bay

Love Begins at Golden Sands Bay

Winter Whimsy at Golden Sands Bay

Sunny Days at Golden Sands Bay

Snow Angels at Golden Sands Bay

The Sunflower Cliffs Series

New Beginnings by the Sunflower Cliffs

LOVE NOTES

LOVE IN EVERY CHAPTER

WHERE ALL YOUR ROMANCE
DREAMS COME TRUE!

THE HOME OF BESTSELLING
ROMANCE AND WOMEN'S
FICTION

WARNING:
MAY CONTAIN SPICE

SIGN UP TO OUR
NEWSLETTER

https://bit.ly/Lovenotesnews

Boldwood

Find out more at www.boldwoodbooks.com

Follow us
@BoldwoodBooks
@TheBoldBookClub

Sign up to our weekly
deals newsletter

Printed in Great Britain
by Amazon

46177428R00169